Manifestation of Prophecy

Manifestations Series
Book 1

MANIFESTATION OF PROPHECY

Manifestations Series

Book 1

Gaius J. Augustus

First Edition

JourneyWorx

Table of Contents

DEDICATION

To every person who made it possible for you to read these words. Especially you. You make magic possible.

ACKNOWLEDGMENTS

Creating a book may start with an author's vision, but many people are involved in making it a reality. The following people may not have written any of the words within these pages, but their contributions cannot be understated.

Fans of my books have joined my Magician's Club HQ, and some of them even further support my continuing work. Thank you to all my Magicians, and an extra special thanks to **Allison Mayle**, a Full Magician in the MCHQ.

No book is complete without its cover, and **Riley Quinn** (rileyquinnart) brought Maliah and Jarith to life beautifully.

Early readers provide feedback with a distinct and necessary perspective on my stories. For *Manifestation of Prophecy*, I received feedback from beta readers and Kindle Vella readers. Their diligence and grace improved this book.

ABOUT THIS SERIES

The Ascension Four prophecy foretells of four generations of a family whose increasing magical power will bring ascension for all in Midrealm. But though prophecy can predict their fate, it can't prepare them for the bending of reality, the battles, or the hard decisions that await them.

The fate of two realities is at stake. While Midrealm awaits ascension as promised in prophecy, the energy beings in Highrealm hope to use the Ascension Four prophecy to solve their population woes. Led by the oppressive Jukartis, the Highrealmers will stop at nothing to ensure their survival.

The Manifestations Series follows those spoken of in prophecy. Across four generations, enjoy stories of acceptance, loss, and love, where anything is possible and everything hinges on the actions of a chosen few.

CONTENT NOTES

This story contains direct or indirect mentions of the following themes. Please ensure you have a care plan in place if any of these items may trigger you. Note that these may contain spoilers. This list may not be comprehensive.

On page death, emotional manipulation, parents forcing a career choice on their child, gender dysphoria, suicidal ideation, child abandonment, physical abuse, emotional abuse, incurable disease, death of a family member, violent death, moral ambiguity, turning against one's friends, and betrayal.

There is also one passing mention of an owl.

Introduction & Pronoun Guide

The characters of the Manifestations Series have been with me for many years, through countless rewrites, several shifts in genre, and an entire upheaval of the worlds and realities that they inhabit. Through it all, their strengths and quirks have persisted. It is these diverse qualities that have allowed me to bring you this story. I'm proud to present the first in the series to you, and I hope you find it immersive, thoughtful, and fun.

Some characters in this work use gender-neutral pronouns. Here is a guide to the usage of a selection of common pronouns.

FEMALE	MALE	GENDER NEUTRAL
She	He	They/Ze/Ey/Xey
Her	Him	Their/Zir/Em/Xem
Hers	His	Theirs/Zirs/Eirs/Xyrs

Examples:

> He/She/They/Ze/Ey/Xey went to the store.
> I want to talk to him/her/them/zir/em/xem.
> This book is his/hers/theirs/zirs/eirs/xyrs.

PRONUNCIATION GUIDE

Below, you'll find a pronunciation guide for common words in this book. The capitalized portion indicates where to add the stress.

Athu Aqatne: AH-too Ah-KAHT-nay

Huleay: Hoo-lee-ay

Jarith: JAY-rith

Jua: JOO-ah

Jukartis: Joo-KAR-tiss

Maliah: Muh-LEE-ah

Meta: MAY-tah

Neferu: Neh-FEH-roo

Omari: Oh-MAH-ree

Whun Miu: W-hoon Myoo, the "h" in Whun is only slightly enunciated.

Ze/Zir: ZEE / ZEER

Xey/Xyr/Xem: ZAY / ZEER / ZEM

1

SEEING THROUGH TO ANOTHER WORLD

The reality known as Highrealm was a place of pure energy, inhabited by beings with advanced knowledge of Nature's workings. However, despite their exceptional intelligence, they had a problem: their numbers were dwindling. This was a total bummer and put a damper on all their energy being activities such as researching things and spreading gossip. Their remaining hope sat with the youngest Highrealmer, Jarith, and a prophecy foretold in a less enlightened and more physical reality known as Midrealm.

Just because the Highrealmers were made of pure energy didn't mean their world lacked structure. To give order and consistency to their lives, they had formed energetic constructs—think of them as buildings. These constructs had once seemed innumerable, each full of vibrant energetic life and all the merriments and petty arguments that came with it. But with the Highrealmers' decreasing population, every structural construct had been abandoned save one, Amandala.

Amandala held all remaining beings of Highrealm. And although it didn't have a physical appearance, it could best be visualized as an enormous, circular structure with towering walls and a central atrium. Within its projected walls were areas for work, play, rest, and whatever the Highrealmers got up to when they weren't working, playing, or resting. You know, like gossiping.

If Highrealm had ever conducted a poll of the greatest advantage to living in a universe of pure energy, most denizens would select the flexibility in how they perceived their surroundings. Many key elements—such as pillars and benches—were experienced consistently by everyone, allowing the inhabitants to navigate Amandala without descending into complete chaos. But within that controlled framework was a flexible environment of infinite possibilities, enabling each Highrealmer to experience it as they wished.

For Jarith, the youngest among them, Amandala was aglow with light. From zir perspective, bright glowing stripes accentuated the information panels secured to the walls. A transparent railing lined the wide, gentle ramp that wound down around Amandala's interior, and the floors were a dark marbled stone with regularly spaced lights to illuminate the walkway.

The immense pavilion at the center of Amandala's rampway was—from Jarith's perspective—lush and green with flora, and ze enjoyed a conjured feeling of dew on zir ankles as ze crossed it.

Ze was headed to the lower levels of Amandala, where the Ascension Project sat. The project's leader—zir parent, who dictated almost every waking moment of Jarith's life—had demanded Jarith's presence. Their relationship was one of control and obedience, but that would change someday. First, however, ze had to endure a ceremony to connect zir to a person in Midrealm through their dreams.

"Jarith," a voice interrupted zir thoughts.

Ze turned to see a familiar someone who projected themself as a small, four-armed creature with orange skin and short red hair spikes.

"Triuv," Jarith acknowledged. "Greetings. How are you?"

"I'm quite well, thank you, young one," Triuv replied.

Even energy beings have to deal with mundane pleasantries, and Jarith had become proficient at masking unfavorable emotions. Ze was already running late, but ze knew better than to rush an elder. And though Triuv's floating form only came up to Jarith's projected chest, they'd existed far longer. In fact, being the youngest meant that, by definition, every other Highrealmer was older than Jarith, almost all very much so. And many beings liked to remind zir of that.

"Can I help you with something?" Jarith asked, projecting a gentle smile to hide zir impatience.

"I hope so. Tanbir told me that Gepli heard from Smuxso that the Ascension Project has taken all necessary steps to connect you to Midrealm through your dreams. Is it true?"

"I don't know," Jarith lied. Ze could have admitted ze was en route to the connection ceremony at that very moment. But then ze would've been subject to Triuv's incessant nagging the whole way there. "Even if it's true, my connection to a Midrealmer is only one step toward fulfilling the prophecy."

Oh, how ze loathed using the word prophecy. But ze had been commanded to lie to the general population by telling them the Ascension Project was fulfilling a future foretold by a long-gone Highrealm prophet. The Highrealmers held a dim view of Midrealm. If they found out a Midrealm prophecy sat at the center of their efforts—well, Jarith wasn't sure exactly what would happen, but zir parent had assured zir it wouldn't be good.

"Yes, of course. We know it's only one step. We do," Triuv said. "We also know the next goal for the Ascension Project is to transfer you—poor dear—to that barbaric Midrealm reality." See? Dim view, indeed. "Last we heard, the project still struggles to calculate the energy costs. We'd all love a progress report on that."

Everyone in Highrealm was aware that in order to send someone—namely Jarith—to Midrealm, there must be an equivalent transfer of energy from Midrealm to Highrealm. However, the nature of that equivalent transfer had so far eluded their researchers.

"I'm curious because," Triuv continued, giving Jarith time to think of a response but not enough time to actually respond, "as you know, we've lost almost fifty people over the last nibroa."

Highrealmers perception of time was convoluted and nonlinear, and there's no comprehensible equivalent to a nibroa. But suffice it to say, Triuv was worried about their impending extinction.

"It would be comforting to know more," Triuv said.

"I wish I had more information for you," Jarith replied.

"You're our first step to bringing new souls to Highrealm," Triuv reminded zir, as if ze needed to be reminded.

"Yes, and I'll do everything I can to make sure that happens," Jarith assured them.

Triuv smiled, somewhat reassured. "Thank you, dear child. This is such a heavy burden on you, but it's also why you were created."

Jarith nodded and projected a thin-lipped smile to the creature. "I must be going. It was lovely to see you, Triuv."

"Always a pleasure."

Then Triuv rushed off as if they had somewhere important to be. Jarith didn't notice because ze was busy trying to get away before anyone else could interrupt zir.

When ze arrived at the auditorium for the connection ceremony, the scientists were still setting up. They were ready to forge young Jarith's connection to a person in Midrealm with their fancy theorems and a proud sense of superiority. All the mathematics, proofs, and estimates were complete. But the scientists of Highrealm were a flamboyant lot, creating unnecessary projections of tubes, machinery, smoke, and, at the center, a single, Jarith-sized pod. It was in this pod where ze would have zir first dream of Midrealm.

Jarith didn't know what to expect from an alternate reality, though ze knew it was grounded in the physical. To a Midrealmer, everything in Highrealm could be considered inexplicable magic. The technological state of the Highrealmers was so advanced that it was simply—or perhaps complexly—impossible for any Midrealm mind to comprehend.

Ze had learned all this in zir studies. Yes, studies. Just because ze was an energy being didn't mean gaining knowledge was easy.

One of the scientists noticed zir standing there gawking and rushed over.

"Greetings, young one."

"Greetings, Chrig," replied the youngest Highrealmer. "Am I early? I thought I was running behind."

"No, no, no. Not at all. You're right on time. Please proceed to the pod," said Chrig, who was never one for small talk.

"You don't need me to do anything for the ceremony?"

"Of course not," they said, although the last six celebrations and ceremonies had required quite a lot from Jarith. "Just enter the pod and fall into a sleep state, as you normally would. We'll handle the razzle-dazzle, as the young ones say."

No one said that anymore, but Jarith chose to leave it at that. No need to ruin their fun.

As ze climbed into the vessel, ze felt thankful not to have to deal with whatever elaborate ceremony the scientists had planned. But more importantly, ze was thankful to have avoided zir parent, whose overbearing oppression shadowed Jarith's life like a cloud blocking out the sun. Not that Jarith knew what the sun was—at least, not yet.

With almost no effort, dreams came. They were light and pleasant, filled with vibrant colors, joyful people, and a cowboy riding a cat while trying to lasso a walrus. Ze would never find out what a cowboy was.

Then, abruptly, Jarith's dreams were interrupted by visions of another world, the reality known as Midrealm. It wasn't at all what ze had expected. Ze was seeing Midrealm through the eyes of an infant who, if her flailing limbs were any indication, had limited control of her physical body.

Not having a physical body of zir own, Jarith didn't understand what these limbs were at first. Ze could hear a gentle voice cooing the infant's name, Maliah, and ze could see chubby arms swinging and legs kicking. She had two of each, which Jarith assumed was normal. This was a correct assumption, unlike Jarith's hypothesis that Maliah would spend most of her life on her back.

The entire experience was unsettling. But no one said it would be seamless to peer into an alternate reality where people are obsessed with the physical nature of things. They said it was "prophecy" and threw around the word "destiny," but no one had ever mentioned "mind-blowing."

After much effort, baby Maliah's hand grabbed onto a fabric doll. She pulled it so close to her face that Jarith couldn't see much else. Ze heard a strange sound that ze later learned was Maliah chewing and sucking on the toy.

Jarith would never forget this moment, and not for its oddity. It was the harbinger of a new life, free from the suffocating surveillance and control that ruled zir in Highrealm. Zir life would never be the same.

Glimmers of light filtering in from somewhere beyond captivated zir, and Maliah's small, sweet sounds brought zir peace. It filled zir figurative heart with a feeling ze had never experienced before: joy. And with the joy came hope.

The scientists had told Jarith that their connection wasn't unidirectional. When Maliah slept, she would see and hear Jarith's world from zir perspective, just as Jarith could experience Midrealm in zir dreams. And Jarith found the idea refreshing. Ze was truly bonding with the small Midrealm creature.

The ceremony was only the first time Jarith experienced Maliah's life. However, with each subsequent dream, Jarith became increasingly frustrated at the limitations of their link. Zir perception of Maliah's world was vague and unsettling. People appeared as glowing blurs of light and shadow, truly the stuff of nightmares. Sounds and touch were varying degrees of muffled. And smells and tastes were downright confusing. Jarith's non-physical mind just wasn't built to perceive these corporeal sensations. Even more frustrating was that ze couldn't access her thoughts or feel her emotions. Still, as the infant grew—a process which was all kinds of disturbing for zir—Jarith tried to understand Maliah and her world as best ze could.

This turned out to be an immense challenge.

Jarith took for granted many conveniences in Highrealm. For example, Jarith could choose a visual form to project to others. One moment, ze could be a floating golden orb with wings wearing a silver crown, and the next moment, ze could project the form of a biped with yellow feathers for hair and deep indigo skin. Meanwhile, those in Midrealm were bound to the form they were born in, which seemed downright cruel. Still, they found ways to express their individuality. Maliah's parents often tied a ribbon in her hair, which Maliah seemed to enjoy pulling off and shoving in her mouth.

Despite their worlds being so mismatched, Maliah and Jarith were tied together through their dreams, and someday—if the Highrealmers could get all their non-physical ducks in a row—they would be brought physically together in one reality. Maybe then all these glowing people, blurry objects, and strange differences would make sense.

By the time baby Maliah was walking and talking, Jarith had learned that her parents commanded the most powerful magic in their world. They lived in Ar, the capital city of the Ledine Empire, a large island nation. Ze had also learned they were part of the spiritual ruling caste of Ledine, known as the Huleay Temple.

Instead of through studying—which was all kinds of boring—Jarith had learned much about Maliah's world through experience. Ze preferred this method, and not only because it made learning effortless. Maliah continued to spark joy within zir in a way nothing ever had, and those feelings grew as time moved forward.

As was typical for families of the spiritual caste of Ledine, Maliah joined the Huleay Temple at the age of six, where she began training as a Young Priest. And when she got into trouble, her mentors and peers never failed to remind her of those pesky responsibilities of destiny.

That was a lot of pressure for a Midrealm child. Jarith had heard her parents regale her with stories of their youth with the Temple, and they were a tough act for any little girl to follow, especially a little girl whose foretold magical powers had not yet manifested.

Jarith understood her worries. Being the subject of prophecy meant a lack of control over one's own fate. And perhaps more disturbing, failure would mean disappointing everyone in a very public way. Maliah expressed fear of her destiny even before she could put words to them, but Jarith didn't need her to spell it out for zir. Ze had the same trepidations.

Perhaps Jarith's strong feelings for Maliah explained why it weighed on zir that the more she learned about her destiny, the more she seemed to dread it. Sometimes, when she was alone, she would whisper to herself—and to zir—her secret wish to be someone else, her vision clouded by tears. It broke Jarith's heart, and ze would have given up zir freedom to grant her wish.

Unfortunately, wishes don't overrule prophecy.

2

Start of Night Ritual

In what felt like the blink of an eye, Maliah's thirteenth birthday arrived. That evening, she would have her "Start of Night" ritual, where she'd acknowledge her destiny in front of her people. The ceremony would be held at the main temple, which sat in the Huleay Grounds at the seat of power in the capital.

Jarith ensured ze was asleep in time to see her don her new dress for the ritual. As ze watched through her eyes, zir joy felt bittersweet. This was a significant event in Maliah's life, but it also shackled her to her predetermined future. Ze was surprised when she smiled as she twirled in front of her bedroom mirror.

"Isn't it lovely?" she asked.

She was alone in the room and couldn't have known Jarith was watching. If someone had walked in on her talking to herself, the situation would have been awkward. But there was little chance of that. She didn't have any friends, and ze later learned that her parents had left hours ago to prepare for the ritual.

Jarith could make out the shape of her dress, though ze couldn't see its fine details. Thirteen-year-old Maliah had spent much of her free time sewing it, and ze thought that she, with her golden skin and thick, dark head of curling ringlets, was beautiful wearing it. However, aside from her, much of Midrealm was still impossible to bring into focus. The edges of the mirror solidified with some effort, but everything else was blurry.

It didn't matter to Jarith. Ze was content with Maliah's smile looking back at zir.

Just because Jarith couldn't hear her thoughts or experience her emotions didn't mean ze lacked insight into what she was thinking. Ze knew her well enough to guess that her smile was directed solely at the new dress, which she had toiled to sew herself. She was dreading the upcoming ritual. It didn't take a genius to deduce this, given how often she had complained about it over the past dozen days.

After another twirl, Maliah regained her composure, collected her things, and hurried out of the house. Jarith was disoriented as blurred buildings, people, and the occasional camel, dog, or donkey whizzed by on Maliah's dash up the hill toward the inner Huleay Grounds.

When she entered the dressing chambers for the Young Priests, she took her place in front of her designated dressing table, where a ceremonial robe and adornments awaited her. She pulled the robe over her dress and adorned herself with an arm cuff, an assortment of jewelry, and a headdress. Each was ornate, covered with symbols and charged gemstones to magnify the magic of the ritual.

"Priest Maliah?" a small voice called from behind her.

That's right, Jarith reminded zirself. Maliah was no longer a Young Priest, despite still being relegated to the Young Priest dressing chambers. She was now considered an adult, and thus would be referred to as just plain Priest. It was a strange hierarchy that ze struggled to understand.

Maliah turned to face the blurry figure who had spoken. Jarith had gotten used to—though was no less annoyed by—the fuzziness of people and objects. Ze could sometimes see the crisp detail of items of magic, such as her ceremonial garb, but people especially appeared as semi-amorphous blobs. Instead, Jarith had learned to concentrate on the auras of those with whom Maliah interacted. The aura of the person in front of her now exuded worry and fear.

"That's me," Maliah acknowledged. "Are you a scribe?"

Jarith knew she was attempting to put the person's mind at ease. Unfortunately, their aura's wobbly undulations indicated they were neither relaxed nor soothed.

"Yes. I was sent to illuminate you with the spells of today's ritual."

The scribe sounded young, around Maliah's age, but with a voice that seemed unsure of its pitch. None of this made them any less blobby to Jarith.

"May I begin?" the scribe asked.

Before Maliah could respond, her gaze—and Jarith's along with it—was pulled away, down the long hall of formless Young Priests, to something out of place and not any of Maliah's business. Nevertheless, she left her dressing table and the scribe she'd been speaking with. The scribe didn't call out or try to follow, which Jarith assumed was because they knew their place.

Watching through Maliah's eyes, each person she passed was an amorphous blur. Yet every detail of the table at the far end of the hall was crisp and clear. Maliah closed the distance, and ze noted a large tray sitting atop the table. On it sat objects for the ritual: several feathers tied together with twine, bowls with powdery or chunky substances, a wooden wand with wire-wrapped crystals decorating its structure, containers with delicate lids, and an urn that Maliah's—and therefore Jarith's—attention was fixated on.

The urn's sculpted lid held the shape of a cat's head. Its brilliant blue color and striking black eyes left Jarith stunned, feeling it sensed zir within Maliah. The urn itself was ostentatious, with intricate decorative motifs lining the top and bottom and detailed images of people illustrated around the center.

It was clearly not something she should touch, yet Maliah's hesitant hand reached toward it. The closer she got, the stronger Jarith could sense the power coming from it, power that some priests could channel in a ritual, but a power that didn't seem quite right for the uplifting ceremony to celebrate Maliah's dedication to her people.

"Young girl, what do you think you're doing?" a shrill voice asked, laced with anger and annoyance.

Maliah turned toward a tall priest. She was just another blobby figure to Jarith, but had an aura glowing in swirls of green.

"The ceremonial artifacts have been blessed for the ritual," she continued. "Only the Exalted Grand Priests may handle them now."

"I humbly apologize for the intrusion," Maliah replied with just a twinge of annoyance, "but someone has made an error. The Ankh of Terunith is meant to be placed on the left side of the tray. You have instead set the Zhur Urn there." Maliah stressed the word you, and Jarith inwardly cheered for her small act of defiance.

Ze couldn't make out the priest's face, but her aura gave off energies of frustration as she reviewed the tray, then surprise when she realized Maliah was correct, and finally embarrassment as she called her aides to fix the mistake. She'd be even more embarrassed when she found out who Maliah's parents were, Jarith laughed to zirself.

The priest showed no appreciation for Maliah's correction and gave no thanks or apology. This bothered Jarith, but Maliah didn't say a word. The birthday girl simply returned to the scribe, who was right where they'd left them.

"Thank you for your patience, scribe," she said, lifting her chin and putting her arms out in front of her. "I stand ready for your illumination."

Maliah's stomach was in knots as she waited for her cue to join her parents on the stage. Covered with magical symbols, she stood at one of the back entrances of the main temple's evening ritual space, a Young Priest to either side. Her parents were on a nearby stage, where the setting sun's rays made them glow with reds and pinks.

This was her Start of Night ritual, one of the rarest ceremonies performed by the Huleay Temple. Though it celebrated the beginning of one's journey as an adult priest, the ritual was reserved for new Priests in unique circumstances, such as Maliah, and for the rare cases where Priests joined the spiritual caste as adults.

Almost every member of the Huleay Temple had been born into their positions, but there were rare exceptions to this. Such was the case for one powerful Exalted Grand Priest who Maliah had only met in passing, but who would soon become an important part of her life.

Mirrors on either side of the stage focused the waning sunlight on the two Exalted Grand Priests on the stage. Their arms, necks, and chests were illuminated with symbols, and as Maliah's mother spoke, the symbols luminesced.

With a dramatic gesture, her father swept his hand across the room, and oil lamps came alive with light. The crowd gasped in amazement.

There was a crowd, Maliah suddenly realized. A crowd who would be staring at her. At the base of the stage, stretching all the way to the back of the sanctuary, the sea of eyes fixated on what was happening on the platform. Although she knew what was expected of her, Maliah couldn't help but worry.

What if she tripped? She looked down at her robe to ensure it wasn't tangled around her feet. Reviewing the ramp up to the platform, she confirmed it was smooth and gentle. If she tripped, it would be due only to her own incompetence. These weren't ideal words of self-encouragement, but they were the best she could do.

Her mother, the night before, had laughed at Maliah's fear of becoming clumsy during her ritual.

"What a day for the most elegant woman of Ledine to become clumsy," she had said, running her hand over Maliah's curls.

"Now, your mother . . . well, let me tell you how she ruined her first public ritual," her father had joked, invoking a quick slap from her mother.

It was easy for them to laugh. There they were, up on that stage, being perfect. Maliah took one deep breath after another. She just needed to keep telling herself she would be fine. If she thought it enough times, maybe she'd even start to believe it.

"We call upon our ancestors," her mother spoke from the platform, "and the spirits of the earth, sky, river, and sun. Grace us with your presence, that we may present to you the one named in the Ascension Four prophecy, the daughter of Exalted Grand Priests Meta and Jua, the mother of those that will change our world." Her mother paused for dramatic effect, her arms out in welcome to the crowd, the spirits, and the ancestors.

Maliah's feet seemed locked to the floor as fear rendered her motionless. An emotional pressure weighed on her. Her parents loved and supported her. They gave her plenty of attention and provided a loving environment. But they also expected Maliah to fulfill her destiny.

One hundred years prior to Maliah's birth, the Ascension Four prophecy had caused an uproar in Ledine. It was such a big deal that the Huleay Temple had publicly declared prophecy to be real in the same breath that they declared prophecy to be the most divisive topic of their time.

Despite the naysayers claiming otherwise, the Ascension Four prophecy was unique. This wasn't one of those streetside predictions, where one might gamble away their camel for a magic bean. No, this was a legitimate divination, foretold by Exalted Grand Priest Emin and promising ascension for all in Midrealm. And it prophesied the future of four generations of her family, starting with her parents.

Like all of Exalted Grand Priest Emin's prophecies, the Ascension Four prophecy was destined to be fulfilled, whether or not Maliah wanted it. And she really, really, REALLY did not want it.

Her mother's voice rang out again, breaking her from her daydream of a much more humble life. "We present to you: Priest Maliah."

Maliah took slow, steady steps forward, just as she had practiced, heading up the ramp to take her place as part of the Start of Night ritual. The two Young Priests at her sides stayed a few steps behind.

As if she were the rising sun, her jewelry and headdress shone in the light of the sunset. Her golden skin was covered in symbols that would be activated later in the ritual. A cool evening breeze flowed through the sanctuary, refreshing those on the platform. When Maliah reached her mark, she put her arms out to the side and lifted her chin.

"Hail and welcome," she said, projecting her voice out to the crowd and spirits.

The people cheered, and she closed her eyes and enjoyed the breeze instead of acknowledging their response. She waited until silence fell over the audience before lowering her arms to her side.

Her mother and father moved in front of and behind her, forming a circle with the Young Priests. They chanted as they circled her once, twice, three times. The Young Priests sprinkled salt as they spoke, careful not to raise their voices above those of the Exalted Grand Priests.

They stopped at an angle so that Maliah could look out over the crowd. Her heart was already racing, so she avoided her mind's tendency to estimate how many people were staring back. She instead gazed at her parents in awe.

Despite her lineage, she was—thus far—a disappointment to her people and herself. She hadn't even been assigned a mentor, which was both embarrassing and nerve-wracking. She assumed she would end up under the tutelage of a minor priest so she could learn the mundane tricks that made the Huleay Temple seem more magical than it actually was. It wouldn't match the big plans the prophecy had for her, but perhaps the change of pace would do her good.

Her parents' disappointment stemmed from her lack of magical ability. They had both exhibited magic talent well before thirteen, and expected the same from Maliah. However, she was utterly magicless . . . well, except for the dreams of an energy being from another world. But that wasn't a useful kind of magic, so it didn't count, in her opinion. And it was a magic she had never revealed to anyone, not even as a child. There were times when she wondered how she'd managed such a thing, but she never lingered on it.

Her mother had all the confidence that Maliah lacked. Meta was a tall, thin, pale woman with cascading brown hair. Considered the most powerful priest in Ledine, Maliah had seen her mother perform minor miracles in healing, prophetic visions, and recharging magical artifacts.

Maliah's father, Jua, was shorter—the same height as Maliah, actually—with dark skin and a rugged handsomeness that Maliah sometimes argued was magical in and of itself. She knew her father had magic as well, but she couldn't recall ever seeing him use it outright. Instead, he used the same tricks of chemistry and illusion practiced by the rest of the Huleay Temple. Maliah's parents sometimes joked about him being too powerful to show his true abilities, but sometimes it was difficult to tell if they were stretching the truth for the joke's sake.

The four people standing around Maliah raised their arms until they were touching hands.

"Priest Maliah," her father spoke, "it is now upon you to choose your destiny. You must choose to use your power in the service of your people, as only you can do."

The four turned with their backs facing her and placed their hands together, again forming a circle around her.

"The people are your witnesses," her mother spoke. "The ancestors are your witnesses. The spirits are your witnesses."

Her parents then shouted in unison. "Choose to enter the start of night, the beginning of the path toward light, a journey to your own true might."

As if from nowhere, the Ankh of Terunith appeared before her. She had been told her father would hand it to her, but now it just floated in midair, waiting for her. Without hesitation, although she was pretty weirded out, she took the Ankh in her hands.

She held the cool metal to her chest, and the symbols on her arms, hands, face, and neck began to luminesce brightly. She glowed with ethereal essence, and the crowd cheered. Even though Maliah knew this was a chemical reaction between the ink on her skin and a fine mist released by the Ankh, to the audience, it confirmed she was a magical being who belonged in the Huleay Temple.

It made Maliah feel like a fraud.

The four priests around her lowered their arms and took several steps away, clearing the audience's view. She looked to see her parents clapping as well, though the two Young Priests who'd come onto the stage with her were not.

The glowing dimmed. The Young Priests exited down the ramp, and her parents led Maliah to a chair at the back of the platform.

"You did great," Jua said.

"Hard part's over," Meta added. "And you didn't even trip."

Once Maliah was seated, she could finally relax. Though she kept her perfect posture and held the Ankh firmly upright, she watched in awe as her parents reviewed the meaning of the Start of Night ritual, made offerings to the ancestors and each realm of spirits, and spoke about Maliah's work as a Young Priest.

"We have one more announcement," her mother said as the ritual came to a close, "before we move on to the festivities in the Huleay Grounds' central pavilion."

"It has been challenging to determine who will mentor Priest Maliah," her father continued. "However, we are excited to confirm her mentorship by Exalted Grand Priest Amun."

Maliah's eyes widened, and the audience's loud murmurs mirrored her surprise. Exalted Grand Priest Amun was the most enigmatic priest of the Huleay Temple. She didn't remember zir, since ze had left the city when she was a toddler. But according to rumors, zir power rivaled her mother's. How was magicless Maliah supposed to train under the second most powerful priest alive?

Maliah's first public ritual was over. She'd accepted her role as Priest and had been placed on a pretty high and wobbly pedestal. And yet, as she followed her parents into the Exalted Grand Priests' dressing room, they had the nerve to act like everything was normal.

"You were right," Jua said to his wife. "Yacob was the right scribe for the job."

"I told you," Meta replied. "You owe me dinner."

He laughed. "I call foul. You left out that he's been doing the priests' illuminations every day for the past lunar cycle."

"Who revealed my deep secret?" Meta asked with feigned indignance.

"Priest Anteri."

"It doesn't matter. A win is a win."

They were ignoring Maliah's sour mood, and she almost cared enough to be offended.

As attendants entered to help her parents undress, she marveled at the pillars that stretched five times her height to the ceilings. The walls held painted murals of people standing at the river, watching a boat go by that held a priest, who was blessing them. Underneath the far wall, an attendant measured out oils and minerals into a large water basin.

She'd visited this room throughout her youth, but its magnificence never ceased to amaze her. It almost distracted her from her anger, too, but someone bumped into her as he entered the room.

The young man apologized. "I was instructed to assist you," he said. "I'll take care of your robes first."

"Priests don't get the royal treatment," Maliah said as she begrudgingly held her arms out.

The boy removed her robe with unnecessary care, then moved on to her jewelry. He was smart enough not to respond to her.

"You're a child of prophecy," Jua said. "That affords you certain benefits."

When the young attendant struggled to remove her armband, she held up her hand to stop him. After removing it herself, she handed it to him.

"But those benefits also come with responsibilities," Meta added.

Ah, the old with great power comes great responsibility speech, despite a noticeable lack of power on Maliah's part.

She looked down at her dress, finding a glimmer of happiness there. The seams were straight, and the fit was perfect. It was such a shame it had been covered by her robe. Her attendant placed her jewelry and headdress in a tray and closed it under a decorative cover. He left the room, but she had seen her parents' after-ritual routine enough times to know he'd be back to remove her illuminations.

And knowing her parents, they'd soon ask about her dreams.

"Maliah, my dear daughter," Meta said with a wry smile, "have you begun to dream?"

So predictable.

"Since you asked last week? No," Maliah lied.

Her mother shot her a disbelieving look. "Now, Maliah. I—"

"Your mother and I," Jua interrupted, "are just concerned for you. We began dreaming of each other when we were children."

"Concerned for me? You mean concerned for the prophecy," Maliah replied.

Much to her annoyance, her attendant returned with supplies that smelled just as bad as she remembered. She obediently held out her arms for scrubbing. Meanwhile, her parents continued to disrobe.

"You know that's not true," Meta said.

"Well, it's a little true," Jua remarked.

Meta shot him a disbelieving glare.

"It is," he insisted.

Her parents stood and made their way to the bath. The attendants helped them remove their final layer of clothing. They offered their hands to assist the Exalted

Grand Priests into the basin. Once seated in the chest-high water, they relaxed as their attendants removed the illuminations from their skin.

They were getting the much gentler bath salts version while she was stuck with an attendant scrubbing at her skin. She puckered her lips in a pout, but no one noticed, which she found quite rude.

"Maliah, this is prophecy. It will happen. And we want you to be prepared," Jua said.

"It's not an easy path," Meta added, "but it's much easier when you don't do it alone."

"Maybe we should wait to start my training. I'm sure I just need more time," Maliah said.

"No, there's plenty for you to learn. Amun returns to Ar tomorrow, and we'll speak to zir then."

Maliah sat in bed, knees to her chest with her arms wrapped around her legs. For her people, dreams meant visions, either prophetic or intuitive, and these dreams were the first signs of latent powers. Though she'd had dreams for as long as she could remember, they weren't prophetic. They were mundane. At least, as mundane as possible for a society with technology far beyond Midrealm's imagination.

Before she joined the Huleay Temple, she'd considered her dreams a secret getaway that her parents might take away. By the time she understood their significance, she was bombarded with other people's expectations of her.

She hated lying to her parents. Although she longed for their perspective, she'd never been courageous enough to tell them about Jarith. This whole prophecy thing was too overwhelming to discuss, and she feared that speaking of it would make it manifest. The powerful abilities she was supposed to attain terrified her. While gaining such power seemed trivial, no one ever explained how she would possibly control it. She couldn't even decide when Jarith came into her mind. Not speaking about her dreams allowed her to dictate one small part of her life.

Usually, by this time of night, she was unconscious, and instead of the nothingness that everyone else in the world—minus certain Exalted Grand Priests—experienced, she would dream. And her dreams weren't exactly pleasant.

Vague people in vague places did strange—and, yes, also vague—things that she rarely understood. Over the years, she'd learned a bit about Highrealm through overheard conversations and rare moments of clarity, but she had more questions than answers.

What came through loud and clear was the care that Jarith brought to zir people. Ze knew everyone's name and listened to their concerns with patience. The others were respectful to Jarith as well. The only outlier was Jarith's parent, but their relationship was complicated.

Some days, she resented Jarith's close-knit community, especially those who worked together on what the Highrealmers called the Ascension Project. She didn't understand what ascension was, although she knew the Huleay Temple sold it as souls drifting into the sky to join the spirits and ancestors.

Most days, Maliah wished she could actually talk to Jarith face to face. As a child, she had tried to have conversations with zir, asking zir questions while hoping ze was watching. Ze had responded on a few occasions, but it still felt distant and cold. So instead, she talked to no one when she needed to, and sometimes, she caught Jarith doing the same.

She slipped under her blanket. Music drifted from the Huleay Grounds' central pavilion, where the Temple was hosting a lively celebration in her honor. She was never one for parties, especially on the evening before an event as important as meeting her mentor for the first time. It was important to sleep tonight. The last thing she wanted to do was give the Exalted Grand Priest the idea that she couldn't take basic care of herself.

Now if only she could take basic care of herself by getting some sleep.

3

THE MASK OF BHRAMADI

Early the next morning, Maliah and her parents left their home for their scheduled meeting with Maliah's new mentor, Exalted Grand Priest Amun. The sun's light peeked just over the horizon, but they weren't alone on the road. Many locals and travelers lined the streets with their camels, donkeys, and offering-laden carts, making their way up toward the Huleay Grounds.

The city of Ar ran along the western bank of the river. The southern edge of the city was lined by a tall hill, at the top of which sat the Huleay Grounds. An outer fortress wall surrounded the Grounds on all sides, the remnant of a long-ago war. The southern wall stood atop a precipitous scarp, so the city had spread to the west and north of the hill.

The inner Huleay Grounds sat within another wall, equally tall but appearing much larger due to the increasing elevation of the slope. Between the inner and outer walls lay the homes belonging to members of the ruling spiritual caste, including Maliah's family. Some attendants were lucky to live near the entrance to the Grounds, though "lucky" was subjective seeing as how this was also where first-generation Young Priests lived and partied. Beyond that, the hierarchy continued, interrupted only by the large market that sat between districts and extended eastward to the river.

Every step of the short walk from Maliah's home to the Grounds brought more anguish to her heart. Her time as a Young Priest had been lonely, since adults expected the best from her and her peers envied her importance. Being a child of prophecy was far too burdensome, in her opinion. And now she'd be adding one more person to her life to disappoint with her mediocrity.

They arrived at the smallest sanctuary on the grounds, typically used for private or intimate ceremonies. Its face held six columns, each with intricate carvings to resemble bundled reeds from the nearby river. They stretched up to a ceiling that was many times Maliah's height and were painted with an elaborate protection spell. Outside the oversized, wooden doors stood an attendant, who bowed as they approached.

"Good day," she said. "Exalted Grand Priest Amun will be with you shortly. My apologies for the wait."

Her parents bowed but did not move, and to keep it from getting more awkward, the attendant slipped into the sanctuary. Within a minute, a priest rushed out the doors, almost running straight into Maliah's parents.

They gasped when they realized who stood in front of them and bowed deeply before continuing their hurried steps away from the small temple.

The door swung open, and the attendant stepped aside to reveal Exalted Grand Priest Amun, who looked down over zir nose at Maliah with the most judgmental glare she'd ever seen.

Maliah wanted to shrink into her dress. No, she wanted to shrink into oblivion. There was no question in her mind that ze was looking into her soul, seeing that she had no magic and was a being of unresolvable contradiction. After all, she wanted to continue as a priest, but she didn't want to be doomed to failure by prophecy.

Exalted Grand Priest Amun's glare seemed to last forever, but it was only mere moments before Amun turned zir attention to her parents.

"Meta. Jua." Ze bowed zir head to each in acknowledgment.

They were both smiling. Yes, SMILING. While their poor daughter was getting hardcore judged. And just when she thought it couldn't get any worse, they both embraced Amun like long lost family.

"It's good to see you again, friend," Jua laughed.

"I'm glad we were able to coax you to return home," Meta joked.

None of this was funny to Maliah.

"Now, now," Amun said, patting the two Exalted Grand Priests on their shoulders. "If you needed me, you could have requested my return at any time."

Ze didn't look any less stern, but Maliah sensed a gentleness in zir voice that was absent in zir facial features. Amun had the worst case of resting stern face Maliah had ever seen.

"Lies," Meta insisted in a teasing tone. "We called you home when Unara was named Grand Priest."

"Well, that's hardly a dire circumstance," ze replied. "But the start of night for one named by prophecy—or perhaps more importantly, the start of night for the daughter of my two favorite people? Now, that's an occasion worth the painful horse rides and scratchy carriage seats."

They all hugged again, and Maliah turned away. Down the walkway in the other direction, the rays of the rising sun painted the clouds in broad, warm tones. She found herself wondering if Jarith was watching. Could ze appreciate the vibrant colors?

When she peered into Jarith's world through zir eyes, color was strange in a way she couldn't describe. She experienced colors she had never seen in her world, that her mind could barely even understand. Yet she saw beauty in it. Did ze see beauty in Midrealm?

Jarith claimed that someday, ze would travel to this world—this reality, as ze called it. And for many years, she had longed for zir presence. Though her heart ached to see Jarith, to talk to zir, to confirm zir existence, the thought now filled her with dread. At some point, she'd have to admit to herself that she was destined to live in her parents' shadow, in her child's shadow, in her grandchild's shadow. They all had purpose, yet she struggled to find hers.

"Maliah?" her father said.

She turned to see three worried faces—well, she assumed that Amun's stern face was also worried—staring at her.

"It's time, dear," Meta said. "We need to prepare for morning blessings."

"You're leaving?" Maliah asked, her racing heart feeling like it had jumped into her throat.

"You'll be fine," Jua assured her.

"You're in excellent hands," Meta agreed.

With that, they were gone. She took deep breaths as she followed Amun into the sanctuary, yet it did nothing to ease the growing lump in her throat. Ze instructed the attendant, who had been waiting inside, not to allow anyone to enter. She closed the door after her, and the bang echoed through the empty chambers.

"Sit," Amun said, gesturing to a chair at the front of the sanctuary's platform.

She sat. What else was she going to do?

Amun stretched zir lips, and Maliah guessed the gesture was supposed to be some kind of reassuring smile. Then, ze left through a doorway at the back of the stage. With no other instructions, she stayed in her seat and looked around.

This sanctuary stretched upward into a funnel shape, ending at a grand oculus that let the natural light in. When it rained, water collected into a wide, raised pond at the center, which drained to storage containers in other areas of the grounds. At the four cardinal directions, enormous stone figures towered over her. They were the embodiments of the spirits of earth, sky, river, and sun. Though their bodies were human, their heads were those of animals, as were other features such as tails, scales, and feathers.

These statues were similar to those throughout the Huleay Grounds. In each temple, the spirits oversaw rituals. However, these sculptures were unique. Along the length of their garments were words, drawn as if they were pleats. It was impossible to read from where Maliah sat, but she correctly assumed they listed the standard appellations of each spirit.

Maliah snapped her head back to the doorway as Amun returned from wherever ze had gone. Ze held a tray with objects hidden under a decorative cover. She looked beyond zir, wondering why no one was assisting the aging priest. When she got up to help, ze shushed her even though she wasn't talking.

"Sit down," ze insisted.

So, she did.

Ze sat the tray on the floor in front of her, then sat on the floor zirself. She had never seen a Grand Priest sit on the bare floor before, much less an Exalted Grand Priest.

Her surprise must have shown on her face because something resembling a laugh escaped zir.

"Don't worry. I'm perfectly capable of getting up and sitting down on my own," ze said. Ze placed zir hands on zir knees. "Now, we're going to start with a few tests, but they aren't the kind of tests that you pass or fail. They merely provide me with information to better understand your level of power."

"I don't have any power," Maliah said, "and aren't we jumping in too quickly?"

"How so?" ze asked.

"I don't know anything about you, and you don't know anything about me."

Ze did a chortle-y kind of thing. Or was ze clearing zir throat? "Very well. What would you like to know?"

She drew in a breath and held it, completely unprepared to be put on the spot. She let it out very slowly, very carefully, as if the act of breathing would trigger some kind of consequence.

"Well, then," ze said when she didn't respond, "what should I know about you?"

Maliah clung to her chair as she tried to think of an answer to the Exalted Grand Priest's question. That she was afraid of failing? That she knew she didn't deserve to be spoken of in prophecy? That she actually enjoyed eating her vegetables?

"I . . ." she began.

That was all she could say.

"Well, why don't I start with what I know about you? You can tell me what I'm missing." Grand Exalted Priest Amun, still seated on the ground, put zir hands together at zir chin. "You are brave enough to speak up when you see an error. You always arrive on time and prepared for your work. When given a task, you complete it with precision and care. Should I go on?"

Little birds had obviously been singing her praises—and ignoring her shortcomings.

"That makes it sound like I don't have weaknesses," she grumbled.

"Priest Maliah, we all have our shortcomings. You, your parents, and me. That's the very reason we work as a collective for the good of our people. We must trust each other to balance our flaws."

"You're asking me to trust others when I don't even trust myself?"

"No, of course not," ze said with a shake of zir head. "I'm telling you that carrying your burden is easier when there's someone else to shoulder some of the load."

She stared deeply into zir black eyes, still looking as if ze was lecturing her instead of advising her. Her mother must have told zir everything, hoping she would listen to her new mentor when she ignored her mother's advice.

"As your mentor, it's my job to support you in shouldering your burden, if you'll allow me," ze continued.

She couldn't help but laugh because she knew she had no choice in the matter. Still, if she was going to be mentored, Amun inspired confidence she had never felt before.

Amun's slightly less stern face made her think ze was proud to have made her laugh.

"Could you please call me Maliah?" she asked.

Zir thin-lipped smile returned. "If you'll call me Amun." Ze placed zir hands back on zir legs. "Now, if I may continue?"

She nodded.

Ze tilted up the cover from the tray, keeping what was underneath hidden, and pulled out three items. After placing them on top of the cover, ze waved a hand over the objects in a clear act of showmanship.

"Pick one," ze said simply.

She waited for more instruction, but she was out of luck because ze said no more.

They looked like normal household items: a hairbrush, a teapot, and a writing stylus. No item was remarkable, but she had to choose one. She held out her hand over each in turn. Unsure exactly what she was searching for, she sighed and pointed at the stylus.

"I choose that one."

"Thank you," Amun said. "Take it."

She picked it up between her thumb and index finger. Nothing happened, so she raised an eyebrow at her new mentor.

"Very good," Amun finally said. Ze pulled out a piece of paper from under the tray. "Now, write your name."

She didn't have ink, but she guessed that was part of the test. So she pulled the paper into her lap and placed the stylus onto it.

Much to her surprise, as she dragged it along the page, her name appeared in dark brown ink. Her eyes gleamed, and her lips broadened into a smile. It was magic. Real magic. And she was doing it.

"Does this mean I do have power?" she asked.

Butterflies fluttered in her gut at the prospect, but she needn't have worried.

"No," Amun replied. "Anyone can use this magical artifact with some training. However, it is impressive that you required no instruction to elicit its effect."

When she was done, she handed the paper back to zir with a smug grin.

"You have poor penmanship," Amun remarked.

Was ze serious, or was that sass? She really wasn't sure.

"I was writing on my lap," she reminded zir.

"Quite true," ze said with a weird smile she would come to recognize as genuine humor.

"So, did I pass?"

"As I said, these are not tests you can pass or fail." Ze finally removed the cover from the tray, revealing a long wooden mask with an oddly shaped face.

"You want me to put it on?" she asked, feeling a bit sassy herself.

"This is a magical artifact, another which typically requires training to use."

"Does this one work even without powers?"

"That is of no matter. I wish for you to tell me its purpose," ze said. "Take your time."

She puckered her lips to the side and furrowed her brow. Her gut told her it was used to filter light, as the eye holes had colored glass fitted into them. However, after seeing the stylus, she wondered if she needed to think bigger, more magical.

Holding out her hand, she asked, "May I?"

Amun nodded, and she picked up the mask. She turned it over to see that the glass was very thick, filling the entire eyehole. Around the edge, symbols had been etched in fine detail.

Some of the symbols were familiar. There were several that she recognized from moon and sky magic, and on the other side, earth and animal magic.

Cautiously, she held the mask up toward the oculus, which was growing brighter with the rising sun, overtaking the glow from the oil lamps in the sanctuary. The light filtering through was odd, but she couldn't place why.

As she looked around the room, she brought the mask closer to her face. Particles of light floated around the statues at the corners of the room.

She followed their movement as the particles drifted downward, resting in a casual swirl around the raised pond at the center of the chamber, then continued their journey toward the platform where she and Amun sat.

When her gaze landed on Amun, she dropped the mask with a loud gasp. As the magic artifact clamored against the floor, its echo reverberated around the sanctuary. Maliah's eyes widened and, with one foot lifted into her chair, she gawked at the Exalted Grand Priest, who remained seated on the ground in front of her.

Ze was smiling, and it looked smug and vile. However, what she had seen through the mask was entirely different.

Her eyes watered. The sight had been so beautiful, she didn't know what to do with herself. She didn't want to speak. There were no words to describe her sense of wonder.

Through the amber lenses of the mask, in Amun's place had been a creature of swirling rainbows of light and sparkling particles. Drifting flows of magical essence were drawn to the figure before her. Ribbons of light wrapped themselves around a form. In place of zir stern face, a benevolent smile had gleamed, leaving her hands tingling. Its impression of comfort radiated within her, even though the vision was gone.

Yet there was another reason the magnificent image had startled her. Though the impression was brighter and clearer, it reminded her of the beings of Highrealm. The swirls of light. The indiscrete forms that she knew to be people. There was a striking resemblance. Suddenly, everything seemed so real, Jarith felt incredibly close, and anything seemed possible.

"Well?" Amun asked. "Do you know what it does?"

"It shows the truth," she said, the words coming before the thought.

Somehow, she knew the mask's purpose, despite not understanding what "showing the truth" meant. Her best interpretation of what she had seen was that Amun was a kind and powerful priest, which was a relief, if nothing else.

This interpretation was wrong.

Amun picked the mask up and returned it to the tray, then began collecting the other items.

"It's the Mask of Bhramadi," Amun said as ze examined each item, "and typically it takes an advanced magic user to activate its power."

"But I'm not an advanced magic user."

"Yet it worked for you," ze replied noncommittally.

"What does this test of yours mean, then?"

"I don't know," Amun said, placing zir hands together on top of the covered tray. "It's clear you don't possess any power of your own, yet your proficiency with these artifacts is encouraging. Perhaps your abilities are locked away, waiting for the right moment to awaken."

She was lost for words. She couldn't reveal to Amun what she'd seen through the mask, not without revealing that she was, in fact, dreaming. Her dreams weren't prophetic, therefore they couldn't be part of her power. Even so, in this reality of dreamless sleep, the fact that she dreamt at all indicated potential within her. As Amun had said, waiting to awaken.

Maliah needed to be careful if she was to get answers from her mentor. If she chose her questions meticulously enough, she could learn something more about her dreams without revealing them.

"I have a question," she said.

"That's wonderful," ze replied. "You must always ask your questions. After all, it's the only way to receive an answer."

Well, wasn't ze a fountain of interesting aphorisms?

"I've heard stories about your power, but do you dream?"

Zir brow drew tight, and ze stood with the loaded tray. Though ze turned as if to leave, instead, ze paused. The room dimmed then brightened as a cloud drifted in front of the sun.

"Not with the proficiency your parents have," ze said. Another minute passed by without movement before ze turned slightly back toward Maliah. "You may not believe it now, but you're destined to do real magic, far beyond what most in the Huleay Temple are capable of. It's a burden as much as a blessing because, despite the great good we can do, we are also capable of great evil.

"Because of this, you mustn't flaunt or share the extent of your power with anyone beyond your family. You are special, but that also makes you vulnerable. Do you understand?"

She'd had this conversation with her parents at least a dozen times, as they continued to hope her powers would awaken. She'd never agreed with it, though she kept that to herself. In her mind, her powers—whenever they decided to show up—were there to serve her people. It didn't make sense to hide them.

Even so, she still replied, "I believe so, but as you've confirmed, I don't have any power."

"Not yet," ze agreed. "But your innate proficiency with magical artifacts is undeniable evidence of latent power that will someday be activated."

"What if I don't want that? What if I don't want my life controlled by prophecy?" she pushed.

It was an outburst she hadn't expected to make, and she felt guilty as soon as she said it. Amun finally turned to look at her. Zir smile almost seemed kind, but it didn't really get there.

"Prophecy guides our circumstances, but not our choices," ze said.

The guilt settled as she took in zir meaning. Just because she was destined to have power didn't mean that she couldn't choose how to use it. With newfound comfort, she bowed her head in thanks.

4

Cut Off From The Dream

The inhabitants of Highrealm needed sleep, but for different reasons from the Midrealmers. They didn't have physical bodies that relied on circadian rhythms and physiological processes to function. Rest was required because their minds required periodic intervals to process the deluge of information they were bombarded with while awake.

They had far more control over their cycles of wakefulness and sleep than Midrealmers. Soon after coming into existence, most Highrealmers could switch between the two states with ease. For that reason, it was difficult to elude someone's request for attention by pretending to be asleep, which was a shame.

Jarith had another reason to rest more often than zir brethren, of course, to feel closer to the young woman ze cared for.

Ze was sleeping when Maliah and her parents left their home to meet her new mentor. As usual, her surroundings were difficult to see, but ze was perhaps too excited to learn more about this Exalted Grand Priest Amun.

However, inexplicably, as soon as the door to the small sanctuary opened, Jarith found zirself awake. With great irritation, Jarith tried to return to the sleepful state. But try as ze might, ze could not return to zir dreams.

Frustration turned to embarrassment as ze wondered if something was wrong. Had ze forgotten how to rest? Trying to convince zirself that everything was fine, ze got into a relaxing energetic configuration—the High-realm equivalent of a comfortable position. Most High-realmers preferred the energetic equivalent of reclining while sleeping, however, there were those who swore by standing up. As they say, there are two types of people in the universe, and Jarith was of the reclining persuasion.

Once comfortable, ze eased into a state of relaxation without forcing the dreams to happen. Rest came easily, but when ze tried to transition to dreaming, ze popped back into wakefulness. This could only mean one thing: ze had been cut off from Maliah.

Jarith was just about to go into full on panic mode when ze sensed a notification on zir communications panel. Ze moved into an upright position. The message appeared on the screen when ze swiped at it, and the words were transmitted directly into zir mind.

"New message from Whun Miu. I have news. Come to the Ascension Project HQ as soon as possible."

Ze could have sworn that their leaders had agreed to establish a better name for their center of operations than HQ. Jarith wouldn't have been surprised if zir parent had overruled the decision in order to focus on "more practical concerns." Or just to be a jerk.

With a groan of annoyance, ze almost responded with an emphatic "No, how dare you ask me to come in on my rest day." But there was nothing to do here except study, and how could ze possibly study without knowing what had happened to Maliah?

Ze turned off the panel and the surface changed to a mirror of sorts. It wasn't actually a mirror, but a mirrored projection of Jarith's current chosen form. Today was a purple day, ze decided, changing zir head to hold a full mane of purple twists.

Once done, ze left and started down the Amandala rampway. With growing speed, ze zipped by others, who each said hello or "slow down, child" or "which young whippersnapper is running in these halls?" Unwilling to break the momentum, ze rushed across the central pavilion, narrowly avoiding an in-depth conversation with an elder about why every room of Amandala should have—but didn't have—a puloni calibrated to the proportional ebb of the Clandinian tides. Not only did Jarith not know what any of that meant, but zir concern was focused on getting this errand completed so ze could return to worrying.

The entrance to the project's headquarters was down another wide, rounded ramp and through a towering archway. At the top of the arch sat a pictorial symbol that was shorthand for the theorem to travel between worlds, called the Athu Aqatne.

As soon as ze entered, the energetics changed. The calm serenity of the upper levels was replaced by people rushing around, holding conversations, arguing over hypotheses, and talking loudly into their communication devices. The high energy wasn't even diminished by the wall installation simulating a beautiful day under a partly cloudy sky with a warm breeze running over a full meadow of grass.

Before ze could orient zirself to today's chaos, Whun Miu popped up from the sea of the Highrealm equivalent of cubicles.

"We found it!" they exclaimed, waving wildly. "Come look. We found it!"

Jarith had no idea what Whun Miu and colleagues had found, but their excited energy was enough to make zir curious. Ze bobbed and weaved through the throng of busy workers, then wound around the cubicle farm until ze reached their workstation.

"I hope you didn't call me here for something you could have just told me," Jarith said with a sly smile.

Whun Miu ignored the friendly jab and pointed at the screen in front of them, really an ultra-thin layer of projected energy that mimicked a screen. On it was the moving image of a woman. A very Midrealm-y looking woman.

Jarith didn't recognize her, although ze suspected why she was important. She was speaking, though no audio accompanied the visuals. Ze leaned closer to try to make out details of her surroundings, but the field of view was too narrow.

"Is that who I think it is?" ze asked.

"If you think it's the sacrifice, then yes," Whun Miu replied.

The sacrifice. Jarith's anticipated transfer to Midrealm required an energetically equivalent Midrealm soul to be transferred to Highrealm. Jarith hated the word sacrifice, though, because it reminded zir of the horrific task required of zir. This woman, whoever she was, would have to die.

"Do we have to call them—her—that?"

Whun Miu shrugged, unwilling to have this argument for the thousandth time.

"Speaking of which," Jarith continued, leaning closer and lowering zir voice, "any news on getting around the whole sacrifice thing?"

It was no secret that Jarith was appalled by what ze was expected to do. Even so, ze didn't want to appear uncommitted to zir role. To do so would bring unwanted attention to zirself.

"Jarith." Whun Miu sighed. They had explained this many times before but were willing to explain it as many times as was necessary. "There's only one way to avoid your task. But if she dies of natural causes, we'd have a limited window to make the transfer. Not to mention that it's completely unpredictable.

"You know as well as anyone the accuracy required of these calculations. Finding an equivalent energetic being was completely theoretical before now. And before you ask, we won't find another match, not statistically speaking."

"So, if I want to go to Midrealm, I'll have to . . ." Jarith couldn't make zirself say the words out loud.

Whun Miu was more than happy to finish the sentence and remind Jarith of zir miserable fate. "You have to kill this person within a short time of your transfer to Midrealm. If you don't, your energy will disperse. You'll return Highrealm, but not in one piece. By all definitions of the word, you'll be lost."

"Lost" in Highrealm essentially meant death. When someone was lost, their energy was no longer a discrete unit with its own consciousness. Though in theory, that energy should become available to create new beings, Highrealm scientists had long ago learned that was not the case. All the energy of consciousness not retained in discrete units—what some might call souls—instead became part of something the Highrealmers called the Source. Counter to its name, the Source was more of a destination because once energy entered, it didn't leave.

The only glimmer of hope was that, when a Highrealmer was lost, a minute portion of their energy didn't immediately travel to the Source. Scientists had developed a method to collect that energy and manufacture a new "child" from it. Jarith was one such child. These children were few, and obtaining sufficient energy for each manufactured child had taken longer than the last. By their most recent estimates, the Highrealmers could only create one more child before every life in Highrealm was lost.

With all that doom and gloom hanging over their non-physical heads, no one really had a problem with Jarith killing an innocent Midrealmer, especially since they weren't the ones who would be getting their metaphorical hands dirty. Jarith, on the other hand, had spent considerable effort trying to determine another way.

No luck on that yet, obviously.

"Anyway," Whun Miu trailed off, "this isn't the only reason I called you here."

"What else, then?" Jarith asked.

Whun Miu grimaced, and Jarith immediately regretted checking zir messages.

"Jukartis requested your presence," Whun Miu admitted.

Any joy in Jarith's demeanor left zir in that moment. Jukartis, Jarith's parent, had called for zir.

This day was about to get much worse.

As Maliah left the preliminary session with her new mentor and headed toward the main temple to volunteer her time, her heart felt light. It was the first time in ages, and she welcomed it.

The weight of acknowledging her role in the Ascension Four prophecy had loomed over every aspect of her life, especially so for the past few weeks. Yet her first lesson with her new mentor brought her a slight comfort about her destiny.

"Prophecy guides our circumstances, but not our choices," ze had said.

If she was stuck with prophecy, she needed to accept it. Even so, she didn't have to let it control her life. She could make choices that seemed right for her.

She wondered if Jarith would have understood Amun's words. Did Jarith also feel like ze was living under a mountain threatening to crush zir at any moment? Unlike her, Jarith seemed fully dedicated to zir role in prophecy. She couldn't hear zir thoughts, but she saw it in the vigilance ze put into zir responsibilities. In some ways, she envied zir devotion to such a dangerous destiny. Jarith's people were hard at work finding a way for zir to travel to Midrealm, where ze would join the spiritual caste as her partner. Then, they would have a child, and—and what? The prophecy didn't say what else she was meant to do.

Her mother had told her that she'd dreamt of Maliah's future. In it, she was powerful, diligent, and just. These were acceptable qualities in an Exalted Grand Priest, in a leader for her people. But Maliah would have preferred happy, carefree, or even content. If she was destined to be with Jarith, would they be joyful? Or would she drown in a pool of her copious responsibilities?

There had to be more to her life than the prophecy, a hidden purpose. Her inability to understand most of what she experienced of Highrealm made these unknown parts of her destiny even more frustrating. If she was supposed to learn something from her time there, she was failing spectacularly.

She refocused her mind on Amun's message.

Jarith was a kind, honest, and intelligent person, which was enough for her. It gave her a sense of security that enabled her to concentrate on her available choices and those that were meaningful to her. That sense of empowerment excited her. Her feet seemed to float as the heavy burden on her future lessened.

As she reached the doorway to an inner hall, she heard her name, but it wasn't someone calling out to her. Because, of course, something needed to come along to ruin her good mood.

"—can't believe Maliah is training with Exalted Grand Priest Amun. What a joke."

The voice was one of a Young Priest. Maliah couldn't see them, but it wasn't the first time she'd overheard one of these private conversations in public areas.

"I can't believe the special treatment she's getting over some vague prophecy. So what? She'll have a baby. So will the rest of us."

"The Huleay Temple is obviously not concerned about the prophecy. They just don't want to upset her parents. It's simple favoritism."

The group murmured in agreement. It sounded like three or four young girls, but Maliah didn't care to find out.

She turned and walked away. She didn't need to hear more. They'd move on to how rude she was when she corrected the errors of authority figures. Next, they'd accuse her of thinking she was better than them when she actually just didn't know how to make friends. They'd all eventually agree to give her the cold shoulder, as if they hadn't done that all her life.

She knew the inevitabilities of this conversation because she'd heard it before. It was hard to blame them for thinking she wasn't enough. After all, she didn't believe she could live up to her parents' reputations. Why expect it from others?

Of course, there's no excuse for gossiping. It's petty and not intended to help anyone. It wasn't as if she was the only person these girls gossiped about, but that was no consolation to Maliah.

Suddenly, the idea of volunteering her time despite having no duties to perform that day seemed less than ideal. So she navigated through side passages toward the entrance to the inner Huleay Grounds, doing her best to avoid others.

The grounds were vast, with lush gardens for different ritual and social purposes, a scattering of administrative buildings, sanctuaries, and random ponds scattered throughout. While many areas were off limits to the public, much was accessible to everyone. The closer Maliah came to the main entrance, the harder it was to find an empty path.

"Excuse me," an old woman said as she passed her.

Maliah stopped to acknowledge her.

"You're Priest Maliah, of the prophecy, right?" the woman asked.

"Yes," Maliah answered with a nod. There was nothing else she could think of to say, and it seemed inappropriate to start crying, which is what she wanted to do.

"Can you tell me, please, what will ascension be like for my children? I'll be in the afterlife, but will I see them again?"

The prophecy failed to give specific details about what ascension meant, so Maliah shared the Huleay Temple's hypothesis on what happened when someone in Midrealm died. She knew this was incorrect, but the truth eluded her.

She said, "Ascension will give purpose to your afterlife. You and your family will be together and fulfilled."

"That sounds lovely," the woman said. "It must fill you with pride to know that you will give our people purpose."

Pride . . . sure.

Maliah forced a smile and excused herself, returning to her attempt to escape destiny for the rest of the day.

5

Jukartis and the Last Child

Jarith didn't care what zir parent was saying on eir call, nor did ze care which political pawn ey was attempting to persuade. It was the act of eavesdropping itself that brought contentment to zir. This was because Jukartis had rarely allowed Jarith any privacy. Zir quarters were full of sensors to ensure that ze acted in accordance with eir will. So Jarith felt no guilt as ze paused outside Jukartis's office and listened in.

"So you're saying the Ascension Project is responsible for fulfilling this Midrealm prophecy?" asked the hologram standing on the desk.

Oh, ey was letting a new pawn in on their little secret.

"That's correct. It's been our focus since our scientists discovered Midrealm," Jukartis replied.

The powers that be had long ago learned about the Midrealm prophecy and recognized the opportunity it brought to solve their population troubles.

However, it was only relatively recently that the Ascension Project, led by Jukartis, had used Highrealm's advanced technology to enhance the powers of two Midrealmers. It was one of the few influences that Highrealm could impose upon its more physical counterpart. By jump-starting the events foretold in Midrealm's prophecy, they hoped to solve their own crisis.

This was why Jarith hated using the word prophecy when speaking about the Ascension Project. It was an elaborate deception to cover up some questionable choices, choices that were out of Jarith's control and made zir non-existent blood boil.

In order to quell any opposition from the Highrealm population, small as it was, Jukartis had insisted that leadership present the project's experiments to the public as a prophecy from a lost scientist. This prophecy was revealed as a revelation that would fix their population woes. The ploy had worked, but newly appointed representatives—such as the one Jarith could just make out from zir vantage point—had to be onboarded once in a while.

"This is incredible," the political pawn said. "I knew the Ascension Project was working to fulfill the prophecy within our limited time constraints, but I didn't realize how much we've been responsible for. It's a scientific miracle."

"I don't believe in miracles," Jukartis replied, "but I'm quite proud of our accomplishments. And we're getting close to several key milestones."

"Congratulations," the pawn said. "What an achievement! What can we do to support you?"

"Support is all we need. That is, the public's support. The timeline is tight, and a public outcry against us could delay our progress and potentially destroy our chances of success."

"Understood. Now, if I may . . ."

Jarith chose this moment to enter the room. Ze had the overwhelming urge to inform this pawn of the less savory truths regarding the Ascension Project. But more so, hearing anyone praise Jukartis was a surefire way to anger zir.

It was all Jarith could do to remind zirself that Maliah could be watching. She already had a difficult enough time accepting their shared fate. It wouldn't be right to worry her by incurring Jukartis's wrath.

Jukartis looked up at Jarith with a furrow on eir projected brow. Eir long red hair was pulled back into a knot that trailed down eir back. Ey projected an androgynous bipedal form with maroon skin and three bright yellow eyes.

The tunic ey wore conveyed a sense of diplomacy, a complete farce from Jarith's perspective. Ze often joked inwardly that Jukartis had a crown somewhere that ey would start wearing at some point. Such was the hubris of Jarith's parent.

"Jarith," Jukartis said in a warning tone. "It's polite behavior to knock."

"I afford you the same courtesy that you provide me," Jarith replied.

This was awkward, mostly for the pawn.

"It appears you have matters to attend to," the pawn said. "We shall talk again soon."

"Yes. Goodbye," Jukartis said.

The hologram dissipated into glowing energy that then faded away.

"How is your counterpart?" Jukartis asked, leaning back in eir chair and placing eir hands together.

The question wasn't intended to show any interest in Maliah as an intelligent, caring young woman. Jukartis saw the Midrealmers as objects, more pawns in an endless game of survival.

"Maliah is well," Jarith replied. Ze was too used to being forced to share these details to argue about it. "She had her ritual into adulthood yesterday, and today she began training with an Exalted Grand Priest."

"A waste of time," Jukartis spat. "Her power will remain negligible until you awaken it."

"Her parents felt it was important."

"Then why are they not training her themselves? There is no evidence of other beings of Midrealm with powers comparable to the first generation pair that we activated." Jukartis stressed the word "we" as if Jarith was naive to zir history.

Jarith didn't have an answer for eir question. Ze knew nothing about this mentor, although ze was beginning to suspect that Amun was somehow responsible for cutting off zir dream. This was an unfounded yet perceptive suspicion, grounded only in the timing of the phenomenon itself.

"Maybe you should tell them that yourself," Jarith said sarcastically.

Jukartis opened eir mouth to reply, but Jarith interrupted.

"We need to discuss this sacrifice thing," ze said.

"Ah, so you heard. Wonderful news, isn't it? All the pieces are finally falling into place."

"I don't want to kill anyone," Jarith said. "There must be another way."

"Well, if you prefer, you can always force yourself on the girl before you are lost."

"How dare you!" Jarith growled.

Jukartis laughed and said, "It's amazing how attached you've become to these lesser beings."

It took everything Jarith had not to attack. Ze knew it wouldn't change anything, but it was still difficult to hold back.

"Maybe if you were being forced to kill someone for an experiment, you'd understand."

"Jarith, our entire universe is at stake," Jukartis reminded zir, "and if you'll remember from your studies, when a being in Midrealm dies, their soul remains trapped in their bodies. The lucky few that are freed instead wander with no purpose. The Ascension Project offers them something more, just as it's going to solve our population issue. We're doing them a favor. If that means taking a few lives, I would gladly do it myself."

Jarith was well aware of Jukartis's cruelty, and the discussion was going nowhere. This conversation wasn't worth the trouble.

"Anyway," ze said, "you called for me?"

"Ah, yes," Jukartis said, eir sly smile stretching across eir face much further than it should have. "I have more good news. The Last Child is almost complete."

While Jarith was watching Maliah pace before meeting her mentor for the first time, Jukartis had received a communication from the research group responsible for monitoring Highrealm's spiritual energy reserves. They had reached optimal levels and could start the process of organizing the collected energy into a conscious being. All they needed was eir command.

Ey had commanded it post-haste.

Now that Jarith was aware that the process was almost complete, zir mind went a million places. This was Highrealm's final opportunity to create a child before they were all lost. Zir parent had a plan in place for the child, just as ey had planned for Jarith. However, those plans had never been shared with zir.

Jarith followed Jukartis deeper into the bowels of Amandala's core, then through a maze of passageways that appeared to be made from rock. It was an odd choice in decor, but it was intentional. Jarith confirmed this by trying to use zir will to change its appearance. Though many elements of Highrealm could be personalized in this way, the brutal rock formation remained as is.

These crazy cakes had actually wanted these halls to feel dark and gloomy. Jarith had no doubt this was a Jukartis Original Design, title case required.

When they at last entered an auditorium, Jarith noted it was underwhelmingly empty, with less than thirty seats filled. On a central stage sat a pod connected by a tangle of wires to three different monitoring stations. The pod was undersized for someone of Jarith's size, but ze assumed it was bigger on the inside.

Jukartis leaned nearer to Jarith and pointed to the pod, whispering, "The Last Child."

Jarith followed em to seats at the back of the auditorium, where they sat and waited.

"What's happening?" Jarith asked after an unbearable stretch of silence.

"The collection process is complete, so they've transferred the energy to the structuring pod."

What a creative name for a pod meant to structure energy into a being, Jarith thought.

"The scientists wanted to have a ceremony, so I promised we would come to witness their achievement," zir parent continued.

"I see," Jarith said, but ze didn't, actually. So ze followed that up with, "And why is the pod so small?"

"We took a different approach for this child than we did for you and the others," Jukartis explained. "Since you were all going to be integrated into Highrealm society, we saw no reason not to structure you as fully formed beings."

"But this child won't be integrated into our society?"

"No, it won't," Jukartis said simply.

Jarith had no idea what that meant, but it couldn't be good. Ze started to ask for more details, but was immediately interrupted.

"Good people of Amandala," a being called out from the platform. "Welcome."

They were a radially symmetric being with four arms and two tentacles, color fading from their orange body to red distally. They didn't have an expressive face, but their gestures were wildly emotive, and they exuded their emotions energetically so that all in the room could understand.

"Since the birth of our previous child," they said, gesturing at Jarith.

Everyone looked, and Jarith gave a small wave. A few people clapped, and as they stopped, another couple of people tried to join in. It was awkward for everyone.

"We've all hoped to avert the extinction of our people. With Jarith, we succeeded in creating a child that flourishes in Highrealm and will fulfill zir responsibilities of prophecy in Midrealm.

"However, we face a crisis. As our numbers fade, so does the nascent energy that we harness to create our children. Our team has optimized the collection procedures, and we are able to present the results of our efforts to you today."

Those in the audience—fellow scientists mostly—cheered, and Jarith clapped, trying to at least appear supportive despite a burgeoning sense of dread and a growing list of questions.

Next, the speaker welcomed guests, one after another, onto the stage: a poet, then several musicians, and then a storyteller.

The storyteller summarized the technical information of the scientists' efforts as if it was the most exhilarating tale of its time, which it wasn't. However, then the story turned its focus to the child.

"The Last Child will be born of light and of darkness, of Highrealm and of Midrealm, and will traverse the in-between while bridging the wall between our worlds and our hearts."

Jarith sat forward, intrigued, but the story continued in riddles.

"There, the Last Child will create and destroy, build and break down, come and go. The result will be a new cycle of life, death, and rebirth never seen in either reality but somehow possible when the universes meet and synergize."

"What are they talking about?" Jarith asked in a whisper.

Ze hadn't really expected an immediate answer, but surprise!

"Why, a pocket reality, of course," Jukartis said.

Jarith wasn't sure ze had heard Jukartis correctly. Ze could swear zir parent had just said something about a pocket reality. These were theoretical bubbles outside of normal space-time where the laws of Nature could be manipulated. The key word there was theoretical.

Jukartis refused to answer any further questions as the scientists and their guests continued treating the birth of the Last Child like some kind of sparsely attended spectacle. For almost any other occasion, Jarith would have been content to watch and enjoy the festivities. But something seemed amiss. Ze struggled to concentrate, zir mind wandering to any wild possibility that came along.

Finally, the lead scientist returned to the stage.

"Thank you all for your attention," they said. "And now, I'd like to present to you our newest child, Jaalam."

The pod hissed, and a thick vapor flowed out from the sides. Two scientists each grabbed a handle, and together, they lifted the top from its housing, revealing a figure that Jarith recognized. Ze didn't specifically recognize the child, but the form that the child had taken was obvious.

It looked like a Midrealm child. Maliah had looked similar when she was a few years old. Ze breathed a sigh of relief. Obviously, the scientists had designed this child to more closely match what was expected for a Midrealmer. Perhaps they had somehow utilized the physics of a pocket reality in order to achieve it, Jarith concluded.

This was wishful thinking and entirely false.

Jukartis stood, and Jarith followed as ey headed into the aisle. However, instead of heading toward the stage as Jarith had expected, Jukartis turned to exit the auditorium.

"You don't want to meet the child?" Jarith asked.

"I merely came in support of the scientists, and I brought you along for the same reason. There's no reason to waste my time."

"What are you talking about? Can you please tell me what is going on?"

"The child won't be socialized in Highrealm for very long. Once we are certain that everything has been prepared appropriately, we'll send it on its way."

Jarith's anger boiled over. Ze was tired of getting the runaround. Ze rushed in front of zir parent, throwing zir arm out and holding em in place.

"Jarith," Jukartis said in a warning tone.

"What are you planning to do to the Last Child, to Jaalam?" Jarith demanded.

With a flick of eir wrist, Jukartis freed emself from Jarith's power, and with a glance, ey threw Jarith against the wall. Zir energy was constricted. Ze couldn't move. In an instant, Jukartis was mere inches from Jarith's face. Try as ze might, zir parent had zir pinned against the rocky wall.

"Child," Jukartis hissed. "You will never use your power against me again. You will ask your questions and receive your answers as I see fit."

The invisible pressure threatened to crush Jarith, but ze refused to cry out in pain. Ze wouldn't give Jukartis the satisfaction.

"I sense your anger, child," Jukartis said. "Have I taught you nothing of emotional control? You could rip your form from existence if left unchecked."

"What are you going to do to him?" Jarith burst out with the last of zir energy.

Jukartis laughed. "Him? You're personifying it. Jaalam is a tool, a mechanism to bring order and life back to our universe."

Jarith was dimming, zir energy fading to nothingness. It was hard to remain present, to hold onto the projection of zirself.

"Once we are sure it will survive," Jukartis explained, "we'll transfer the child to a pocket reality. And as soon as that's done, you'll be transferred to Midrealm. The child will live in solitude until your offspring is born, who we will also transfer to the pocket reality. That's all you need to know."

The grip on Jarith's being loosened, and ze dropped to the floor.

"Stand up," Jukartis said.

Easier said than done. Jarith felt fractured, and zir thoughts were fixated on retaining zir projected form. It was an experience more painful than was possible with human nociception because it was as if Jukartis had reached into zir soul and shredded it into ribbons.

"I said STAND," Jukartis commanded.

With every ounce of effort ze had and a resolve ze didn't know existed, Jarith complied. Jukartis's firm grasp on the science of reality translated into a strength of power Jarith couldn't hope to match. But every act of cruelty left a mark inside zir.

Yet Jarith's mind wasn't on zir own suffering. Zir very being twisted in knots at the Last Child's future. The Highrealmers planned to condemn an innocent child to isolation, just as they had condemned Jarith to the fate of a murderer.

Ze thought of the long night between birth and zir first encounter with Maliah. She had brought with her a light that burned brighter than any collection of photons. Now, hardening zirself against Jukartis's cruelty, ze chose zir own path, a path of kindness and love.

The Highrealmers had forced the prophecy into reality. Jukartis would have Jarith believe ey was powerful enough to change fate. But as Jarith glared into eir three yellow eyes, ze knew that this was destiny.

And ze intended to destiny like it had never been destiny-ed before.

6

Six Years, Six Lunar Cycles, and Six Days Later

Six years, six lunar cycles, and six days later, Maliah again sat on a chair in the smallest sanctuary of the Huleay Grounds. Across from her, Amun again sat on the ground with legs crossed and holding a covered tray.

Ze pulled three objects from the tray and told Maliah to choose. These tests had become a common occurrence, popping up at random intervals of her studies. Sometimes, months would pass between them, but once, Amun had brought in items two days in a row. However, like every other time she had done this, she sensed nothing from the items. Instead, she made a logical choice: a mirror.

Amun never provided a method for this decision, and she was never certain what task Amun would ask of her once she chose. Sometimes, ze just asked her to hold the item. Other times, ze instructed her to stare at it. Maybe those were days when she'd chosen wrong.

But most often, Maliah was expected to complete an exercise with the object. One time, her selection of a v-shaped artifact had required a two-hour ritual. In the end, the artifact turned out to be a simple knife-sharpener. Because of that, Maliah had formed a strategy for these decisions. Namely, she chose the object with—in her opinion—the least likelihood of requiring a complicated procedure.

Aside from the mirror that Maliah chose, Amun had presented a children's toy—a ball on a string connected to a paddle—and a large coin used in rituals to collect intentions from those who held it. She didn't wish to play with the toy, and she could only imagine horrible things from dealing with an intention-laden coin.

Thus, the obvious choice was the mirror. What else would ze ask of her than to look in it? Even if it reflected something horrific, it was still a simple mirror that she could put down when her task was complete.

Amun rarely repeated an item once she chose it, though she never questioned how ze obtained so many new artifacts. It was possible that many of these objects were merely random items Amun had collected on zir travels, but if they were, ze had never admitted it.

"Pick up the mirror," Amun said.

It was far heavier than it looked. She gripped it with both hands to hold it steady. The reflection was dark, and as she moved it closer to her, she realized she could see through it. Turning it over, she verified that the back was solid metal.

"What do you see?" Amun asked.

She tilted the mirror this way and that. "I think I can see the room through it," she said, then added a qualifying, "sort of."

"Anything else?"

Tilting it back down to the seats, she paused when she saw movement. She leaned toward it, then checked the room without the mirror. Verifying the difference, she stood and took careful steps forward.

"There's a string," she said, squinting her eyes as if that would help.

"A string?" Amun asked.

"Yes."

"What do you think it is?"

"I'm not sure. Perhaps a connection of some sort? It's pulsing, as if something is passing through it."

As she neared the string, it seemed to pull apart, showing her it was made of many smaller fibers just like a physical string. She sensed that the string wanted her to pull at the fibers and manipulate it somehow.

Reaching out to touch it, her hand went right through.

"Can you see where it ends?" Amun asked.

She followed the string to the main entrance of the sanctuary. Instead of leaving to follow it further, she turned around and walked along it in the other direction. The closer she got to it, the sharper it appeared. It was golden and as thin as a silk fiber, even thinner when it unwound itself. She soon found herself standing in front of her mentor.

"You're at one end," she said. "The other end is outside the sanctuary. Should I see where it leads?"

Not that she wanted to follow the mysterious string. She was very happy to stay right here and continue their lessons, which had become an empowering home for her to develop her knowledge.

"No. That's quite enough." Ze put out their hand for Maliah to return the mirror.

"What is it?" she asked as she handed it back. "The string, I mean. Do you know? Is it something you should be worried about?"

"Not at all," ze assured her. "It's a spell, one that I cast several hours ago. It's still in its maintenance phase. You remember the phases of a spell, correct?"

"Yes. First come the preparation and the enactment phases. After a spell is cast, there's a variable maintenance phase, during which the spell is actively transmuting the environment. Then, during the residual phase, after effects of the spell may be felt."

"Very good," Amun said, sounding impressed although zir face was as stern as ever. "Your studies are going exceptionally well. Once your powers awaken, you'll find the burden of training lessened by your diligence."

"If I ever actually get powers."

"They will come," Amun assured her. "They are destined to, though I sometimes get the feeling you don't want them."

It was true. Maliah had grown in her knowledge and confidence, however, instead of learning to accept her role in the prophecy, she dreaded it more than ever. The burden of responsibility and her imminent failure made her sick.

"Maliah, what did you feel while you were visualizing the string?" Amun asked.

She took a long moment to consider the question. Mostly, she had merely seen the string. She hadn't considered any physical sensations that came along with it. However, now that she focused on it, she did remember a tingling, though she couldn't work out where the feeling originated.

When she told Amun as much, ze said, "That's quite normal at your current level of ability. I'm impressed that you honed in on that feeling and described it."

"So, that mirror tracks the source of a spell?"

"Yes. That's exactly what it does," Amun said with pride. "Or should I say, that's what I designed it to do."

"Wait," Maliah said. "You created that artifact? You can do that?"

Amun laughed zir strange, stern laugh at Maliah's amazement.

She had seen her mother recharge artifacts before, but she didn't remember her ever creating an original one. She also didn't recall anything called "Meta's Comb" or "Meta's Lucky Dice" or whatever.

Did this mean that Amun was more powerful than her mother? Was that even possible without everyone in the temple knowing it? The thought rattled her, though she wasn't sure why.

"Of course I can," Amun replied. "Where do you think our artifacts come from? Almost every one was created by Exalted Grand Priests."

"I just thought artifacts were really old and created by dead people," Maliah replied, feeling a bit embarrassed at her own naïveté, though obviously not enough to hold her tongue.

Amun gave a vague nod of zir head, as if ze was considering the idea.

"Historically, very few priests have had magical abilities as strong as your parents and I. We are truly blessed at the Huleay Temple to have accumulated so many artifacts. So, I can see how it might seem as if creating them is a lost art, but I am happy to dispel such a myth."

"Will you teach me how to make artifacts?"

"I've already taught you many of the concepts needed to create them, but the practice will come when your powers awaken."

"Of course," she said begrudgingly. "My powers."

The mirror she had just used seemed useful, but Amun had never mentioned it before. Now that she thought about it, since she started training with Amun, ze had often introduced her to obscure yet remarkable items.

Most of the artifacts used by the Huleay Temple were actually mundane, at least once one knew the trick to them. Hidden compartments, chemical reactions, and tricks of the eye were the basis of most of the so-called magic conducted by the spiritual ruling caste.

It was this way out of necessity, according to Amun. People with magical gifts were rare, but there were always people who needed the sense of purpose that the Temple provided. In order to retain the people's respect, the Huleay Temple had to empower followers who lacked their own magic.

Thus, they had expanded their study of magics—what in Highrealm they referred to as science or mathematics or a whole slew of other fancy words—to find patterns of Nature that could be used either in service of the people or in service of keeping the Temple in power. It was a candid lesson that Maliah had been surprised to receive.

If a child showed any magical ability, the Huleay Temple conscripted them with haste to begin training. Her parents were the most recent children to have gone through this process. Despite being brought into the Temple later than most spiritual caste children, both had become Exalted Grand Priests by the time they were twenty years old.

Amun had been a priest far longer than her parents, although Maliah didn't know how much longer. Perhaps ze was also planning to teach her parents how to make artifacts.

"Do others know you've created artifacts?" Maliah asked Amun.

"Only the Exalted Grand Priests know," Amun said simply.

Maliah had come to recognize that Amun's usual stern expression was an indication of a somewhat playful mood. The look that Amun now held was pretty much the same, but after years under zir tutelage, Maliah now recognized the nuanced change in zir features.

Amun's voice was gravely serious.

"Maliah, you're getting access to this knowledge because you'll one day be an Exalted Grand Priest in our Huleay Temple. It's important that you understand your history because you'll be even more powerful than your parents."

"How do you know that?" she asked, a sudden panic clear in her voice.

She didn't wish to be that powerful. With that kind of power, everyone would expect perfection from her. And it was impossible to be perfect.

Amun had also frequently made it clear that she was expected to conceal the extent of whatever power she would possess. More than anything else—more than a fated partner from another universe, more than becoming far too powerful, more than potentially disappointing her people—she despised the idea of hiding her powers from people who needed them.

Many desperate for help arrived on pilgrimages to the Huleay Grounds of Ar. She had seen Priests give prayers and charms to followers. She couldn't bear the thought of knowing she could do more, but being compelled to hold back that help.

It would be better to be devoid of power.

"How do you know how powerful I'll be?" she asked her mentor again.

"The prophecy has become clearer," ze said. "We know more now. For instance, I know you've been having dreams and have been lying to us."

All her muscles stiffened, and she drew in a sharp breath.

"And I know the name of your beloved."

She waited, hoping beyond hope that ze would guess wrong. Maybe Gideon. Oh! What about Quay? That was a nice, strong name.

Instead, Amun clearly stated, "Jarith."

Maliah couldn't move. Her mentor, and likely her parents, apparently knew everything. They knew her secret, that she was seeing Jarith in her dreams, and they knew her future, that she would be more powerful than her parents. She wasn't sure which terrified her more.

Her grip on the seat of her chair tightened, and her jaw hurt as she clenched it closed.

Thoughts spiraled out of control. Did they think she was hiding her power, too? Were they going to expect her to do impossible tasks? Would she be forced to embarrass herself in front of her parents, or worse, in front of her people?

"Maliah," Amun said, zir voice so low that the echoes of the room didn't hear it.

She gathered her courage and looked up into zir eyes. Instead of anger or disappointment, zir stern gaze was tinged with worry.

"I'm sorry I didn't tell you," she said, fighting her frozen body to say each word.

"You don't owe us that," Amun assured her. "You and Jarith share a special bond, and that is your own private business. I can't speak for your parents, but I'm not upset. You arrive every day, do your best, and appreciate the knowledge you're being granted. I brought this up because I know the truth, and I don't want to hide that from you any longer."

"I don't have any power," Maliah insisted. "I swear it."

"Yes. I'm aware. My tests don't rely on your honesty." Ze paused, and the tension in the room built.

It was the kind of tension that, if allowed to continue, would get awkward, but which is very difficult to break. Amun took on the challenge.

"If you want to discuss anything, I'm here," ze said. "I understand it may seem daunting to discuss things with your parents. Therefore, I vow to keep our discussions confidential."

Maliah forced an accepting smile, but her soul wasn't comforted. The end of her innocent days was nearing, and she had delayed her true start of night as long as possible.

"Do you still believe I have the power of choice?" she asked.

"I believe as I've told you before, yes. Prophecy is a powerful tool, but it never contains all the details. That is impossible because our every choice is a drop in the ocean of possibilities. All prophecy does is identify points of convergence across timelines."

Ze held up the index finger of both hands. Slowly, ze moved them around in random patterns.

"Your parents were destined to meet. But individual choices made in every moment create a dynamic system of randomness."

"Stochasticity, right?" Maliah asked.

Amun had taught her that word, and while she didn't understand its exact meaning, she understood it had to do with randomness.

"Exactly so. The stochasticity of existence leads to many parallel paths, but those paths converge . . ." Ze brought zir index fingers together. ". . . at points of destiny. Your parents could have met anytime in their childhood, but they were destined to meet."

"Then how do I have any choice?" The question came out with more desperation than she intended, but she couldn't take it back. Maybe there was a parallel path where she kept her composure.

"Dear Maliah, your life is about your choices. Prophecy can only predict points of convergence, accumulations of choices. Each individual choice is your own."

"The prophecy says Jarith will travel here and we'll have a child," Maliah said.

"Does it say that you'll love Jarith? Or when you'll give birth? Or under what circumstances?"

"Well, no."

Maliah didn't like what Amun was suggesting. She had seen Jarith living zir life. She knew zir, and she trusted zir. Her heart was torn between wanting to be with zir and wanting to delay the prophecy, but that wasn't because of Jarith. It was her own insecurity.

"But Jarith wouldn't hurt me," she continued.

"Jarith is dedicated to fulfilling prophecy," Amun said.

"Does the prophecy dictate how you will raise your child?" Amun asked.

"I'm expected to raise her for prophecy," Maliah argued.

"But you have a choice," Amun said. "You will choose to raise her for prophecy. Or you will choose to give her freedom."

Maliah wanted to believe Amun. She wanted to have some level of control over her life. Pushing away doubts, she nodded her agreement and lied.

"I understand. Thank you."

That didn't mean she didn't have questions.

"Amun, regarding the prophecy, there's something that I've always been confused about." She took a small corner of her dress and twisted it between her fingers. "What is the point of the Ascension Four prophecy?"

She knew the Huleay Temple's hand-wavy explanation, but it had never sat right with her. She wanted the truth.

Why were dreams an important part of the prophecy? What was the connection with Highrealm? Why did it take four generations to fulfill?

Surely, Amun could provide the answers she needed.

"What is ascension?" she asked when Amun didn't respond.

Amun had always encouraged her to ask questions, and ze had never refused to answer her. Until now.

"That will be all for today," ze said, placing the items onto the tray and standing.

"You do know, don't you?" Maliah asked, taking steps toward zir when ze stepped away. "Amun!"

Ze paused, as if considering how to respond. Maybe ze even opened zir mouth to offer words of wisdom, but ze had turned away from her.

"Tell me. Please," Maliah pushed.

It was one push too far. Amun left the sanctuary, and Maliah didn't follow.

If Amun knew the truth, was ze not allowed to say it? And if it was forbidden, was ascension something unspeakably bad? Was she destined to bring the downfall of her people?

This kind of downward spiral often leads to irrational behavior and ankle inversions, both of which may have happened if Maliah's day had ended here.

But it didn't.

7

THE ASCENSION FOUR PROPHECY

As the transfer ceremony neared, Jarith found it difficult to concentrate on the preparations. All the proofs had been proven. All the calculations had been calculated. All the accomplishments had been celebrated. The only thing left was the unnecessarily elaborate ceremony where they'd send Jarith to Midrealm. That would start soon.

Jarith had solidified a projection consistent with Midrealm and should have felt prepared to live as a Midrealm man. After all, though he was still getting used to his new masculine pronouns, he wanted to be with Maliah. He longed to touch, to smell, to hear, and to see her with his new masculine body.

However, any joy he had about his coming transfer was dampened by the circumstances.

His first task upon arriving in Midrealm was to find and ceremonially kill the sacrifice. He would appear close to her location to make it easier to complete his task. Jukartis had insisted that he memorize her features, but Jarith was afraid her death would be burned into his memory. He couldn't accept it. He wanted another way.

Unfortunately, the Ascension Project team still didn't know how long he could exist in Midrealm without completing the sacrifice. Their best estimate was seven days, but they followed it up with a large confidence interval that rendered it useless. This unknown solidified the terror within him, the yearning to continue to exist. After all, his life was only just beginning.

But even these challenges failed to occupy his mind. He was consumed by a different ceremony, the recent one to transfer the Last Child, Jaalam, to a pocket reality.

At the ceremony, the scientists had spoken at length about the reality. It was semi-physical in nature, with weather, linear time, and natural resources. Jaalam would have to hunt and farm for food and prepare for cold and wet seasons. The creatures were non-sentient, so he would be alone, at least until Jarith's child was born.

It seemed an exceptionally cruel fate, and the Ascension Project team's pride in being a part of it sickened Jarith. He had wanted to save Jaalam from that place, to shelter and love him as Maliah's parents had done for her. Yet he'd done nothing.

Had Jarith had a stomach, it would have left him feeling nauseous. Instead, guilt, shame, and fear fought for space in his mind as he tried to focus on Maliah. He grasped for some semblance of a silver lining in this impossible situation.

He could barely believe he had allowed Jaalam's transfer to take place. But he was trapped in Highrealm, just as Jaalam was now trapped in the pocket reality. His only hope for escape was Maliah.

The thought left him troubled. Had he truly stood by only to save himself? If that was true, it changed everything about how he saw himself. He wasn't risking a transfer to save his people. He was escaping a prison to save himself.

His thoughts were interrupted by Jukartis. "It's time," ey said.

Jarith took his projected place on the projected stage in front of a crowd of projected beings, but he wasn't fully there. As speakers spoke and performers performed, Jarith was consumed with despair. Scientists scrambled around, preparing his pod for the upcoming procedure, as he wondered what would happen if it failed.

The procedure deconstructed his energy and transferred it to Midrealm. If it failed, he would be destroyed.

Part of him wished for that.

When instructed, he stepped into the pod. Through the transparent material, he saw the symbol of the theorem, the Athu Aqatne, labeling walls, platforms, and even inside his pod.

He had spent his entire life in service to the theorem and its supporting scientific theories, to the hope it held for his people. Perhaps his people deserved to go extinct. If they were willing to go to these lengths to ensure survival, what else were they capable of?

He sank deeper into melancholy as he questioned what he was capable of.

With everyone projecting smiles and many projecting cheers, the final projected button was pressed. Everything around him faded into bright, white nothingness.

The first sensation of Midrealm was heat. The sun on Jarith's skin was burning him. Wait, no, he wasn't on fire. Or was he?

Suddenly, the world seemed to spin, and he hit something with his bum. Spoiler—it was the ground. Not used to balancing a body against gravity, he'd fallen.

Everything around him was a dark red—not at all how it was supposed to be. He brought his hands up to his face, which he found with ease. His eyes were closed.

How to fix that? He concentrated on finding his eyes, and abruptly, they popped open.

It was so bright, it hurt. He covered his eyes as he closed them. Then, he slowly opened them again, allowing the light in incrementally. Despite the sandy earth beneath his rear, he refused to believe that he had fallen to the ground.

He had totally fallen to the ground.

Orienting himself to up and down, he rolled onto his stomach, his side burning as it pressed against the sandy earth beneath him. He flinched, but finished his roll. When he touched the skin under his shirt, he found dried blood and ink. It was part of the transfer process, but he hadn't realized it would hurt.

Slowly and methodically, he pushed himself to his feet. There was a wall nearby, and he fell against it for balance. After a few moments to get the feel for this standing up thing, he allowed himself to get distracted by his surroundings.

He was standing in the middle of a small pedestrian road, lined on both sides with mud-brick walls that were painted in reds, yellows, and blues. The colors were dazzling. Every reflected photon his eye and brain converted into an image was extraordinary.

Beyond the walls and up the hill, there was at least one enormous building. Framing two tall pillars were massive sculptures—likely five times his height—of two humanoid figures with animal heads. He had a vague understanding of Midrealm animals, but throughout his studies, he'd never seen anything like it, especially not so large.

Before fear could take over, he was distracted by the gate just in front of him. It was a few heads taller than him, made of wood stained a deep, rich brown, and finely engraved with symbols he didn't recognize. He assumed this was the home of the woman he was meant to kill.

Despite not having become a murderer in the last few minutes, he felt fine physically. His clothes felt weird on his body, and his body felt weird in his clothes. But there were no signs of losing his shape and dissipating into pure energy, though what signs one might expect, he wasn't sure.

He considered leaving and getting as far from this home as possible. However, he decided to peek at the place, just to say that he had.

The gate had a handle, but it didn't open with a simple push or pull. He placed his hand at its edge and slid it around, pushing small reverberations into the structure to see where it was stuck. He sensed the hinges on one side, and on the other, a physical locking mechanism.

With a mere thought, he moved pins out of place, unlocking it. It was a trivial matter of applying a force against them, just as he had applied a force against the wall to stand up. He pushed open the gate a crack and peered through. Far off voices drifted from within.

He crept inside and closed the gate behind him. Staying low and quiet, he slunk through a lush garden and over to a window of the house. Within, a man and woman sat on a couch. The room was a comfortable size, with several closed doors along the far wall. The couch wasn't alone. There were many pieces of furniture around the room, each ornately carved and finely adorned.

Jarith recognized the woman. She was the sacrifice.

"You've seemed weaker recently," the man said.

"I'm not as young as I used to be," the woman replied. "You worry too much."

"You would tell me if anything was wrong, wouldn't you?"

This didn't seem like a casual conversation to Jarith. He only half-listened as he tried to decide what to do.

If he barged in there now, he'd have to kill both of them. Cornering her when she was alone would be preferable, but where could he lie in wait? The walls surrounding the house were pretty high, so he couldn't really watch from a distance.

This wouldn't have been an issue with Highrealm technology. A simple psychic drone could transmit her activity. Or he could have used a biosensor to alert him when she was alone. From his limited understanding of Midrealm technology, nothing close to this was possible.

No, he'd have to do this the old-fashioned way—or whatever you call the way people do things in primitive worlds. Anyway, he would watch her carefully and wait for his chance.

Before he could make his retreat, a noise from behind startled him.

"Who's there?" a voice called.

Jarith whipped around to confront his opponent. With precise movements, he lifted his arm to lash out and silence the person.

Don't worry. He was planning to use non-lethal force. One murder was more than enough for him, but he also couldn't afford to let anyone keep him from reaching his goal.

He stopped mere inches from her neck, recognizing her curling locks, the golden skin, and every point of her face.

Her eyes were wide and her lips parted. She was beautiful.

"Jarith?" she asked.

Tears formed in his eyes, and he pulled in a quick breath to keep from weeping.

"Maliah," he said.

She threw her arms around him and buried her face in his neck. With as much gentleness as he could muster, he held her tightly against him.

He could barely think. Her smell was a mix of the incense burned throughout the Huleay Temple and of a fragrance she applied daily. The warmth of her skin was mesmerizing. Her soft, full hair brushed against his face. She seemed so small in his arms that, for a moment, he worried he had chosen too large a form.

He tried to find an explanation for her presence. The chances of such a coincidence were immeasurably small. There had to be more to it.

Perhaps she had sensed his arrival and come looking for him. It seemed a reasonable assumption at first, but then, how had she gotten through the gate? Had he failed to lock it behind him?

Yes, he had failed to do so, but that wasn't why she was here.

"I can't believe this is happening," he whispered.

Abruptly, she pulled away and stepped backward.

"Why **are** you here?" she asked. "How did I not know you were coming? How did you find my home?"

"Your home?" he asked.

She took a few more steps back. "And why were you looking through our window?"

Jarith's mind reeled as he tried to make sense of her words. But before he could even consider answering her questions, the nearby front door opened.

"Maliah, is something wrong?" a voice asked.

Jarith looked for somewhere to hide, but there wasn't time. The door was open, and the man from inside was looking right at him.

The man's eyes widened just as Maliah's had. In fact, many had commented on how similar Maliah's eyes were to her father's, which is who this was. But Jarith hadn't pieced that together yet.

"You're Jarith," Jua said. "Meta's dream was correct. You're here."

Jarith hadn't yet deduced who this was, but the man's voice sounded familiar. The Highrealmer's mind was moving slower than usual—the limitations of a Midrealm brain. But he wasn't a lost cause. He just needed time.

If this was Maliah's home, then this must be her father, Jua. But that would mean the woman he was tasked to kill was . . .

Maliah's mother?

Horror filled Jarith, and his stomach twisted into knots. This was impossible. The world seemed to spin, and he grabbed his head in an attempt to quell his vertigo.

"Come inside," Jua said with a complex smile that left Jarith wondering if the invitation was genuine. "Please," Jua added when he noticed Jarith's hesitation. "We welcome you with open arms. You're practically family."

"Dad!" Maliah hissed.

Jua laughed and stepped out of the doorway to welcome their guest into their home. Jarith couldn't think of anything else to do but follow Jua's guiding direction.

There she sat, the sacrifice, one leg tucked under her as she relaxed on a long wooden couch with a seat cushion made of animal hide. Her hair was pulled out of her face, but most of it cascaded over her shoulders. Her linen dress was embroidered with intricate designs of animals at the edge of a river. Gold and gemstone bracelets graced her arms, complementing the rings, necklace, and earrings she wore. Her presence demanded attention, which sat in contrast to the crooked smile she was giving him. It wasn't as complex as the smile Maliah's father had worn. Her smile made it clear she'd been expecting him.

His heart raced, and his throat went dry.

"Hello, Jarith," Meta said. "Welcome to Midrealm." Her smile turned to her husband as it morphed into something even more mischievous. "And you, my dear husband, owe me a drink."

Jarith didn't register her casual manner. He was far too distracted. Maliah's mother was the sacrifice, the woman that he was tasked with killing. If he didn't, he'd dissipate into pure energy, return to Highrealm without his consciousness intact, and lose his people's only chance to avoid extinction. But this was the woman who'd cared for Maliah all her life and who was a beacon of hope to her people.

The decision to kill her or to die himself was too heavy.

She urged him over and pulled him down to sit next to her. As she introduced herself and her husband, Jarith reviewed the home. The common room seemed larger than it had from outside, and he guessed that the doors around the room led to living quarters. The strategic placement of windows brought a breeze through the house with ease, keeping it fresh and airy.

"You look just as you did in my dream," Meta said. "The prophetic dreams get no less intimidating, you know."

He wasn't sure what she meant by this. Did she think he was intimidating?

She pointed to her husband, who was leaving the room to grab the wine she requested and looking quite unamused. "Jua didn't think you'd come this soon. He thought you'd wait until after Maliah's powers awakened."

"But you knew?" Jarith asked. "You saw that I was coming?"

"Yes, and I bet him one of his favorite wines that I would be right." She was smug, but in a playful way that set Jarith at ease.

He noticed Maliah standing just inside the front door, arms holding each other and lips tightly drawn. Despite it not being sensible, Jarith wondered if she knew the horrific task he was supposed to complete. It was unclear if she was aware of the sacrifice, though he'd tried to keep mention of it to her waking hours. Yet her gaze was unsure and somewhat cold. Could she somehow see through him?

"Do you drink wine, Jarith?" Meta asked.

"We don't need sustenance in Highrealm," Jarith said, turning his attention back to her.

"Well, you should try it tonight. You'll be staying with us here."

He considered arguing with her, as he didn't want to intrude. However, he needed to keep an eye on her, and he didn't have anywhere else to go. So, as she voiced that she was insisting, he gave a simple nod.

"Now, I really must know. How did you get here?" she asked.

His scientific explanation was incomprehensible to her, so, as Jua poured her the first cup of wine, he attempted to simplify the complex process.

"Imagine two different vibrations exist. One is Highrealm and the other is Midrealm. The process makes the traveler move at the right vibration so they can pass through the barrier between realities."

This interpretation was so simplified that it bordered on a lie, but it was the best he could do.

"Your people made that vibrational shift happen?" Meta asked as she relished a sip of wine.

"I'm the first," Jarith said. "It's taken us a very long time to engineer, but I'm here, so I guess it all worked out."

Meta offered everyone a cup of wine. Jua begrudgingly accepted, and Jarith tried a sip. It was very bitter, and he declined to drink more.

When asked, he went on to describe the Highrealm culture and the Ascension Project, leaving out his murderous intent. There are few ways to more effectively lose favor with your future in-laws.

Meta and Jua had many questions but none directed to Maliah. Jarith knew Maliah hadn't told her parents about him or Highrealm. But he was here now, so why was she still holding back?

Jarith walked the treacherous line between sharing what he had learned about Midrealm and not letting on just how long he and Maliah had shared lives through their dreams. It didn't help that Maliah was watching him with an intense gaze that he didn't know how to interpret. Had she even blinked? As if in response—but actually just because she needed to—she did blink, and he breathed a figurative sigh of relief.

"You've heard about our prophecy?" Jua asked when it came up in the conversation.

Jarith was used to speaking his mind freely in Highrealm, and he found lying troublesome. However, the one thing he was proficient at lying about was the Ascension Project and its underlying prophecy. That didn't mean he liked it, though.

"Yes, though I admit I don't know the details of your prophecy," Jarith answered.

"The core prophecy is quite concise," Jua said.

"Would you like to hear it?" his wife asked.

Jarith had never heard Midrealm's prophecy before, and he wondered if Maliah had. From an early age, she found the whole ordeal overwhelming, so it wouldn't surprise him if she knew every word by heart. As Meta began to recite it, a shiver ran through Jarith, and his skin tingled, as if something was pulling it tighter around him.

"Four generations, one mind.

"It begins with the sun. The sun sets, and with darkness come dreams. The visions of night come to those named. Visions—dreams—give glimpses into godliness."

She placed her hands in her lap, loosely holding her cup as she recalled the words.

"The first will arrive from beyond the Huleay Temple. Power not seen in many generations.

"The second will bring the traveler. Set the stage with brightness and wisdom.

"The third will carry the darkness. Creation of nothing among the everything.

"The fourth will make the connection. Ascension beyond Midrealm.

"Each generation requires a key, a lock, and a sacrifice. All are required for the spiritual evolution of Midrealm."

Meta opened her eyes and relaxed back into her seat, wiggling against a pillow behind her to find a comfortable spot.

"And that's it," she said with a smile.

"But it didn't mention any of you by name," Jarith pointed out.

"Over the years, we've received further information regarding the details of the prophecy. The priest who brought Jua and I to the Temple was a prophet who saw our names."

"And Meta foretold your arrival," Jua added.

"So random people just get glimpses into the future?" Jarith asked.

"No. It requires a level of magic only found in our highest level of priest, the Exalted Grand Priests. But there have been several among us whose visions have added value to our interpretations," Jua said. "Maliah's mentor, for example."

Jarith found himself tense at the mention of her mentor. He'd never been able to dream of Maliah when she was with zir, depriving him of precious time with her. Jarith might have a grudge against zir for this, although it wasn't something he would have admitted.

"Surely you and your people have more detail you could share with us," Jua said. "What's the prophecy in your realm like?"

Oh, great.

These two had a knack for asking difficult questions requiring not-so-subtle lies. Jarith felt torn between telling Maliah's parents that the whole prophecy was a sham and repeating the falsehoods he'd been forced to tell his people.

"Well," he said noncommittally.

Meta and Jua's eyes were locked on him, and Jarith realized that they'd been aching to ask about Highrealm's prophecy all evening. They'd skirted around the topic, and he'd just been too distracted to notice.

The idea of telling them the truth made him uneasy. If he told them Highrealm was responsible for fulfilling the prophecy, would they continue to believe he was there in good faith? How could they trust him if they couldn't believe in the prophecy? Maybe they'd send him away. Worse yet, they could convince Maliah to forget about him.

On the other hand, if he lied, how long would he be stuck living with it? He had hated lying to his people. He didn't want to doom himself to another life of perjury. This was supposed to be a fresh start. He longed to live a good, honest life here with Maliah.

Maliah let out a long groan.

"You have been pestering Jarith for hours," she said. "I'm exhausted. Let's stop this nonsense for tonight."

Jarith tried to make eye contact with her, to gain some understanding from her gaze. Was she genuinely tired of the conversation, or was she attempting to help him out of the troublesome situation?

"But—" Meta started.

"Maliah's right," Jua interrupted. "We haven't even eaten dinner yet."

"I'm not hungry," Maliah said. "I think I'll go to bed early."

"Are you sure?" Meta asked.

"Absolutely," Maliah replied before her mother could protest. She placed her hands to her forehead and bowed her head. "Blessed start of night."

"Blessed start of night," Jua replied before his wife could protest.

Without missing a beat, Maliah entered one of the attached rooms and closed the door.

It was then that Jarith realized one downside to being in Midrealm. He had become used to seeing Maliah's life, but now he was restricted to his own physical perspective. If he wanted to spend time with her, he'd need to earn her trust.

Like a normal person.

8

New Dreams of Sleep

Maliah leaned against the door as she closed it behind her. Her heart raced, and she felt light-headed. It probably wasn't the best idea to skip dinner. Her stomach grumbled its agreement, and she rolled her eyes at its betrayal.

Her mind was reeling. She'd dreamt of Jarith for as long as she could remember, and she'd wanted to be close to him—he had mentioned he was using male pronouns now. Yet, only after feeling his warm touch, smelling his fresh scent, and hearing his calm, gentle voice did it become real.

When she had seen him in the garden outside the window, she wanted to hold him and never let go, as if holding him meant holding on to her autonomy. She left his warm embrace fully aware she could no longer hide from the coming change. Even so, she wasn't ready. Not ready to get married, to have a child, to take on more

Temple responsibilities, or to do whatever else everyone expected from her.

Her mind wandered as she changed into a nightgown and retreated into bed. Magic hour lit the sky in blazing hot pinks, but the room was dark. A small lantern sat on a dresser nearby, but there was no way to light it. Her parents could light a flame with a spell, but the attendants regularly forgot that she was without these abilities.

With a sigh, she covered her head with her blanket, plunging herself further into darkness. She wondered if, when she fell asleep, she would see through Jarith's eyes.

When she thought of Jarith, her face felt hot. His form had been dynamic in Highrealm, and she'd never known how he would appear each night. Because of this, she had never associated him with a specific physical appearance, especially not one as masculine as his Midrealm form.

Instead, she'd become accustomed to what his energy felt like, and she had immediately recognized it when she encountered him. He exuded immense magical power, strong enough that she couldn't ignore it, however that power was contained within a timid wrapper that kept his energy from being oppressive.

But her mind wasn't focused on understanding how she'd so easily recognized him or even her surprise at seeing the dark, muscular form he had taken. It was something else that held her attention. When their eyes met the first time, his gaze had been consumed with longing.

She hadn't been prepared for his arrival, but if there was something she'd been especially unequipped to deal with, it was her body's sensual reaction to the look in his eyes. Despite hours of watching her parents barrage him with questions—which is a huge turnoff—the feeling was still fresh.

His dark brown eyes expressed complex emotions of caution, fear, and love. The firmness of his muscles had surprised her, and she had felt small in his arms. She ached to feel his lips on hers, to relax into his strong arms, and to lose herself in passion.

He was entrancing, and that terrified her.

She closed her eyes in the darkness and settled into a calming, distracting meditation with practiced intent. The gentle passing of time rocked her blissfully into sleep, soothing her mind with beautiful images of sunshine, flowers, love, and magic.

Unfortunately, a night of tender rest was not meant to be.

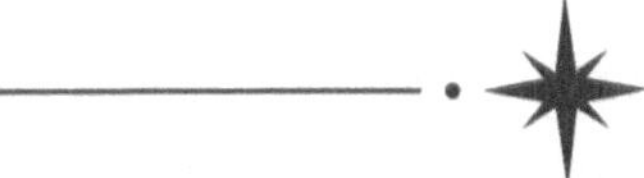

Sparks, flashing, dancing across an unseen surface.

Popping sounds, intermittently interrupting the long intervals of silence.

Flakes of ash, drifting upward in a spiraling cloud.

The earthy aroma of sage, strong and thick.

Flickers of flames, rising from the darkness with purpose. The intention to find.

But find what? Something? No. Someone.

A feeling of overwhelming dread as the heat from the fire rises. Burning.

Gusts of winds. Spirals of debris. Suffocating smoke.

All around. In front. Behind. Above. Below.

Inescapable.

Words.

A spell.

An ending.

A beginning.

After a tour of their property, Jarith had enjoyed a Midrealm meal with Maliah's parents. It was simple yet delicious. The texture of the food in his mouth, the process of chewing, and the sensation of swallowing all were new to him. It took him a few tries to perfect it.

Key lesson for the day: he could fit far more food in his mouth than he could swallow.

Somehow, he lived through the meal, and it was probably for the best that Maliah wasn't in attendance.

Afterwards, Jarith wandered up to their roof patio, where there was a couch and chair, a small table, and a rug. He leaned against the parapet as he looked out over the landscape. Up the hill, the silhouettes of Huleay Temple buildings were flattened against the outer wall of the grounds. The detail he was just getting used to faded with the dying light. Down below, lamps flickered from homes and businesses of the city of Ar. But above him, the sky was coming to life.

He had never considered how many stars could exist in a physical universe. And, according to the scientists of Highrealm, many stars had planets that contained life. In Highrealm, his people were aware of other beings beyond their borders but had always remained separated from them. He didn't know why, and he'd never questioned it either. But now, confronted with the vastness of the universe, the question weighed on his mind.

He heard steps behind him and turned to see Meta appearing from the stairs. She held an oil lamp with both hands, and the white stone walls of the lamp glowed, bathing Meta's face in warm light.

"Enjoying the view? It's not ideal at this time of night, I suppose," she said.

"You must be joking. It's amazing," Jarith replied, smiling with a genuine innocence anyone would have found adorable. "The city looks vast. How many people live here?"

"We had about 400,000 citizens at the last census." She placed the lamp on the small table before joining him at the parapet. "But the city of Ar is the center of the Huleay Temple, so hundreds of thousands of people travel here on pilgrimages each year."

"That's . . ." Jarith trailed off.

He didn't have a word to describe how overwhelming those numbers were. Jukartis had spoken of the Midrealmers as if they were an untapped, limitless resource to pull souls from. Jarith had regarded this as an exaggeration, but now, he wasn't so sure.

"And there are other nations, right? Outside of Ledine?" he asked.

"Yes, many. And this is only one city in our empire. Ledine is a vast territory stretching far beyond the horizon."

"I can't even imagine that many people," he whispered. "Maybe this is the answer, after all."

"The answer?" Meta asked.

He was hesitant to look away from the fading, picturesque view, but he looked over at Meta, who patiently waited for an answer to her question about an answer.

"In Highrealm, our population is fading. Soon, we'll be extinct."

"Hence why you're here, I suppose," Meta said in an odd, sly manner.

Jarith didn't know what to make of it.

He knew Maliah's mother had a strong playful streak and was rarely serious outside of her duties as Exalted Grand Priest. For example, once, when Maliah was a child, the young girl dawdled as they were crossing the street. A passing cart nearly ran her over, but it swerved out of the way just in time. Maliah was terrified and began to cry.

Meta had laughed, which only made Maliah cry harder.

"Maliah, love, don't you see?" Meta had said. "It's a sign from the spirits that you shouldn't wear white today."

Maliah had looked down, and through her eyes, Jarith had seen that her dress was covered in mud. She looked back at her mother as she knelt to meet Maliah's gaze.

"We can't have that, can we? How about we go get you a new dress?"

Maliah was laughing again in no time.

Thinking back, Jarith couldn't help but wonder if Meta had used her abilities to protect her daughter from a cart-ly demise? Or was she really that flippant? Earlier that evening, she had pushed him to answer questions about Highrealm, but her current crooked smile made Jarith wonder if she knew more than she let on.

"Yes," he replied. "Our population crisis is why I was sent here."

"I still don't understand the connection between your population issues and our spiritual evolution," Meta said. She laughed and added, "Disregard that. I made a bet with Jua that I could keep myself from pestering you for answers."

Her shoulders suddenly slumped, and she moved to sit on the bench. Jarith joined her.

"Well, instead of explaining that," he said. "I'd like to make my intentions clear. Because even though I was sent here with a purpose, I came here for Maliah."

"My, you are quite dedicated," Meta said, the glowing aura of her smile having faded without reason.

"I'm not sure about that, but I do know that your daughter is a unique person who has always inspired me."

She reached out and placed her hand on his knee.

"Me, too," she said.

Despite having seemingly run out of energy, her smile shone through. Its warmth permeated him and made him feel whole and loved. He wondered if this was part of her ability.

The human brain is an amazing thing. Sometimes, in the middle of a perfectly normal conversation, the human brain will pick the worst thought imaginable. What popped into Jarith's mind was the reminder that in order to survive, he would have to kill Meta.

The thought sent him reeling through every memory he had of his investigation into alternatives. Every avenue of inquiry had led to an unequivocal zilch. Nada. Nothing. Over time, the Highrealm scientists had begun shutting him down at the mere mention of the topic. Even his last hope, Whun Miu, had long ago given up on finding an answer.

But they hadn't really understood what they were asking him to do. None of them had known who he was preparing to kill.

The sacrifice was Maliah's mother: a funny, intelligent woman with the power to heal. She was a woman who dedicated her life in service to others. The idea of committing murder had been difficult to accept when the victim was a faceless stranger, but this? This was devastating.

There had to be another way.

"I worry about Maliah, though," Meta said as she shifted positions on the rooftop bench. "I know her destiny has always been difficult for her to accept. Now that you've arrived, I hope she can find her way to the path." Her wry smile returned. "Because believe me, if she doesn't, the path will find her, and it won't be fun."

"How do you know?" Jarith couldn't help but ask.

"That's what happened to me." She laughed. "I'm sure you know this, but prophecy doesn't always charge us with tasks we enjoy. Sometimes, it calls on us to do dreadful assignments for incredible reasons, and we complete them. Not because we're instructed to, but because it must be done."

"I don't understand," Jarith admitted.

"That's fine," she said. "Someday it'll all make sense. When it does, come reveal your epiphany to me, and I'll remind you that I was the one who informed you of it in the first place."

Jarith couldn't help but smile in amusement.

Meta leaned forward and pushed herself up to stand. She looked unsteady, but held her hand up when Jarith reached out to help her.

"Don't fuss," she said. "I'm just tired. It was a taxing day."

"At least let me help you down the stairs," Jarith insisted.

"Nonsense," she argued. "Enjoy the view. Jua has prepared the guest room for you. It's the one with the open door." She nodded at the lamp. "Now, when you retire for the night, don't forget the lamp. And before you sleep, quell the fire by turning this knob."

"No need," Jarith said.

He held up his index finger and spun it in a tight circle. The lamp's fire extinguished itself. With another, less visible gesture—because they were now in darkness—the flame burned anew.

Meta's jaw hung open.

"You're able to do magic?" she asked.

"It's not magic," he said with a laugh. "I just deprive the flame of oxygen."

Then, abruptly, she was laughing with him. He wasn't sure what exactly she found funny, but her joy made him laugh harder. Her eyes watering, she lost her balance.

As he had with the flames, Jarith could sense the shifting forces at work. He reached out with his mind and applied an opposing, cradle-like force to allow her to regain her balance. Still chuckling, she put a hand to her chest and wiped her eyes.

"Blessed start of night, Jarith," she said, placing her hands to her forehead and fighting back another laugh.

He returned the gesture and words and watched as she descended the stairs.

"And be prepared to show me that trick tomorrow," she called up.

"We'll see," he replied, a lilt in his voice to denote that the comment was in jest.

She was laughing again as she entered the home's rear door.

9

A Midrealm Morning

Jarith awoke to sunlight and voices. With an immediate sense of panic, he jumped to his feet and toward the open window. The door to the room was closed, an obvious violation of his person because he had left it open. Movement caught his eye as he examined the room for intruders, but the only thing moving was his reflection in a mirror.

Staring back at him was a muscular man of deep brown complexion with a red undertone, hair separated into twists that fell across his shoulders past his collarbone, a trim face, and widened dark, brown eyes. It took him several seconds to recognize this man as himself.

His unfounded distress subsided as he recalled where he was and how he got here.

He placed a hand on his chest. Was this really how he had imagined himself? It seemed odd to be trapped in this body. It was a bit too masculine for his taste. The feeling of trousers between his legs was disconcerting, and he found his arms touching his clothing uncomfortable.

Leaning closer to the mirror to examine himself further, he pouted at how messy his hair was. Running his hands along each twist of hair, he rolled it until it was smooth. Then he pulled two twists back and tied them around the others.

There was a bowl of water and a towel on the dresser. He remembered Maliah cleaning herself each morning and did his best to mirror what she had done. For his first birdbath, he did an okay job. If he survived, he'd probably want to get advice on this kind of thing.

A thought disturbed him as he scrubbed at the crust in his eyes. He hadn't dreamt. He had closed his eyes the night before, and then he had woken up this morning. He didn't remember anything in between.

In Highrealm, he had been in full control of his dream state. But here in Midrealm, he'd involuntarily drifted off to sleep and had been met with nothingness. He hadn't detected anyone entering his room, even though the newly placed bowl of water proved that someone had been here.

His stomach turned. It was disturbing to think that while he slept, his body—what? Shut down completely? Did he breathe while asleep? Was there any brain function?

He took a moment to acknowledge gratitude that he had awoken. It would have been quite the conundrum if he hadn't, after all. He couldn't help but wonder if Maliah deactivated in the same way that he had. They were both asleep, so there wasn't anything to see. But was there more to it than that?

In his life before Maliah, his mind had gone to fantastical places as he slept. The impossible had always seemed possible in his young mind, and his imagination had dreamed up experiences that couldn't exist in Highrealm. When he had loosened his control, his dreams seemed to put his life on shuffle, rearranging experiences into new and interesting contexts. Relaxing to sleep had always been part of a ritual to process his thoughts, and he'd never considered what life would be like without dreams.

To be fair, he'd only spent one night in Midrealm. This not dreaming thing could've been a complete coincidence. But that was no consolation to the Highrealmer.

He exited his room, noting again to himself that someone had shut his door. A shiver ran through him.

Maliah and her parents were sitting at a table at the far end of the common room. Maliah cocked her head to the side and gave Jarith a measured once over. She murmured something to her parents that he couldn't hear, and they added two more overs to Maliah's once.

He looked down at himself. He was wearing a baggy, sleeveless shirt held together with laces at the front. The laces were loose, leaving a gap at the center where his chest showed through. It was made of animal skin—or so he thought—and blended decently enough with his light, natural-toned slacks. They weren't much to look at, but he'd never seen clothing much outside of

Maliah's dresses and ritual wear. It had been his best estimation of Midrealm garments.

One look at the family made it clear that his threads were not sufficient.

"You're fine," Jua said, sensing his hesitance. "Come sit and eat."

"Maliah was just admiring your muscles," Meta laughed.

"No, I wasn't," Maliah said, trying to act nonchalant with an eye roll despite too conspicuously averting her eyes from his form.

"I think we all can appreciate how well-toned Jarith is," Jua said as he pulled items from the central tray of food onto his own plate.

Suddenly feeling shy, Jarith tugged his shirt closed—which was useless because it immediately opened again, as if some race of energy-based beings who'd never worn clothes before had designed it. There was a setting waiting for him on the table, and another in front of each additional empty chair. He reached out and took bread and fruit before using a spoon to scoop beans onto his plate. Jua poured a beverage into a cup and placed it in front of Jarith.

That would be good to have if he choked again. Luckily, Jarith was a fast learner and did not further embarrass himself.

"I suppose it's silly to ask if you dreamt last night, Maliah," Meta said.

"Seems unnecessary at this point," Jua agreed.

"I did, actually," Maliah said sheepishly.

Meta dropped the food she had been preparing to put in her mouth, more dramatic than was necessary. A small, round fruit bounced from her plate onto the table, rolled along the edge, and fell to the floor, where it continued its journey for another few moments before finally resting under Jua's chair.

She looked to her husband, as if to get some validation, but he held the exact same expression pointed at her. With a slow turn back to her daughter, she asked, "You dreamt?"

She waited a whole five seconds for Maliah to explain, but no explanation came.

"Well? Let's hear it," Meta urged.

"Please," Jua added politely.

Maliah had spent her entire life lying to her parents about her ability to dream, so Jarith was as surprised as anyone at her declaration. He sat in silence as she either masterfully built suspense or reflected on whether she'd made the right decision by saying something.

"My dream," Maliah explained, pausing to form her thoughts, "was really vague. Or. I mean. Well, there were a lot of details, but I don't remember them."

There was a lot of looking around as Meta and Jua nodded at each other while Maliah and Jarith tried to figure out why her parents were doing so.

"Our early premonitions were the same," Jua finally said. "Don't worry. They'll become clearer."

"I am so proud," Meta said, almost shaking with excitement. "My little girl is having premonitions."

"We don't know that they're clairvoyant," Maliah argued. She looked to Jarith for support, then added, "They could be like the dreams in Highrealm."

At her parents' questioning gazes, Jarith explained, "Our dreams don't usually tell the future."

"How interesting," Meta said, sharing a look with Jua.

"What are they like?" Jua asked.

"Pretty random, I guess," Jarith said in the most obscurely vague way he possibly could. "Last night was strange for me, too, though. I didn't dream at all."

Maliah's hopeful gaze drifted away, replaced by a frustrated glower.

"That's normal," Jua said.

"You don't have other dreams?" Jarith asked.

"No," Meta said. "Only prophetic ones."

Jarith distracted them from Maliah's discomfort by sharing examples of dreams he'd had in Highrealm, but he was confused as to why she'd admitted to dreaming if she didn't want to be told her dreams were prophetic.

Attendants returned as they finished eating. The hectic energy of preparing for the day overwhelmed Jarith, so he retreated to the rooftop patio. A cool breeze drifted down the hill, but it was already warming up as the sun beamed down.

He met the family at the front gate. As they walked down their street, Jua explained the layout of the city. They soon turned the corner onto the main road, where travelers, followers, and workers cluttered the stone path.

But Jarith didn't notice. His eyes were drawn upward. Up the hill but not far, the two towering, animal-headed figures flanked the gates into the Huleay Grounds. His head tilted back as they drew closer, entranced by the enormity of their presence. Each wore a golden helmet and held a golden item. The sunlight gleamed off of them in stark contrast to the dark red pigment that painted their skin. He wondered how the Midrealmers had accomplished such a thing, but he was struck speechless.

"Welcome to the Huleay Temple Grounds," Meta laughed when she saw his wide eyes.

He looked at Maliah as if to ask why she wasn't gaping like a tourist. She grinned at his expression.

"There's a lot of larger-than-life art here," she said. "The Temple likes to impress."

"I am thoroughly impressed," he said as he fell into step beside her. He lowered his voice. "By the way, I'm sorry if I put you in a tough spot with your parents earlier."

"Don't worry," she replied, giving him a gentle nudge. "I guess I expected you to have dreamt last night, too."

"No, just . . . nothingness. It was terrifying."

"I suppose it would be scary for someone who hasn't experienced it before. But it's normal here."

"I must admit," Jarith said, "it's strange being here. This world, this body, and the way I perceive them aren't what I expected."

"How so?"

"I'm not sure how to explain it. It just feels so . . ." He paused, made a gesture with his arms as if presenting the world, then continued. ". . . real."

"Yes, it's quite real," she said with a laugh.

"Well, not everything feels real yet," he said. "May I?"

He held his hand out, and she hesitantly put hers in it.

"I can't believe I'm here. Finally here," he whispered. "I've wanted this for so long." He turned his gaze to her, despite only being about fifty percent sure there wouldn't be anything to run into while he spoke. "Didn't you?"

"Yes," she said. "But we're also in such a complicated position."

"You mean because of the prophecy."

She nodded. "I don't intend to blindly follow it. I need to make choices that are right for me. Yet, even thinking that feels as if I'm denying my duty to my people. I'm being selfish, aren't I?"

Jarith couldn't bring himself to tell her that her words rang true for him as well. The battle waged in his heart, torn between his duty to kill Meta and save his people and his selfish wish to not become a murderer.

Both Jarith and Maliah wished for choice, which isn't really that selfish. However, with lives dedicated to serving others, even their simplest wishes became out-landish. Unfortunately for Jarith, his options were mutu-ally exclusive. Kill Meta and live, or don't and die. Un-less he could find another way.

"You're doing your best," he said. "And we'll get through this together, without giving up who we are."

He really meant "I hope we will."

Jarith wanted to believe it, but the universe seemed so immense from this small, physical body.

In Highrealm, he had been capable of thinking and acting in ethereal and abstract ways. Yet now, he wondered how medium-sized mammals on a small, blue planet in an arm of a spiral galaxy could hope to change the nature of reality. Not that the people of Ledine knew they were on a small, blue planet in an arm of a spiral galaxy. But Jarith knew because it was part of his studies of Midrealm.

The Huleay Grounds continued to get grander as they neared, and Jarith's stomach was in knots as he tried to find an excuse to stay with Maliah. He was surprised when she laid her head on his shoulder.

"Thank you," she said.

"For what?" he asked.

"When you showed up, I became afraid that you weren't the person you portrayed to me. I thought, per-haps, you weren't the compassionate person who I've come to know. I couldn't help but wonder if I could trust you."

He replied to the suggestion that he was untrustworthy with a small, sly grin. "You're welcome, I guess."

She laughed. "I'm thanking you for being yourself." She squeezed the hand she was holding. "And for being real."

Words sprung from him before he could resist them.

"I have to admit something to you." He didn't wait for her permission before continuing, fearing he'd lose his nerve. "My whole life has been dedicated to my duty. I spent every spare moment studying and training, and I've done my best to do everything expected of me. But sometimes, I wonder if fulfilling the prophecy is worth it."

He'd been afraid to say the words out loud—especially while in Highrealm under the scrutiny of Jukartis—but he felt at ease with Maliah. He wanted to tell her everything, to share his fears and ambitions. But there's a right time and place for these things, and this wasn't it.

Her eyebrows were raised in surprise, and she stood back up straight to look at him squarely. A glimmer of doubt in Jarith's mind sparked within him, threatening that she would judge him harshly for his words.

"You're serious?" she asked.

"Yes," he assured her.

She let out a long sigh, and the tension seemed to melt away as her whole posture shifted. He tried to peer beyond her, at her aura, and found it widening from a restricted warmth to a more relaxed coolness. Admittedly, he was surprised that it had worked, as he hadn't seen an aura since he arrived in Midrealm. Even so, every time his power worked as he expected, he felt immense relief, much like Maliah appeared to be feeling now.

"I know what you mean, about wondering if it's worth it," she said.

"I'm glad," he said. "But I want you to know that even though I have my doubts about the prophecy, I've never questioned whether **you** are worth it. Meeting you here, sharing this time with you, is worth everything."

She hid her face from him, and he realized he'd said something embarrassing.

Instead of waiting for a reply, he added, "We should have a proper talk. About everything."

"I'd like that," she replied. After a moment, she finally looked back at him with what appeared to be new-found determination. "I have some hard questions, too."

"Such as?"

"Such as the meaning of the words 'spiritual evolution' and 'ascension' in the prophecy."

He wondered if this was confirmation that she didn't know Highrealm's plans, but he told himself not to make assumptions that could bite him in the bum later. He didn't actually know how much she had seen or heard. So, he decided to find out the only reasonable way he could: ask. Groundbreaking idea.

"It's a long explanation, but I'll tell you what I know," he replied.

She stopped walking, and he turned to face her. He realized they were under the massive gate that led into the Huleay Grounds. She was still holding his hand, but her stance made it clear that they would not be staying together.

"Let's talk more tonight," she said with a forced smile. "I have to take care of my duties."

"I've actually never seen your mentor," Jarith said, hoping to elicit an introduction.

She raised an eyebrow in surprise. "Ze will be at dinner tonight, so we can do a proper introduction then."

A sense of dread beset him as she pulled her hand from his. As he watched her rush off toward one of the larger structures, he noticed her parents speaking with a figure with an overwhelming aura.

He hadn't tried to see it, but its glow was so powerful that he couldn't help but be aware of it. Tendrils stretched out into the surrounding environment, as if seeking out an enemy to destroy. At its center was a person who seemed more like a black hole than a well of energy. The feeling made the fine hair on Jarith's arms stand up.

He pushed the ability back, willing the aura to clear so he could make out the figure. Slowly, a form emerged, and with it, two deep, black eyes staring right at him.

10

KING YEMOMON

Maliah's day began with shadowing Grand Priest Omari in her daily duties. She was an older woman and very set in her ways but was deeply connected to her spiritual self.

As soon as Maliah arrived, they did a grounding meditation, which she desperately needed. Although better than earlier that morning, Maliah remained anxious. She wondered if Grand Priest Omari sensed that or if this was a new daily ritual for her, but she gladly sank into her center as Grand Priest Omari spoke rhythmic chants.

Maliah's racing mind quieted, and the conflicting thoughts of here and there were replaced with resolute focus. Grand Priest Omari must have noticed because her demeanor softened once the meditation ended. Or maybe she was an anxious mess just like Maliah.

Either way, they walked together to the Arathu Temple, a sanctuary with a capacity of up to fifty. Despite the small size, the architecture was grand and elaborate, like everything in the Huleay Grounds.

The spiritual caste that ruled Ledine was nothing if not flashy.

They approached from the rear, but the line waiting for audiences curved around the building. Maliah was overwhelmed by the mass of people. With deep breaths, she pulled her attention to her duty.

Grand Priest Omari instructed Maliah to sit on a hassock next to Grand Omari's throne-like chair. Beside her, woven baskets held common charms. Maliah recognized them all, but Grand Omari reviewed them with her anyway. Once satisfied, the Grand Priest took her place on the throne. She lifted her hand, and her attendants allowed the first group to enter.

The purpose of this chamber was twofold: resolving local disputes and providing prayers or blessings under the guidance of the earth spirits, who ruled over the Arathu Temple. Maliah paid close attention to Grand Priest Omari's words and demeanor as she handled each case with concise decisiveness. When instructed, Maliah dispersed the appropriate charms to the visitors.

Every visitor left seeming relieved and gracious. Maliah was surprised as their tense muscles relaxed and their tight expressions loosened. Grand Priest Omari was masterful at handling matters under the earth spirits. She had spent much of her life studying the texts specific to the earth, which described its tempers, moods, flexibility, and resiliency.

After the last case was handled, Maliah excused herself to help with the midday ritual at the main temple, which occurred with precise timing as the sun shone through an oculus and set a central bowl aglow.

Attendance at midday ritual was low, as usual. So, Maliah focused on her participation in the ritual while attendants led people into the sanctuary beforehand and out afterward.

Back in the preparation hall, Maliah was just removing her last piece of ritual wear when Amun appeared to escort her to her daily lesson. Though ze never participated in rituals at the Huleay Temple, ze always looked ready for one. Zir long tunic was embroidered with ornate patterns and figures, and ze wore a gold-trimmed headdress with a delicate circlet on top. Like all higher priests, ze embellished zir facial features with makeup. Maliah had once asked how long Amun spent getting ready each day. Zir response was that it took as long as it took.

"Good day," Amun said when Maliah approached.

"Good day. Are you well?"

"I'm very well. It's wonderful to see you assisting with midday ritual again."

They exited the main temple and weaved their way through corridors and passageways toward their usual temple of practice.

"I wanted to apologize," Maliah said as they walked. "Yesterday, I asked an inappropriate question, and I pushed you for an answer. I'm sorry I made you uncomfortable, especially if you felt you couldn't come to dinner last night because of it."

Amun ate with her family almost every evening. Ze had once told her that, since ze didn't have a family of zir own, it comforted zir to be around their bright and uplifting energy.

"I had another matter to attend to. No need to apologize, dear," Amun said. "Although, I must admit, I was unprepared for such lines of inquiry. There is much we don't understand about the Ascension Four prophecy, and the things we do know are somewhat vague. Our visions aren't as straightforward as we'd like."

"What do you mean?"

"Well, for example . . ." Amun paused as a Young Priest walked by, then continued once they were out of earshot. "Your mother once had a vision of fifty pieces of paper stacked together. On each was one of four symbols and a number. When she chose from the stack at random, the paper had a two and a heart."

"What did it mean?" Maliah asked.

"None of us knew at the time," ze replied. "But you were born two years later, to the day."

"I was? I've never heard that."

Amun laughed zir weird laugh. Despite sounding sarcastic, Maliah knew it was genuine. Over the years, she'd come to find zir odd expressions refreshing and zir company pleasant. She looked forward to her time with the Exalted Grand Priest, strange humor and all.

"We've always told you that your birth was foretold."

"I thought you meant in the Ascension Four prophecy."

"This is why you must leave nothing to assumption." They reached their destination, and an attendant opened the large doors for them. Amun didn't continue until the doors were closed behind them. "You see, our visions don't always give us the clarity we desire. Sometimes, they leave mere impressions of emotions, colors, or scents. These are burdensome to convey and are sometimes unpleasant."

"Are you talking about the Ascension Four prophecy? Is ascension a bad thing?" Maliah asked.

"You're extrapolating and making assumptions, Maliah," Amun warned. "I'm merely explaining the difficulty in transferring the knowledge we obtain through visions."

She tried to sort her thoughts. Amun had often encouraged her to ask questions, but it was rare to receive straightforward answers from zir. Maliah wanted to understand Amun's warning regarding the prophecy. At least, she thought it was a warning. But who knew with all zir cryptic crap?

Wasn't there a perfect question somewhere that would force Amun to tell her everything ze knew about the prophecy? If there was, it would seem she wasn't clever enough to figure it out.

"So, you're saying you won't answer my question," she said plainly.

"There are some questions broader than the mind can hold, and there are answers so narrow the mind cannot comprehend them," Amun answered.

A "no" would have sufficed.

"Now, if we may begin," ze said, pointing to the chair in the middle of the platform.

Maliah took her seat, listened to Amun's lecture, watched zir demonstrations, and answered zir questions.

"Excellent work today, as always," Amun said. "Shall we try a meditation spell for concentration?"

Maliah agreed and found a comfortable position.

Amun's tone shifted to one of calm. "Woathu athuas woardias m'e bidi m'e wolele, leat athuguhuatas bi fiar at fil'e. Athune asatatle ne'at ciniciarat peleatas nedi asnedi dias bi."

She knew there were more verses, but she didn't hear them.

Instead, her mother appeared before her, engulfed in flames and flailing in pain. The fire clung to her curves, smothering her with intense heat. Her mother reached, clawed, and grasped at an invisible barrier, but her efforts were in vain. She was consumed in what felt like forever just as much as it felt like a moment. Every cell of her body disintegrated, breaking down into molecules, then into atoms, then to nothing. From beyond, her vibrant soul glowed, pulsing with life. But as the forever moment stretched on, it too dimmed into nothingness.

Maliah gasped and jumped to her feet. An uncontrolled cry escaped her, and she clasped her hand over her mouth in surprise at herself. She swallowed, trying to ease the nausea that threatened to bring her breakfast back to see the light of day.

"What's wrong?" Amun asked as ze rushed to her side.

"I . . . I saw . . ."

Her legs wobbled beneath her, and she shook all over. Tears fell from her eyes. Pulling her into zir arms, Amun whispered soft words of comfort. Ze couldn't erase the images of her dead mother, of course, but the embrace soothed her somewhat.

When she settled down, she described her vision. Amun's usual levity was absent as ze listened with intense concentration.

"What does it mean?" she begged.

"I'm not sure," Amun replied.

This same terror had awoken her the night before. She had cried herself back to sleep and felt compelled to mention it to her family this morning.

"I think I dreamt of this last night. But why now?"

"Something must have triggered it."

"Is Mom alright?" she asked. "Are you sure you don't know anything?"

Amun paused a few moments too long. "Maliah, what else is going on? Has anything changed?"

"Well, no. I mean . . ."

Her mind was reeling, and she couldn't think straight. But she took deep breaths to calm herself. It was only then that she remembered Jarith's arrival.

She had already normalized him as part of her life. Her mind had already envisioned daily meals arguing across the table about which food was the tastiest, watching the sunsets every evening as the sky lit up the city like fire, and holding each other at night as the chilly breeze drifted through the house. It seemed impossible that he'd only arrived yesterday, that she could feel so close to him so quickly.

Yet here she was.

"Jarith is here," she breathed. She was almost afraid the words would send her back into her vision, but the terrifying imagery didn't return.

"What?"

Amun seemed genuinely surprised, and Maliah couldn't believe it. She had assumed ze would know already. Between her parents' gossiping streak and Amun's . . . well, Amun-ness, she didn't think there would be any hope of hiding it.

But why was she wondering now if she should have concealed it?

Her thoughts were scattered. So much for that concentration spell.

"When did Jarith arrive? Today?" Amun asked.

"He showed up at our home yesterday afternoon."

"He?"

Maliah furrowed her brow at the odd response.

Ze pivoted to a different question.

"And what has he done since he arrived?"

"I don't understand," Maliah said.

It wasn't like Amun to be this intrusive with zir questions. Unless ze thought that Jarith and her vision were connected somehow.

"He's staying with us, and everything is fine," Maliah said in her most reassuring tone. "You'll meet him tonight."

Amun's tight, intense expression worried her.

"Really, Amun. Jarith is wonderful. You'll see. Say you'll join us for dinner."

As if distracted from a distant memory, ze turned zir attention back to her. "Yes, of course. I'll attend as per usual."

When Maliah arrived home that afternoon, Jarith was on the rooftop patio. His gaze was locked on the city, and he didn't react when she entered the front gate. Deep in thought, he didn't address her when she reached the top of the stairs.

Unsure what to say, she leaned against the parapet next to him. His attention drifted to meet hers, and she smiled. His eyes were dark, even with the western sun beaming into them, and every delicious muscle of his form seemed relaxed with contentment.

Even though she struggled to understand Jarith's relationship with his parent, Jukartis, she knew it had been complicated and tumultuous. Jarith had always seemed in a heightened state of stress. Seeing his relaxed composure sent her heart racing.

She pulled in a deep breath and held it, willing her heart to slow and chill out. The effort was not effective.

"Welcome home," he said finally.

His voice was deep and rich, and the way his mouth formed around each syllable reminded her of an instrument's smooth transition from note to note.

She thanked him, then asked, "What did you do all day?"

"I watched your world, mostly," he replied. "Listened to people in the streets. Felt the sand drifting in the breeze. Smelled all kinds of things, and a lot were pretty bad, if I'm honest."

Maliah laughed. "Did you eat a midday meal?"

As if hearing her words, his stomach grumbled. Jarith placed his hand over it. "Well, that felt exotic," he commented. "Bodies are weird."

"It's true," Maliah said. "Dinner will be awhile, so why don't we walk down to the market? You could try some local dishes."

She looked him over. That morning, she had realized his clothing wasn't what one would expect for someone in the spiritual caste. Jua had offered to find him some options on the Grounds, but she thought it wise to allow Jarith to develop his own tastes.

"Maybe we can pick up a few other items as well," she suggested.

"Sure," he replied. "Sounds good."

Once they'd exited the front gate, Maliah pointed down the hill, where the outer wall of the Huleay

Grounds separated the homes of the spiritual caste from the rest of the city. When they reached the main road, five archways became visible, each with an enormous lifted gate. Between the archways stood four statues, similar to those up the hill but not as tall. Maliah saw Jarith's jaw go slack as they neared the wall.

"Is the wall getting bigger?" Jarith asked. "Everything here is enormous." He gestured to the statues, each standing at least twice his height. "Is our perception really so awful that these giants seemed shorter from up the hill?"

"I've never thought about it," she said with a laugh, "but the walls are tall because this was once a fortress that withstood many battles."

"Battles? Against who?" Jarith asked.

Maliah placed her hand to her chin in thought. "Our neighbors mostly. Before what we call the Spiritual Revolution, wars were rampant around the world. Ledine conquered her enemies through violence and intimidation. And other nations attempted to do the same to us."

"And then?"

Maliah was suddenly glad she had paid close attention to her history lessons.

"Well, then came the last king of Ledine, King Yemomon, who had no heirs to the throne. His advisors predicted panic if he didn't choose a successor, and they begged him for years. Ultimately, a civil war broke out as the most powerful candidates to become the next king tried to take out the competition."

"Sounds productive," Jarith said.

Maliah smiled, and her movements became more animated. "King Yemomon had a very loyal royal guard, who commanded a very loyal army. The king condemned the fighting and refused to choose. He said choosing the wrong heir was worse than choosing none at all.

"Then, one gloomy day, as his advisors argued with each other in the throne room, King Yemomon noticed one who simply watched and listened.

"He called upon the advisor, asking for their counsel. Should he yield to the one who had accumulated the most wealth? Should he choose the one who had conquered the most land? Or should he listen to the one who had gained the most favor?"

She paused as they reached the gates. Placing her hands together, she gave a reverent bow to each of the four statues, saying each of their names in turn.

"Arathu, guardian of earth." Arathu's statue had the head of a canine and a horse tail. In its hands, it held a spear and shield.

"Arvoar, guardian of river." The fish scales on Arvoar's crocodile head matched those on its hands and feet. An oar was propped up in one hand while the other held a reed.

"Kuay, guardian of sky." This statue's head was that of a falcon, sharp painted eyes commanding attention. Its tail was angled down, but the feathers were spread to reveal peacock coloring. Kuay's arms were out in front of it, holding a bow and arrow.

"Asne, guardian of sun." Asne's lion headed statue stood with its mouth open mid-roar. Its toes and fingers held claws, and a thick tiger tail wound around its body. It held a tablet of paper in one hand and a stylus in the other, its calm task in stark contrast with its fierce expression.

When Maliah returned her gaze to Jarith, he had a questioning look.

"The four pillars of our religion," she said.

"You didn't bow to them," Jarith said, pointing up the hill at the two massive statues at the inner gate.

"Those are decorative," she stated, as if it was obvious. She held her hand out to present the four statues. "These are embodiments."

Jarith shifted his gaze back and forth between the statues behind and in front of them before returning his confused expression to her.

"These are infused with protection magic," she added.

She really hoped that was enough because she wasn't sure what else was different about these four. It was tradition, so she followed it.

Jarith seemed sufficiently satisfied, and they continued on their way through the gates.

"So the king called on the quiet advisor. What did they say?" Jarith asked, getting back to the story.

"Nothing."

"Nothing?" Jarith asked.

"Not a word," Maliah assured him. "And this angered the king. So he asked again, 'Do I choose the strongest, the most wealthy, or the most powerful?' But again, the advisor gave no response.

"Livid at this insubordination," Maliah continued, remembering this next part word for word from the stories she'd been told, "the king threw out his arms and commanded his royal guard to take the advisor as a prisoner. Three guards pushed through the crowd, roughly tossing people this way and that. The silent advisor didn't try to run. They didn't even flinch as the guards drew near. In exquisite coordination, they all reached their target at the same time, and grabbed at their arms."

Maliah swiped her hands out in front of her.

"But their hands were empty. The advisor had disappeared. Everyone was stunned, and the entire room became quiet. Then, outside, the clouds parted. Light shone into the chamber and onto mirrors that illuminated four statues of Arathu, Arvoar, Kuay, and Asne. And from behind the statues, the missing advisor stepped into view. It was Exalted Grand Priest Dukar Bhramadi."

"A priest?" Jarith asked in amazement.

His exuberance was infectious, and with an amused smile, she nodded.

"It had been an illusion cast by Exalted Grand Priest Bhramadi," she said. "But now, they spoke. They said, 'Just as you were focused on my illusion while I stood here, you also focus on illusions to solve your problems. You've asked which candidate you should choose based on what they have obtained when you should ask what they have given.

"You, my king, have spent your life truly serving your people. We have flourished in health, prosperity, and peace thanks to your guidance. I implore you to ask yourself, who will lead us to the future you wish for your empire?'"

"Bhramadi was put to death, weren't they?" Jarith asked with a wry smile.

Maliah couldn't help the laugh that escaped her, but she gave him a push for the rude interjection.

"No!" she exclaimed. "King Yemomon proclaimed that a king would no longer rule the empire. Instead, the spiritual house of Ledine, the Huleay Temple, would guide the people's future."

His disbelieving stare gave her pause. She rolled her eyes.

"After he thought about it for a few weeks while Exalted Grand Priest Bhramadi was detained," she admitted reluctantly.

Jarith guffawed. "I knew it." He laughed so hard, he almost lost his balance.

She rolled her eyes again in feigned annoyance, just in case he didn't see the first time. "Anyway, there's the market entrance." She pointed straight ahead, where a banner hung above the main road that read "*Ar Central Market*" in large, bold lettering. "And I know exactly where we should go first."

That first booth happened to be a local baker. The bakery itself was another ten-minute walk past the market, but the baker's two daughters took turns carting baked goods from the shop to serve at the busy—but more convenient—front booth. Maliah especially wanted to share a honey cake with Jarith. Despite the long line, the cake was perfect, providing just the boost they needed to continue shopping.

She took his hand and led him from booth to booth, starting with carts that sold fresh produce and more baked goods and then to clothing boutiques that sat inside permanent buildings. At one point, a row of booths distracted Jarith. Loud salesmen promised love and fortune, and eager people of all ages crowded around.

When he asked Maliah about them, she said, "They sell magic items and charms. Growing better crops, telling your fortune, helping your love life, giving you luck. That kind of thing."

"Do they work?" he asked.

"If they did, those peddlers would be priests in the Huleay Temple."

"So the temple sells magic items?"

"No. We **provide** magic items to those in need."

The vendors sold a wide variety of items, from those promising the world to the items that bordered on petty. Maliah saw the doubt in Jarith's eyes as he pointed to a nearby charm hanging on a nail.

"Love charms?" he asked.

"Among others." She tried not to sound defensive, but failed.

"And do those from the Huleay Temple work?"

"Well . . ."

She'd been indoctrinated so thoroughly to lie that she found it difficult to form the truth into words. Not only did most charms from the Huleay Temple fail to do what they claimed, but most did nothing at all. In the case of love charms, this was probably for the best.

"No," Maliah finally answered after doing all the mental gymnastics she could muster and still not finding a viable answer.

"Then why do it?" Jarith asked.

"Because it gives people hope. Often, they merely need encouragement and agency, and we provide that. Many of our Priests study the magics, and when we have advancements that can help our people, we share them. But we're much less sophisticated than Highrealm. We can't solve most everyday problems."

"Your mom was surprised when I started and snuffed out an oil lamp's fire. I can see auras, too."

"Mom can start small fires like those in our lanterns at home. Both of my parents even claim they can move things with their minds. But the things that are possible in Highrealm, well . . ." She shrugged as she tried to figure out how to describe just how weak it made even her mother look.

"I guess I misunderstood what it meant for you to have powers," he said when she didn't continue. "I knew you couldn't do everything I was able to in Highrealm, but I wonder why I didn't realize how limited your society is. So how powerful are your parents?"

"I don't know how to answer that."

"Yeah. It's probably difficult to describe without some kind of scale."

"No, it's just that I've never asked. We're not supposed to show our power too openly."

Jarith looked genuinely shocked. "What? Why not?"

She shrugged. "It's dangerous. At least, my parents and Amun think so."

"Isn't all this about helping your people?"

As his shock turned to disappointment, Maliah couldn't contain her happiness. His question was often at the forefront of her mind, and no one else seemed to share this opinion. Tears came to her eyes, but she hid her face from him.

"I knew you'd understand," she breathed. Her heart was racing again, and she felt ridiculous for it. She wiped her eyes. "I don't know what kind of powers will be awakened within me, but whatever they are, I want to use them to help my people when they're in need."

"Who knew you were such a rebel?" Jarith joked.

She didn't even try to fight back her smile.

Every particle of her being told her to trust in this man, and it almost, just about, very nearly drowned out the inner voice telling her to stay vigilant.

11

An Awkward Dinner

By the time Maliah and Jarith started the uphill trek toward home, Jarith had eaten too many snacks, and Maliah had bought him more clothing than he needed. She couldn't explain how it had happened, but they both held bags overflowing with goods.

Now that they were away from the market crowd, silence hung between them. Maliah wanted to enjoy being together, but she couldn't shake off her curiosity. She needed to understand what Jarith knew regarding the prophecy, and she couldn't deny the weight that this unknown was putting on her.

So, as they walked toward the Huleay Grounds, she dropped the bombshell. "I had a vision today, while training."

Jarith gawked at her, but his reply was calm and gentle. "Like your dream last night?"

"I believe so."

"Is that good?"

"I don't know. It showed something—" A shiver ran through her as the memory of her mother burning to nothingness welled up in her mind's eye. "—something terrible happening."

He set his gaze firmly on the road ahead of them. She had hoped he'd ask for more details because she didn't want to spill it all without prompting. That would be almost as embarrassing as crying in front of your mentor, which she'd already done.

Definitely enough embarrassment for one day.

"It got me thinking again about what ascension might mean," she said when she gave up waiting for a reply.

"That's right. I said I'd tell you."

"Yes, you did."

He looked around, then lowered his voice as if not to be overheard. "Right now, when someone dies here in Midrealm, their soul usually stays trapped in their body. The afterlife promised by the Temple doesn't exist."

Maliah nodded. "I know that much. You and Jukartis talked about it sometimes. I didn't believe it at first, but after helping with burial services . . ." She trailed off as she remembered her first burial service with the Temple. As the priests chanted a spell to free the person's spirit from this world, she had sensed a heaviness from the body. It was as if the flesh, which had once been the soul's window to the world, was now a prison. "I don't know how to explain it," she continued, "but it's just obvious once you understand the truth."

Jarith nodded and continued. "At first, we didn't realize it either. We assumed your souls dissipated after death and that energy then formed into another soul to live a new life."

"We call that reincarnation," Maliah said. "So that doesn't happen either?"

"If it does, it's very rare. But before we knew that, we hoped to learn how it was possible. You know, so we could apply those principles in our reality. That didn't work out, of course, but somewhere along the line, we realized there was another answer."

"Ascension," Maliah said.

"Yes."

"And that is what, exactly?"

"The transfer of souls from Midrealm to Highrealm," Jarith said.

"Transfer? Like how you came here?"

"It's much more complex than that, but essentially, the souls of the dead here, instead of being trapped, would transfer to Highrealm."

"And do what?"

"Live a new life."

Maliah had been ten years old when she'd realized the Highrealmers were right about the dead. Many sleepless nights had followed, during which she worried about her fate and maybe worried a bit about the fate of her people. She was still in that egocentric stage of childhood development, so cut her some slack.

She had grappled with the Huleay Temple's lies. Everything they had taught her about an afterlife was concocted to ease the minds of the living. With this new information, her mind was no longer at ease.

The ability to transfer those souls to Highrealm seemed too good to be true. It would be a genuine afterlife, but there had to be a catch.

Before she could ask, Jarith said, "I've been wondering something, too, about where we stand. Our relationship, I mean."

They had just turned from the main road when he said this, though she could hear the shudders of a horse and cart going way too fast down the hill behind them.

"I know what destiny has in store for us," Jarith continued when she didn't answer. "But I want to know your feelings."

She wanted him to say more, though she couldn't explain why. Instead, he waited for her response like the patient person he was. Nervous butterflies filled her stomach as she opened her mouth to respond, not knowing what was going to come out.

"Jarith, I don't know what you want me to say," she said when nothing that came to mind seemed appropriate.

"Are we strangers? Friends? More? This morning you held my hand, but this afternoon, you've been more reserved. I don't want a misunderstanding, and I don't want to overstep your comfort level."

Maliah's face burnt with embarrassment as she faltered. "What about you?"

He let out a chortle and, with a dopey grin on his face, said, "I love you, Maliah. I've looked forward to this moment my entire life, and you've exceeded my expectations. You're thoughtful and cautious, passionate and outspoken, gorgeous and elegant. I'd dedicate my life to being by your side with no hesitation."

He opened his mouth to say more, but she held up a hand.

"That's enough," she said. "Too much, really."

"I'm sorry." He looked away with an expression that hinted of self-consciousness but not regret.

She put her hand on his chest and drew herself closer.

"Don't be sorry," she whispered. "This is difficult for me, but . . . "

He was leaning toward her, and her gaze darted between his eyes and lips. The tips of two of her fingers touched the skin on his chest, and thrills ran through her. She allowed her hand to move up to his neck and trace his jaw.

As she leaned closer, her breath quickened. His arm wrapped around her. He placed his hand on the small of her back but didn't pull her in. She was in complete control, yet her body wasn't acting in accordance with her brain.

His hot breath teased her lips as she closed the distance. Her heart pounded as something noncorporeal within her reached out to connect with him.

Her fingers moved to the nape of his neck. She pressed her body against his. He flinched with pleasure, and she pulled him closer.

"Maliah?" a voice called from down the road. "Is that you?"

It shocked Maliah, pulling her out of her fantasy-turned-reality. She jumped away from Jarith, who staggered back a step. They both looked toward the source to find Amun standing just outside the gate of Maliah's home, hand raised in greeting.

Her legs trembled, and she felt unsure about taking a brave step forward. As if sensing her struggle, Jarith placed a hand to her waist to steady her.

The bags she'd been holding were slumped in a pile on the ground. Had she gotten that carried away? She didn't even remember them slipping from her grasp. Before she could reach down, Jarith grabbed them and gave her a knowing smile. What he knew was anyone's guess.

"I'm glad you could make it," Maliah said when they reached Amun.

She introduced them to each other, sensing none of the worry that Amun had expressed earlier about Jarith. Or maybe she was misinterpreting Amun's subtle facial expression altogether.

Before she could wonder any further, Amun suggested they go inside, and she followed without question. Something within her sensed a shift in the air, but she wasn't skilled or powerful enough to recognize it. All she felt was a powerful urge to follow Amun into her home in a quiet procession, where an awkward dinner awaited.

At Amun's recommendation, Jarith retreated to the guest room to change into something more appropriate. As soon as he closed the door, the atmosphere changed. He stumbled over to the bed and fell onto it, allowing the bags he was holding to spill their contents onto the floor.

He knew from the moment he saw Amun that ze was powerful, but Jarith had just experienced a feat of magical engineering. Without a second thought, he had followed Maliah into the family home. Jarith only now realized what had happened. Amun had triggered a compulsion in his mind, the sudden urge to follow zir inside.

Midrealmers hadn't reached the level of scientific maturity to understand how their brains functioned. So how had Amun learned such a thing?

Having experienced its effects, Jarith was certain he could counteract it if it happened again. He had sensed the changes Amun had effected in his body. Now that he was aware of those reactions, he could ward off future attempts. After all, he'd learned to do that long ago to keep Jukartis from having complete control over him.

Getting Maliah and him inside was a rather innocuous use of such power, but Jarith couldn't help but wonder how often ze had used it before. He shuddered at the thought of what other powers Amun may command.

He rolled over and sat cross-legged on the bed, concentrating on his physical form. He sensed the tether between his body and his soul and visualized its fragile connection. It would become solid once the transfer ritual was complete and Meta was dead. If he could bring himself to kill her, that is.

He closed his eyes and focused on how his energy flowed within and around him. His physical form was connected to the physical world, and they interacted through conduits of energy and force. While these interactions were pivotal to staying grounded in the world, they were also points of weakness that could be exploited. It was through these weak points that Amun had controlled them.

Jarith had never thought too hard about Midrealm's connections between the physical and the metaphysical. It had never come up in his studies, either. But as he reached out with his mind to memorize the complex interlacing of these conduits, he constructed the scientific and mathematical proofs necessary to protect himself.

With precise intent and careful concentration, he weaved an energetic barrier around himself. He layered overlapping, complex patterns one after another until the barrier strengthened into a shield around and through himself. It wouldn't stop a physical attack, but it should provide adequate defense against magical assaults.

Of course, hopefully he wouldn't need it. But it never hurts to be cautious.

As soon as the shield was set, he could feel the cost. It required a constant draw of energy. His body felt heavier as he forced himself to stand.

He breathed a sigh of relief as he pulled off his pants and secured a wrap skirt around his waist. If the shield was going to distract him, he could at least be comfortable. His body still felt foreign to him, and the pants had accentuated his awkward relationship with it.

He'd taken note of the clothing worn by the denizens of Ar. Most who presented as feminine wore dresses, usually down to their ankles. Those of the Huleay Temple wore overlays of beads or gold. The more masculine presenting citizens wore shirts and pants while members of the Temple wore tunics or wrap skirts.

He had believed his choice of attire was suitable when he transferred. Now, he understood the concerned looks the family had given him that morning. Clothing was a symbol of status here. The whole concept of a caste system was confusing to him, much like gender.

Becoming male was the right choice for the prophecy, but after a day of being a man, he couldn't say it felt right for him. His physical form was limiting. He missed the ability to change his appearance with his mood. Though his body felt foreign, he concentrated on his gratitude for more comfortable clothes. Now wasn't the time to worry about this, not with a suspicious priest trying to control his actions only minutes prior.

He returned to the main living space of the home. Meta and Jua were arguing playfully about something in the kitchen area. Amun stood nearby, agreeing with both of them in a teasing manner. Maliah sat at the table, so he joined her.

"Are you alright?" he asked.

"Of course," she said. "Why wouldn't I be?"

"Maybe because your mentor just mind-controlled you into your own home?" Jarith decided not to say. Instead, he went with, "Well, we were interrupted. And you didn't answer my question."

Her parents let out a loud laugh, and she smiled at their overwhelming joy. She waited for the laughter to diminish.

"Don't worry," she said. "I won't abandon you. But I do need time to figure out how I intend to move forward." She reached over and put her hand over his. "No matter what, you're part of my family. You always have been and always will be."

Her touch calmed him, and he had just started to smile when that powerful aura reached out to force them to separate. Maliah moved her hand from his, although Jarith was pretty confident she didn't know why.

"So, Jarith," Amun said as ze joined them at the table, "you are a 'traveler.' Just as the prophecy predicted."

"As if there was any doubt," Meta said. "He came from another world, just as my dreams foretold. From a place called Highrealm."

"Is that so?" Amun asked.

"Yes," Jarith replied succinctly, not feeling very generous with his information.

"And why did you come here?" Amun asked. "I assume you didn't end up here by happenstance."

"No. I came here to be with Maliah, the woman of my dreams."

"Woman of my dreams" wasn't a colloquialism in Midrealm, but its sweet connotation wasn't lost on Meta.

"What a romantic way to put it," she cooed.

"Quite," Amun agreed. "And how did you find your way here?"

"What do you mean?" Jarith asked.

"I'm inquiring about the methodology. I presume you don't merely wish it and make it so."

"No," Jarith said. "My people . . . " For some reason, it felt odd to say the words "my people" to Amun, but Jarith wasn't sure why. ". . . have advanced technology that allowed me to come here."

"That's wonderful," Amun said, though zir face didn't reflect the levity in zir voice. "I'm sure that required some convincing."

When, the previous evening, Meta had asked Jarith why he came to Midrealm, he had seen no reason to lie to her. However, being challenged with a similar question from Amun gave him pause.

The Exalted Grand Priest had just tried to control his physical body a second time. However, Jarith now questioned whether Amun was aware of what ze was doing.

Ze may have been more in tune with Nature than zir level of scientific knowledge. If that was the case, it was theoretically possible to affect zir surroundings subconsciously. It wasn't common for someone to be able to feel their will into existence, but Jarith couldn't deny the potential. Especially for someone so highly regarded by the family. A family that, according to Maliah, he was now a part of.

Jua sat the large tray of food at the center of the table. "Let's allow the man some breathing room and enjoy the meal."

Maliah laughed and said, "You're only saying that because you and Mom did the same thing last night."

"I'd be a fool to deny my guilt," Jua admitted with a smile.

"And what did you learn?" Amun asked.

"That Jarith is a trustworthy man from a very remarkable place," Jua replied. "And who needs to slow down when he eats."

Meta laughed when Jarith grimaced at the comment. She and Jua took up the torch, telling Amun everything they knew and even more that they assumed based on the previous night's conversation. And though the family had no doubts about the honor of Maliah's mentor, Jarith couldn't quell the uneasy rumbling in his stomach no matter how much food he shoved into his body.

He started making his own assumptions about the priest. Perhaps ze was a spy from a neighboring country, or maybe ze was dabbling into power that shouldn't be touched. Well, that last part was definitely true, since, in Jarith's humble opinion, it was never acceptable to control others through one's abilities. Even if done unintentionally, Jarith wasn't sure he'd be able to stay silent the next time it occurred.

As the night's darkness crept into the house, Amun rose to excuse zirself.

"I'm afraid I must retire," ze said.

"But tomorrow is our rest day," Maliah said.

"Unfortunately, I have much to do tomorrow, and I hope to complete it all before dinner so that I may join you again." Ze turned zir stern eyes on Jarith. "Jarith, I welcome you into my home. If you intend to stay here indefinitely, your room should be properly dressed for someone of your station."

"Station?" Jarith asked.

Amun opened zir mouth to speak, but Maliah interrupted, "Let's not get ahead of ourselves."

Jarith didn't mind Amun's offer at all. In truth, seeing Amun's property would be the perfect opportunity to figure out what made zir tick and what, if anything, ze was hiding.

"Thank you for the invitation. I think that would be great," he said.

"You do?" Maliah asked, far more surprised than Jarith would have expected. She covered her mouth. "I mean, of course. Amun's home is beautiful. You'll love the fountain in zir garden."

Jarith's brow furrowed.

"*It doesn't bother you, does it?*" he wondered.

Her eyes widened, and she sat up straight. She broke off eye contact.

"Then it shall be," Amun said. "Come, dear child. It's a short distance from here, but the night draws ever closer and thus, so does my weariness."

Jarith waited another moment for Maliah's attention, but when it didn't come, he stood.

"I'll see you all tomorrow," he said.

Amun bowed with zir hands to zir head and said, "Blessed start of night."

The family returned the gesture, and Jua walked them to the front. With one more wave, the gate closed behind them, and Amun led onward into the darkness.

12

A Walk in the Dark

As Jarith kept pace with the nimble Amun moving briskly towards zir home, he noted the darkness of the street. Amun either had incredible night vision or knew the path in astonishing detail. A lump formed in Jarith's throat as he tuned his attention to Amun's shuffling footsteps. He reached out to the side and breathed a sigh of relief when his hand touched a wall.

He much preferred his experience in Highrealm, where he chose how he saw the world. But this wasn't the first time he'd felt out of his element. He had once swapped personal aesthetics with Whun Miu in the central atrium of Amandala. The shift to Whun Miu's preferences was far more drastic than Jarith had expected.

A sky full of stars was interrupted by a glittering nebula and a low-hanging moon. The grass was dewy under his feet, just as Jarith liked it, but luminescent flora lined the paths instead of small balls of light. Whun Miu glowed, too, with a ghostly aura. It was awe-inspiring but far too overwhelming for Jarith. He couldn't imagine how Whun Miu knew what to do or where to go.

"The same way you do," Whun Miu had explained when he asked.

Which was pretty much the most useless answer possible. Though the darkness had triggered the memory of his friend, Jarith's mind turned to improving his current perception. Though he was still grappling with the extent of his abilities, he was certain a better solution existed than wandering aimlessly through the darkness.

Unfortunately, this particular walk was too short to figure that out, and even if it hadn't, his problem solving was interrupted by Amun.

"I know I promised not to pry, but I do have one more question," ze said.

"Which is?" Jarith asked.

"Were you told the risks of fulfilling the prophecy?"

Jarith was suddenly glad it was dark because he did a double take. His foot caught on a loose rock, and he would have tumbled right onto his face had he not applied a force sufficient to catch himself.

When the Highrealmers spoke of risk, they'd always referred to the residual risk, that is, what was left over after mitigation. There were many risks in prematurely sending Jarith to Midrealm and creating the pocket reality for the Last Child, Jaalam. And there were even the unnecessary risks involved in the corny presentations given to the public by the scientists. There's a limit to how many times one should say "Wow" during a presentation, and they often exceeded it. Very dangerous to one's state of wakefulness.

But according to the project team, they had identified potential hazards to their ultimate goal early on, before Jarith was born. Those risks had been accounted for when the goals of the Ascension Project were defined. Although he wasn't aware of every plan the Highrealmers had considered, he knew they regarded their plan to be ideal. As far as Jukartis was concerned, as long as everyone played their part, the only risk was a total project failure, leaving Highrealm with no options but extinction. This had been eir obsession as long as Jarith had known em.

Jarith stopped in his tracks at a realization. "How are **you** aware of the risks?"

Amun's steps slowed, and the sliding sound that followed indicated to Jarith that ze was turning.

"Some of my visions regarding the prophecy have been . . . disturbing," ze said.

Jarith couldn't explain it. He couldn't even pinpoint the exact sensations in his body. But somewhere, somehow, his physical form was telling him that this was a lie.

He waited for Amun to say more, but ze didn't. A cool wind blew sand into the air, and Jarith threw his arm up to form a shield of air that kept his eyes sand-free. Best to keep them clear just in case.

Of course, he still couldn't see, but that wasn't the point—not Jarith's point, at least.

"Hmm," Amun mumbled.

The shifting sand was a prelude to receding footsteps.

Jarith hesitated.

Should he return to the family's home? His mind returned to dinner. Amun's expression had never changed from zir stern gaze, yet Maliah and her parents had often laughed and smiled as if everything was normal.

They had known this priest for many years. Jarith had known zir for mere hours. A twinge of guilt nagged at him for being so suspicious of someone the family trusted, and Jarith wondered if Jukartis had instilled this mistrust within him. Or maybe he was projecting his self-doubt onto Amun. After all, he was the one with the deadly secret and the murderous intent.

He drew in a deep breath of the cool night air and followed the footsteps beyond. As he caught up to the crunches of feet on sand, the footsteps stopped. A lamp began to glow from Amun's hands, illuminating zir.

"Here we are," Amun said, opening the gate.

Zir face, with its innumerable wrinkles and tight features, was eerie with the light coming from below, and Jarith waited to be welcomed before stepping inside.

As they crossed the threshold, lamps lit themselves across the garden. Reflections flickered in running water, bubbling in a central fountain. It was grander than Maliah's garden, with well-tended flower beds and seating areas. A small pond sat near the far wall, though it was somewhat obscured by the darkness.

He had cursed his physical limitations many times since he arrived, but he did so once more for good measure.

"It's beautiful," he admitted out loud.

"Thank you," Amun replied, leading Jarith through the ornate front garden. "I spent many years traveling, and I brought back many artifacts and mementos. My home is quite eclectic. I like to think of it as a curated art installation. Of course, I must attribute most of the credit to my attendants from the Huleay Temple property management team. I only guide the design."

When they entered the home, the lamps of the garden snuffed themselves out while several interior lamps began to glow. This was definitely what Midrealmers called magic, and was not trivial. Affecting localized temperatures of dozens of specific points simultaneously was no easy feat. To the untrained eye, they were simple flames, but the calculation and intention necessary to control so many was significant. Amun really was quite powerful. How had Highrealm been unaware of zir?

"Any open door is yours," Amun said, handing zir lamp to Jarith. Ze bowed with zir hands on zir forehead. "Blessed start of night."

"Blessed start of night," Jarith replied, mirroring the gesture as best he could with one hand.

Amun nodded approvingly and retreated into zir bedroom. All the lamps darkened except for Jarith's.

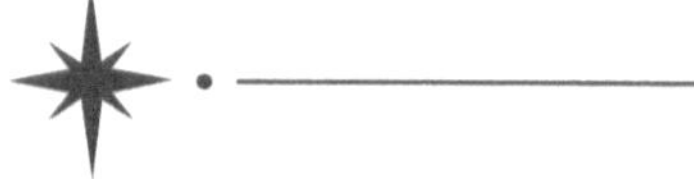

Maliah's parents waited mere moments after the front gate closed behind their two guests to confront Maliah. It was a miracle they'd held in their questions for so long, and had Maliah been less stressed about answering them, she would have been proud of them.

"So," her father said, drawing out the word as he sat next to her on the couch.

"How long have you known about Jarith?" Meta asked.

Maliah didn't know how to respond, but her parents were skilled at getting answers.

"When did you first dream of him?" Jua asked.

"I don't remember a time when he wasn't there," Maliah admitted, her gaze focused on her hands.

"So you've seen him in your dreams all your life?" her mother asked.

She nodded in agreement.

"And what did you see? Was it a certain future event?"

"No," she whispered.

"Then, you saw the past?" her father asked.

"No, that's not it."

"Then what was it?"

"I saw his life," she explained, "through his eyes, as he was living it."

It sounded insane when she said it out loud. If she hadn't seen, heard, felt, smelled, and almost tasted Jarith in Midrealm, she would've questioned her own sanity.

But if he was here, and he'd shared her experiences while he slept, her memories of Highrealm had to be real.

"That's . . ."

"Amazing."

She looked up at her parents, who were sharing an expression of excited wonder.

"I'm so glad," Meta said.

"What a comfort that would've been as a child," Jua agreed. "Although, you were a ruffian, dear, so perhaps I would've been more anxious than I already was."

"Me? A ruffian?" Meta asked, feigning offense. "I've always been a perfect lady." She began laughing at the absurdity of the sentence before even finishing.

"Beautiful? Yes. Ladylike? Not so much," Jua said, then he was chuckling, too.

Maliah expected them to dig deeper by asking more detailed or invasive questions, but they just continued their playful banter. A part of her was relieved, but she was overwhelmed by her fear of the unknown.

"That's it?" Maliah asked, her hands shaking. "That's all you wanted to know?"

"We needed context," Jua said. "But it's your life. You're an adult, and if you'd prefer to keep the details to yourself, we respect that."

Her mother, surprisingly, nodded her agreement. Even so, suspicions about her parents' motives worried her.

"You aren't upset?" Maliah asked.

Meta leaned closer and took her daughter's trembling hands in hers. She gave them a comforting caress.

"Maliah, we trust you to understand your boundaries and to request our assistance when you require it." Her voice was uncharacteristically solemn, though she was smiling. "You never should feel burdened to carry your load alone, but you are the judge of your own scale. It's up to you to determine when you're overburdened."

Maliah's eyes watered. By the time she wiped away the first tear, more streamed down her cheeks. She fell into her mother's arms.

"I had a vision today, while in training," she cried through her sobs. "Mom, you were dying. It was horrible and terrifying. It was so awful."

The sudden outburst surprised Meta, but she soon pulled her daughter closer.

"Visions often aren't as they appear," Jua said, rubbing Maliah's back. "Their meaning may be cloaked in symbolism."

"I don't want to go through that again," Maliah continued. "I don't want to do this."

"Oh, Maliah. My poor baby," Meta cooed with the gentleness of a parent that doesn't often tease their daughter. "I'm so sorry this is difficult for you."

"Have I ever told you about the Drought of Harnarim prophecy?" Jua asked.

Maliah sniffled, and her mother wiped at her tear-streaked cheeks. Unable to speak, Maliah shook her head.

"It was my first vision that wasn't about your mother," he explained. "I was working in the field when I came across a wounded animal. When I called out to my older brother, he took one look at the poor creature and told me we could do nothing to save it.

"Although I was very young, I understood the implications. Before I could react, the entire world around me changed. The field became a barren landscape. The sky turned dark. A portal appeared above us and drew all the clouds into it.

"The next thing I knew, I was in the field again, floating just above the ground along with my tools. My parents called for a Temple priest at once.

"My brother wrapped up the creature and brought it to the house, waiting for the priest from the nearby village. The vision was over, but its vivid detail haunted me."

Maliah sniffled, then asked, "What did the priest say when they arrived?"

"Ze said that my vision foretold a drought for the village of Harnarim. The creature was of a type seen exclusively in the region around the village, and the retreating clouds were a common symbol of lessened rainfall. The priest instructed my family to care for the creature and nurse it back to health."

"To stop the drought?"

Jua smiled. "No, of course not. You know the Huleay Temple looks down upon that kind of large-scale intervention. No, the priest didn't explain why. Ze merely bade us to do the task and let the Temple handle the drought."

Maliah sat up straighter, far more invested in the story than in its meaning.

"But I thought your brother said the creature was too far gone," she said.

"That he did," Jua agreed with a nod. "Before the priest left, ze taught us a spell and instructed us to repeat it each night. When the priest returned a lunar cycle later, the creature was healed."

Maliah understood the implications. "You did that, didn't you?"

"Yes," Jua said. "The priest said it was a sign for me as a new Young Priest. A message directly from Arathu, Arvoar, Kuay, and Asne."

"What was the message?" Maliah asked with impatience.

"That the darkness of night is a beginning, and what follows is the glory of daylight, a daylight that we help to create."

Maliah's smile fell as she sensed the connection to her own worries. Why couldn't her father's story have just been a nice, irrelevant tale with a happy ending?

"What you've seen is a burden," Jua said. "A burden we all share. But we have these abilities for a reason, for a greater purpose, which will bring daylight to our people."

Maliah was sobered from her sobbing and despair, but not comforted. As a matter of fact, her hatred of the prophecy may have just reached a new height.

Amun sat in an armchair of fine wood, eyes wide and focused. Intricate carvings of flora decorated the chair's sides, rails, and legs. The cushioned seat and back were lined with soft animal hide. It was meant for relaxing, yet Amun sat up straight with zir feet planted on the floor.

Each toe pressed deep into the woven rug, the darkness of the room hiding its reds and blues. The night's sliver of moon hung low in the sky, but provided little light. Not that Amun needed it.

Ze took deep breaths in, then released the air back out. Zir open eyes saw little of the physical world: the edge of the windowsill, the flicker of a flame up the hill, the endless sea of stars. Instead, zir stare was transfixed on the metaphysical world, a level of existence that ze had trained zirself to see through years of practice.

Though zir hands were palms up on zir lap in a welcoming gesture, Amun had placed them in the precise location necessary for zir intent. And with each breath, zir focus intensified.

Golden strands of magic peeked out from under zir toes. They stretched out, twisted around each other, looped through and into themselves. They formed bundles and knots in an intricate pattern about Amun's feet. Then outward they spread, glowing with ethereal intensity yet not illuminating their physical surroundings.

With alternating condensing and stretching motions mirroring Amun's deep breaths, the strands lengthened. They reached past the rug and across the plaster floor.

Amun allowed zir consciousness to extend beyond zirself. Ze had done this many times before, but not with tonight's intent, never with harm in zir thoughts.

Reaching zir mind outward, ze could sense the residences of others in the spiritual caste. Families in nearby homes slept soundly. An infant cried as her father rubbed her head to soothe her. Ze had reached too far, so ze pulled zir consciousness inward.

An owl perched in a tree at the edge of the garden. Its eyes were sharp and focused on any movement on the ground below. Insects scurried through the foliage.

Ze pulled further inward, into the walls of zir home, across the central living space, and through the closed door of the other occupied room. The golden tendrils of magic were creeping ever closer to their target, advancing with each breath Amun took. There was no sense of urgency. Just cool, calm breaths.

In and out.

In and out.

In and out.

The strands of magic crept beneath the door, across the ground, and up onto the bed. There, a sleeping body lay, the body of Jarith, the traveler from another reality.

Amun heard a whisper. Pausing to listen, ze was distracted yet held the golden tendrils steady. They pulsed with zir beating heart, but didn't advance any further.

The whisper was soft yet clear, a voice Amun recognized and understood. It was a voice that no one else could hear, and some might argue it wasn't there at all. But it had been there, once. With the fuzziness that was the reality of alternate realities—each of which held dimensions upon dimensions—perhaps the voice still was.

With renewed determination, Amun returned to zir task, wrapping the golden strands of magic around Jarith's arms, legs, neck, and torso. They unfurled and uncoiled, poised to go deeper into his spirit, to his very core. Amun could sense the delicate connection that held Jarith in this world.

The tendrils reached out, nearer and nearer as their ends grew sharp and rigid. At Amun's direction, they leapt to rip Jarith's soul from the physical world, intent on returning him to Highrealm and not caring how many pieces he returned in.

Just short of their goal, an invisible barrier curled their acute edges back on themselves. He was protected. Amun reached further, exploring every crevice of Jarith's essence. Every soul was connected to the world, and it was next to impossible to close oneself off completely. Yet ze found no opening in Jarith's armor.

The golden strands, with their brilliant metaphysical glow, retracted, and the safety of the darkness returned.

13

ANOTHER ABILITY

Jua and Meta lay in bed, enjoying the music provided by insects beyond the walls of their home. The moon's sliver of light drew silver lines on the window's edge. He held her in his arms and stroked her soft skin.

"Was I too harsh?" Jua asked, referencing their earlier conversation with Maliah. "Perhaps it wasn't wise to share that particular lesson."

"It was the lesson you learned at a much younger age," Meta noted. Her dark brown hair was pulled around her shoulder, and she ran her fingers through it idly.

"Indeed, but the priest told me that my own daylight would follow the night. Instead, I spoke only of the daylight of our people. I wish I could grant her a life with only daylight, but we must always remain focused on our duty."

"Maliah already appreciates the benefits of being a priest. It was a fine reminder of the scope of her duty."

"I'm not so certain," Jua said with a sigh. "I hate to see her so upset."

"She can't avoid the truth forever," Meta replied in her usual flippant tone. "It's our fault for allowing her to think she could escape her fate. I always thought I'd toughen up once she started dreaming, but now I realize I waited too long. Maybe we should've performed the awakening ritual years ago."

"And forcibly awakened her powers?" Jua asked. "When she's already so apprehensive about her role in the prophecy?"

"It likely wouldn't have even worked," Meta said with a chortle. "We always suspected that only her beloved could perform the ritual successfully. But it would've been worth an attempt."

"She would never have forgiven us."

"We're her parents. It's our duty to push her beyond her comfort level."

"No," Jua protested. "Our duty is to prepare her for her future."

Meta turned toward him. His dark skin blended with the night, but she could make out his intense gaze.

"You're far too soft," she said with a sly smile.

He ignored her jeer. "I don't know how to convince her that the prophecy is a blessing. The responsibility and burden is immense, but it's changed our lives for the better. She didn't grow up on a rural farm or in the slums of Ar. We've raised her to want for nothing. You and I have the context to understand how fortunate we truly are."

"You think she sees the prophecy as a burden?" his wife asked. "She's not dim, Jua. Maliah understands her role and is dedicated to performing it. That's all that matters. Whether or not she accepts her gifts, they will come to her, and she'll fulfill her destiny. It's up to her to make the best of it."

"I want her to be happy," Jua insisted. "Even now, I watch her resist her feelings for Jarith as if to spite the prophecy."

Meta chuckled. "She's always been one to swim against the current, hasn't she?"

"In her own way, I suppose."

"But she always does what's necessary for our people in the end," Meta insisted. "You'd be wise to re-member that, Exalted Grand Priest."

Jua rolled his eyes despite knowing that she couldn't see the gesture. "And what of Jarith?"

"What about him?" his wife asked.

"If Maliah refuses the awakening ceremony, he won't perform it."

"Yes, he would respect her decision. But she won't refuse. I've seen it in my dreams. I don't know the circumstances, but she'll concede."

Jua sighed and rolled onto his back. He stared at the ceiling, which was as dark as the rest of the room. "You aren't worried at all?"

"You know me," she replied. "Our futures are written in the stars, and our actions inevitably lead us to our predefined destiny. All we can hope to do is find comfort, joy, and humor in our daily lives."

"Maliah's vision, though."

The quiet dragged out, interrupted only by the insects continuing their nightly symphony outside.

"Meta?" Jua asked when there was a lull in the music.

"Let's not worry about a vision that we could not see and have no hopes of interpreting. Maliah doesn't yet have the proficiency to communicate what she experiences. Amun will work with her to refine her skill."

"What if it's an impending threat?"

"What would you have me do?" she asked in her facetious manner.

"I don't know. But it plagues me, and it obviously haunts Maliah."

"It does us no good to worry about things we can't understand." Meta put her hand to his chest. "Instead, find comfort in knowing that no matter what, I love you and Maliah. I'm not minimizing what she told us. But every day brings me immense joy, and I wouldn't give up our time together for anything."

She leaned toward him to share in a passionate kiss. Then, with one last glance at the dull moonlight, she lay down to sleep. Jua, less than comforted, closed his eyes to attempt the same.

Maliah awoke with the sun after a night of dreams she couldn't remember. They were prophetic dreams, of course, but they don't do much good if they're forgotten.

She could sense that her night hadn't been empty. Had she taken a moment to reflect on her hours of sleep, she might have even thanked the spirits and the ancestors for whatever part they played in her forgetting. However, at the moment of her awakening—that is, her daily awakening, not her powers awakening—something else entered her mind instead.

"Good morning."

The words came as clearly as the night before, when she'd heard Jarith ask a question without speaking the words aloud. His voice rang in her head. She looked around to ensure he wasn't in the room as she gauged just how strange the situation was. Categorically, it was very strange.

"Good morning?" she said in a questioning tone aloud. When there was no response, she formed the words in her mind instead.

She could sense him nearby. It was effortless, so much so that she didn't notice it at first. But then she felt him smile, a warm, loving smile that sent shivers through her body.

"What is this?" she asked. *"Where are you?"*

"Come find me," he replied.

She rushed out of bed. Passing the soap and water she usually cleaned her face with, she opened the door she usually only left once dressed. She raced to the front door. Attendants were bustling around the kitchen, preparing the morning meal for the family, but she paid them no mind. She threw open the door and peered out into the garden.

Racing around hedges, her bare feet padded against the soft, manicured ground to a small, secluded pond where, as if she'd known just where to go, she found Jarith sitting on a wooden bench.

He was wearing a light, tailored linen shirt with loose-fitting sleeves and delicate embroidery over a proper wrap-around skirt fastened with an ornate belt. It was an outfit she'd bought for him the day before, and it suited him gloriously. His twists were tied into an intricate braid that rested on his shoulder.

Her heart filled with joy. It was an odd feeling because it wasn't only her own emotions. Jarith's elation at seeing her intermixed with her own, and the meld of their excitement was breathtaking. It took everything in her not to run into his arms.

She did have some dignity, after all.

"What are you doing here?" she asked.

"I woke up and wanted to see you. So here I am."

"Why can I . . ." She paused, pointing to her ears. ". . . hear you?"

"I think it means you love me," Jarith said with a twisted grin.

She put her hands to her mouth to stop the laughter from escaping, but it came anyway. "You've already spent too much time with my mother, I see."

He took her hand in his and smiled up at her. "How did you sleep? More soundly, I hope."

It was the wrong question, and Maliah didn't want to spoil the mood. "I don't want to talk about it."

"I see. What would you like to talk about?" he asked.

"We should discuss what we're doing today."

His smile widened. He held her hand out away from her body. Her nightgown was translucent, and it rippled just above the ground as a gentle breeze drifted through.

"Perhaps you should get dressed first?"

She slapped his hand away playfully. Turning on her heels, she rushed back toward the house. Her father appeared in the doorway as she approached.

"Maliah?" Jua called.

She laughed as she rushed past him. "Jarith is joining us for breakfast," she sang.

"Were you outside in your nightgown?" he asked, but she had already closed the door to her room.

Soon after, they were all sitting around the table, once again enjoying a morning meal together. Maliah couldn't believe how normal this seemed, nor could she express how much it comforted her.

"Priest Anteri told me that the Ar theater group is presenting a new play at the market stage this afternoon," Meta said.

"That's the same group who performed the Divination of the Anunsi Bowl last year, isn't it?" Jua asked.

"No," Maliah chimed in. "That was the traveling group based out of Intonalia. The Ar group did an interpretation of the Rimah prophecy. They requested assistance from the temple for the stage effects, remember?"

Jua nodded as he chewed. "Even better. Shall we go after midday ritual?"

Everyone agreed except for Jarith, who looked more confused than anything. Maliah wondered if he had ever watched one of the performances through her eyes, though his raised eyebrow made her pretty confident the answer was no.

She stood, having finished her plate of food, and held her hand out to Jarith.

"Come help me pick out what to wear."

She smiled when he slipped his hand into hers and pulled him away from the table.

Jarith was as good at helping Maliah prepare for her day as he had been for himself. With little prompting, he pulled out a dress and shawl from her wardrobe and selected jewelry from her collection. His hands were gentle but firm as he tamed her curls into a loose, braided bun at the back of her head. He adorned her hair with decorative pins and an ornate comb she'd forgotten she had, pulling motifs from the shawl.

Maliah always refused help with her makeup from the family's attendants. This day was no different, but the request prompted her to show Jarith the proper techniques for the Huleay Temple. After she demonstrated on him, she instructed him on how to apply hers.

He bit his lip as he concentrated on each stroke. She was pretty sure she had never seen steadier hands. His warm breath brushed across her face to dry the ink around her eyes before he stepped back and surveyed his work.

"I don't think they're even," he said.

She looked in the mirror and laughed.

"That bad?" he asked.

"No," she replied. "I just never took you for such a perfectionist. It looks amazing."

By the time they exited her room, the attendants had left for morning ritual.

"Sorry," Maliah said to her parents when she found them waiting in the garden.

"Wow," Meta called, looking her over with an approving gaze.

"It's all Jarith's work," Maliah admitted.

Meta's sideways smile crept onto her face. "Looks like I need to upgrade my attendants to compete with my heirs."

Maliah laughed with her mother as Jarith's face lit up with pride.

"You look ready for the high priesthood," Jua said, then added "on the only day of the week you aren't participating in a ritual."

Maliah rolled her eyes, though she made no attempt to hide her smile.

"We should go," she said as her parents shared a laugh at her expense.

There were many benefits to being part of the ruling spiritual caste of Ledine: priests and attendants lived very close to the Huleay Grounds, the compensation was quite generous, and it was never difficult to get a table at a fancy restaurant or to pick up a date at a bar.

One unexpected benefit to being in a party with two Exalted Grand Priests was priority seating at all public rituals in the crowded sanctuary of the main temple.

The grand entrance sat at the center of a colonnade of pillars that stretched up to an incredible height. She had once tried to guess how tall the ceiling was, but when she reached five times her height, she found it difficult to measure further. To ease her curiosity, she had asked Grand Priest Duvramhi, a historian and the oldest-looking priest she knew at the age of seven. He had told her how many spans it stretched, but it was so beyond her understanding at the time—seeing as how she was only three spans tall—that she promptly forgot.

She saw the same question in Jarith's eyes as they walked through one of the oversized doorways and into the inner courtyard, and she really hoped he wouldn't ask her.

Very few people remained in the courtyard, most having entered the sanctuary. Those left were likely visitors from beyond Ar, people caught up in interesting conversations, or attendants doing their work.

Maliah and her family walked straight through and into the hypostyle hall that stood between the courtyard and the sanctuary. They veered to the left, where a guarded door hid a stairway up to a balcony area. Just as the door opened, a voice called out.

"Exalted Priest Jua," the voice said.

Maliah's entire party turned to see a priest about Maliah's age rushing toward them.

"I'll leave you to it," Meta said, turning back to the stairs.

"I'll go with you," Jarith added.

Maliah's father made a gesture that encouraged her to stay. She thought there was a hint of "whatever this is will be good for your career" in his eyes, but he turned back to the young woman without saying a word.

"Good day, Priest Neferu," he said, and she seemed surprised that he knew her name.

She bowed her head and said, "I'm very sorry to bother you right before morning ritual."

"Is one of the temples out of a certain spell again?"

"No, I'm afraid it's nothing that simple."

Her father's composure changed, and his expression became stern.

"You see," she continued, "an item has been stolen from the artifact library."

14

Residue of Essence

At the news of a theft, Jua's eyes grew wide, and Maliah brought her hands to her mouth. Their reactions weren't uncalled for. This was more than a surprise. It was impossible.

The Huleay Grounds hadn't had a security breach in over fifty years, and the artifact library, which held the most dangerous artifacts in the world, was the most well-guarded location in Ar. Two guards were always stationed at the entrance. Furthermore, a spell on the door should have alerted the guards to an intrusion.

"What was taken?" Jua asked.

"We don't know yet," Priest Neferu replied. "I was informed and immediately sought you out. Grand Omari said you were the best person for the task."

Jua nodded, his features grim. "Lead the way."

"What task?" Maliah asked as she kept pace with her father and Priest Neferu.

"Essence tracing," he replied. "Wherever we go, we leave an echo of our essence behind. That residue fades over time, and how fast it decays depends on the emotions and individual it's tied to, so we must act quickly."

"What information does the essence hold? Can it determine the culprit?" Maliah asked.

"It's only a residue, so it rarely holds enough information to identify someone, although there are some historical exceptions. But most importantly, we can typically create a trail of sorts. If we can identify the unique signature of the essence, we may be able to trace it back to its origin."

"That's amazing," Maliah said.

They came to an intersection with one of the main walkways of the Grounds. Most visitors were at the morning ritual, but enough wandered about that Priest Neferu pushed through with a polite "Excuse us."

Once they had returned to the smaller paths, Priest Neferu said, "Grand Omari said you've done this before. When was that?"

"When I was much younger," Jua said, as if he was some old geezer and not an incredibly handsome middle-aged man. "I was involved in a series of murder investigations. My heightened sensitivity to the residue of essence helped identify the culprit."

"You've never told me that," Maliah said, her eyes wide with wonder.

"It's not something I particularly enjoy discussing. Although I'd absolutely perform the task if necessary, it's not an experience I wish to relive."

Maliah furrowed her brow. There were many things she didn't know about her parents, many things she'd never asked about. The more she learned, the more she realized how difficult the priesthood had been for them. Yet they persisted. More than that, they excelled. The nation had expected the best from them, and they certainly received it.

Maliah couldn't help but wonder when they had gotten their power? Her father had mentioned having his first vision as a young child, but when did he gain the ability to detect a person's essence? And how would Maliah reach their level with the limited ability she had so far?

They rounded the final corner, where a crowd of guards stood in a semicircle around the entrance to the tall, windowless structure that was the artifact library. Maliah thought the impenetrable wall of guards was an odd choice, seeing as how the theft had already occurred, but she thought it best not to say that out loud.

Grand Omari broke through the line and reached out to Jua. Her typical calm demeanor was absent as she grasped at his arms.

"You found him," she exclaimed with immense relief. "Wonderful. Thank you for coming, Exalted Grand Priest Jua."

"Jua is fine," he replied.

Maliah knew full well that Grand Priest Omari wouldn't dare call him that, and she was sure her father knew that, too. However, she was also keenly aware that Jua hadn't made the same offer to Priest Neferu. Had he suggested it to Grand Omari knowing she wouldn't do it? Or did it simply annoy him that she used the full title every time? Maliah couldn't be sure.

"Please come in," she said as if inviting her father into her home, if her home had happened to be on fire. It was a tone of intense worry suppressed by a practiced temper of hospitality.

After judging the glances the two senior priests gave them, Priest Neferu stayed put while Maliah followed her father past the guard barricade.

"Are you sure?" Grand Priest Omari whispered, gesturing to Maliah.

She clearly didn't think Maliah should be involved, but if she thought she was being discreet, she was totally wrong. Maliah could see and hear her just fine. Her father, on the other hand, pretended he hadn't heard or seen anything. It wasn't often that Maliah saw this side of him. He was typically the kind of man who befriended everyone. However, when it came to questioning his ability or actions, he refused to concede.

They reached the threshold of the library, and he stopped so sharply that Maliah almost ran into him.

"Maliah, do you sense anything?" he asked.

She took a deep breath, opening her senses to any input, just as Amun had taught her. But as had been the case for her entire life, she sensed nothing.

"No," she said.

"Good," he replied. "Stay near the door. If any sensations come to you, alert me with urgency."

"I understand."

"Grand Omari, you've done an initial scan, I assume?"

"Yes, Exalted Grand Priest Jua. I kept it brief to avoid contaminating the area, but I made one pass widdershins around the periphery of each room."

"Perfect," he said. "Anything?"

"Just the whispers," Grand Omari replied.

With a nod, Jua stepped inside.

"Whispers?" Maliah asked.

"The whispers of the artifacts," Grand Omari replied.

Maliah had never heard of such a thing before. It sounded creepy, but she told herself not to jump to conclusions. Maybe artifacts whispered wonderful affirmations like "you've got this" or "what a fine hair day."

"What do they whisper?" she asked.

"These artifacts?" Grand Omari shook her head. "Things too horrible to mention."

Exactly what Maliah wanted to hear before entering the library. So much for affirmations.

Jarith glanced toward the balcony entrance for the hundredth time. The morning ritual was well under way, but Maliah and Jua hadn't yet joined them.

He had been surprised when, despite the numerous chairs, he and Meta were alone on the balcony. Prior to the start of the ritual, he had asked who else she expected.

"This seating is only for Exalted Grand Priests and our guests," she had mused. "We tend to prefer being in service to watching from above."

"Then why are we here?" Jarith asked innocently.

He had assumed they were required to attend, given the family's status. It would have been preferable, he thought, to explore the city further.

"Many reasons," Meta had answered. "But mainly because the spirits told me we needed to be here."

"So you don't come to every ritual on your days off?"

"Jua and I make the effort to attend at least one ritual on days we aren't in service," she explained. "You never know when the spirits will reach out to you."

Jarith didn't think the spirits were really there, or if they were, that they were doing much reaching out. However, that line of conversation didn't seem appropriate at the time.

Now that the priests had begun to chant on the platform stage below, he had a million burning questions, but he continued his diligent glances over his shoulder at the door.

Meta slapped him on the leg. "You're making me nervous." Despite her words, her tone was playful.

"They'll return soon. The priests often see us arrive and request our assistance."

"On your day off?" Jarith asked in a whisper.

The whisper was unnecessary. Below, the chanting was building as the voices of the priests were joined by the hum of the entire crowd below, repeating the words in unison. The floor buzzed with energy under his feet, and he wondered just how sturdy this balcony was.

He leaned forward and looked over the railing. Below, an aura of swirling color was building. It amazed him, especially since he knew the aura was invisible to the crowd and most of the spiritual staff. Stretched out from the bubbling energy were four long strands, like glowing strings, each leading to a statue at the corner of the room.

Jarith had, of course, noticed the enormous statues of animal-headed people with large, creepy painted eyes staring down at the sanctuary. Since entering the inner Huleay Grounds, he'd wondered how this technologically young race built such massive structures.

But now, with every passing moment, the statues were changing. It was almost as if they were coming alive. Not moving or breathing or metabolizing. But somehow living. Or perhaps channeling power from elsewhere, some place he couldn't detect or comprehend.

He stood and leaned to look at the statue closest to them. It was Asne, a physical representation of the spirit of the Sun. Although it had a lion's head, claws, and a tiger tail, the rest of its body was human. In its hands, Asne held a stack of paper and a writing stylus. It wore a ceremonial dress and sandals similar to what the Exalted Grand Priest below was wearing. Vibrant colors adorned every span, yet even that color seemed more vivid than before.

The chanting rose, and the building's undulations intensified. The aura bubble below decreased in size but grew brighter, as if becoming more dense. Jarith could just make out a faceted ball at its center, sparkling in the sunlight being reflected onto it. The ball rose slowly into the air, hovering above the priest.

The floor and walls of the sanctuary shook as the chanting continued. Jarith gripped the railing to keep his balance. He could have sat down to keep from toppling over, but the floating ball commanded his attention.

He suddenly realized that the glowing strands of aura surrounded physical strings, which were being pulled taut in order to lift the ball. They were almost invisible in the dimly lit sanctuary, especially with the reflections on the faceted sphere casting light elsewhere.

Smiling and content at having unraveled a mystery, he sat down and leaned back in his chair.

The Exalted Grand Priest lifted their hands into the air as the chanting grew ever louder. When they gestured at the not-floating ball, the strings detached from it and retracted into the eyes of the statues. The sphere fell into the priest's outstretched hands, and the room fell silent.

Jarith stayed seated, but leaned forward in hopes that he could confirm his hypothesis for how they had performed this trick.

The faceted ball that now rested in the Exalted Grand Priest's hands had connection points where magnets were embedded. The statues housed retractable strings with small slices of metal at the ends.

Before the ceremony, the strings were connected to the ball. Then, at a predetermined point in the ceremony, the strings disconnected from the ball and retracted back into the statues. It did this very quickly, so Jarith assumed incorrectly that it was a tension-triggered device. In reality, a system of interconnected gears and axles allowed one attendant to turn a crank and pull the strings, releasing the ball to drop into the hands of the priest on stage.

What puzzled Jarith was why this fooled the audience. His vertically superior position obscured the fact that from below, the strings were undetectable. The sound of the mechanism was masked by the loud chanting. The result was a very convincing feat of "magic" that was characteristic of the Huleay Temple.

Jarith gave himself a figurative pat on the back as he realized he was literally witnessing what Jukartis had always called "the indoctrination of an entire world." Even so, he couldn't deny that it was captivating.

"Five out of five stars. Would recommend," Jarith thought.

Five priests formed a circle around the Exalted Grand Priest and knelt as the arms holding the faceted ball stretched toward the ceiling. They moved their hands in a wavelike motion, and the Exalted Grand Priest appeared to be floating in a river of human arms.

"As Asne travels across the domain of Kuay, so do we travel across the domain of time," the Exalted Grand Priest said, their voice echoing through the chamber. "We thank the dark of night for watching over us. We welcome the light of day ahead."

"Thank you, night," the priests led the audience. "Welcome, day."

Jarith placed his elbows on his legs as he leaned forward, almost forgetting that Maliah hadn't joined them.

15

Artifact Library

Inside the artifact library, regularly spaced shelves held items placed with generous gaps between. The comfortable spacing made the room feel rather empty and allowed Maliah to watch as her father walked each aisle.

Along the walls, set between dim lanterns, hung old, faded paintings illustrating a vibrant history of the more interesting artifacts housed in the library. Maliah knew little of those stories. Amun had often tested her with artifacts, but she'd never thought to ask about their origins or histories. Ze must not have thought it important.

Maliah couldn't say she felt nothing when she crossed the threshold into the artifact library, but she wasn't sure she was feeling something either. It was a general feeling of something nothingness—or was it nothing somethingness. Either way, she couldn't pin it down, but she was confident that the energy was different than outside the library.

"Whoa," she said.

"Ah, you sensed it," Jua said, his tone revealing a sense of pride. "Very good."

"What am I feeling?" Maliah asked.

"A history of magic."

"What does that mean?"

Jua paused whatever he was doing, which looked suspiciously like pretending to be busy, and looked at her.

"Priests created these artifacts, and each was designed with a specific purpose," he said. "Magic is our way of influencing Nature. Therefore, every item is attempting to exert its influence on the world."

"So, the artifacts are all trying to affect the environment at the same time?"

"Exactly. And that's an energy shift that anyone can sense, no matter their level of sensitivity. Most people wouldn't recognize that. They'd just feel . . . uncomfortable."

Yup, she was definitely uncomfortable.

"Amun has told me you're adept at using artifacts, even though your magical abilities have yet to surface," Jua said, going back to whatever he was doing. "Do you agree?"

"I believe Amun," Maliah said noncommittally.

Jua laughed. "That's fair."

Having circled the room, he picked up a lantern near one of the three rear doors and lit it with a nearby match. He waved for Maliah to follow and instructed her to stay by the door to the first storage room.

Unlike the entrance chamber, this room's shelves were tightly packed. Maliah felt claustrophobic as soon as she stepped inside. Cluttered aisles sat between the shelves, and although the floor was clear, Maliah wondered how her father could fit. Handles, blades, arms, and more protruded into the aisles, and many artifacts sat in haphazard stacks.

A shuffling caught her attention from the right-most aisle, but when she looked toward it, nothing was there. Her father wandered through each aisle, his footsteps silent.

The noise came again, louder this time. Maliah took a step toward it.

"Maliah, don't leave the doorway," Jua said.

"I heard something from over there," she replied, pointing.

It came again. Louder. But this time, she recognized it not as shuffling, but as a whisper.

"I heard it again," she said. "It's . . ."

The hair at the back of her neck stood on end. Her heart raced as the whisper became clearer. She gasped as it spoke, still not wanting to believe what she heard. But it returned. The words were crystal clear.

"You're killing her."

Maliah screamed as the words rang over and over, louder each time.

"You're killing her."

Without being told, she understood who the voice spoke of.

"You're killing her."

It was her mother.

"YOU'RE KILLING HER."

Clenching her hands and closing her eyes, she tried to block out the voice. She wasn't doing anything. Her mother was fine. She wasn't going to hurt her mother. She would never—

The voice continued to get louder.

It was inside her head. The words remained the same, but the meaning shifted.

"YOU'RE KILLING HER!"

No longer a suggestion, it was now a command. A command from a whisper that screamed inside her.

Then, only moments later, the words no longer came from a whisper. Instead, the thought was her own. A thought intent on committing an atrocity.

"YOU'RE KILLING HER!"

Maliah looked at her hands. They buzzed with energy, as if they held a power she'd never possessed. It threatened to explode, and she fought to hold it in, to keep her control over it. The strength surged into her arms, her torso, her legs, and up into her head.

With every passing moment, her power reached further from herself. It collected the latent energy in the air, in the plants, from the people, from everywhere and sapped everything dry. Her physical body was paralyzed in fear while her spiritual body clawed its way closer to her mother.

"*YOU'RE KILLING HER!*"

She was killing her mother. She couldn't comprehend how or why. But it was happening.

She could do nothing to stop it.

Maliah abruptly fell backward, thrown to the ground. She looked up. Her father stood over her, having shoved her down.

Did he know what she was doing? How could he?

What had she done?

Had any of it been real?

What was she doing just a moment before?

"Maliah, is it gone?" Jua asked.

She paused.

It was quiet. The voice, the power, and even the emotion of the last few minutes had all disappeared. Like the distant memory of where she put that one thing so that she'd never lose it, the voice and the echo of its message had faded away.

"Maliah?" he asked again with greater intensity.

"I'm sorry," Maliah said. "Yes, it's . . . it's gone."

Jua breathed a sigh of relief and helped her to her feet, keeping her well away from the doorway.

"You must be more proficient than Amun believes," he said. "The Ash of Ger is incredibly dangerous, but only to those who can hear it."

The Ash of Ger. That sounded ominous. And Maliah wasn't in the mood for ominous.

She wrapped her arms around herself and collapsed her shoulders inward. The whole experience was fading, leaving only an unnerving perception of lost time. The memory of what she had been trying to accomplish drifted from her mind.

"So that was from an artifact? It was so intense, and now it feels like it never happened."

"You'll learn more about its power in due time," he interrupted, grabbing her by the shoulders. "For now, just know you did exactly as instructed. Great work."

"How are you able to handle that?" she asked.

He pulled her into a protective hug. It wasn't something she needed. The memory had faded to a dull speck at the back of her mind.

"That's not important right now," he said. "All that matters is that you're safe."

Regaining his composure, he returned to finish his review of the room, giving Maliah strict instructions to stay by the artifact library's entrance.

He didn't have to tell her twice.

When he finished his initial scan of the three back rooms, all of which were overstuffed with artifacts, he rejoined her. Grand Priest Omari was speaking to one of the guards when he emerged.

"What did you sense?" she asked.

"Would you prefer the good news or the bad news?" he replied.

She crossed her arms and waited, refusing to answer the question. Maliah wondered if her father found it amusing to push Grand Omari's buttons, but if he did, he wasn't letting on.

"Well, the good news is," he continued, "we can track the residue. The bad news: I know what they stole."

"How is that bad news?" Maliah asked.

Jua raised an eyebrow and looked to Grand Omari to guess.

"They stole something awful, didn't they?" Grand Omari asked, clearly annoyed at Jua's guessing game.

He nodded. "The Dwesdar Dagger."

Maliah had never heard of this artifact, though the name Dwesdar sounded vaguely familiar. Truth be told, she was finding her knowledge of artifacts to be lacking. She made a mental note to ask Amun to rectify this as soon as possible.

"I apologize, Exalted Grand Priest Jua," Grand Omari said. She bowed her head, seeming actually as sorry as she sounded and not just apologizing to save face. "I find it difficult to keep all the weapon artifacts straight. Which is the Dwesdar Dagger?"

"Later," Jua said. "Right now, all that's important is that it's dangerous. I must identify a traceable pattern in the residue as rapidly as possible."

"I understand. What should I do?"

"Summon an investigation squad and divide them into three groups. The first group should work with the Huleay Governmental Council to uncover any domestic or international intelligence about this theft. Then, another group should speak to everyone who has set foot within the Huleay Grounds over the last two days. I'm interested in any suspicious behavior in recent weeks, no matter how small."

"Any particular suspicious behavior?" Grand Omari asked.

"I'm not sure, but my intuition says that whoever did this is a magic worker."

"A magic worker?" Maliah asked. "Do you think a priest did this?"

"We won't jump to that conclusion, but we can't rule it out either," Jua replied with strict discipline. He turned back to Grand Priest Omari. "We need to gather as much information as we can. Our primary goals are to identify the thief and determine what they intend to do with the Dwesdar Dagger."

"I understand," she replied. "And the third group?"

"The third should report directly to me. Only non-spiritual caste individuals and Grand Priests who've completed their artifact training. No one in between."

She nodded and started to turn, but he held his hand up and waited for her full attention to return to him.

"Let me make this clear," he said. "Once we have the trail, no one should pursue this person until I can accompany them. I don't wish to see anyone harmed out of recklessness."

"Yes, Exalted Grand Priest Jua." After confirming there was nothing else, she rushed off, probably to tell Priest Neferu to do the grunt work for her.

Jua then turned to Maliah. Butterflies fluttered in her stomach as she wondered what work he would assign her.

"Go back to your mother and tell her what's happening," Jua said.

Perhaps she shouldn't have been surprised at his simple command, but a small part of her was disappointed.

"Any instructions? Can we do anything to help?" she asked.

Jua shook his head. "Your mother won't follow any instructions I give her, so there's no point. But if you can convince her to relax on her day off, that would be amazing."

"You don't want her help?"

Maliah was full of questions, but that one seemed the most pressing. Her entire life, her mother had been the center of all magic activities, with her father playing a supporting role. She'd rarely seen her father take a leadership position, such as he was doing now.

He looked at her with reluctance, and she almost took back the question.

Before she could, he said, "Your mother has been exhausted recently. I'm worried she's overdoing it and needs some true rest." A crooked smile came to his face. "And I have a feeling you and Jarith need a chaperone."

Maliah found herself laughing, and she couldn't help but wonder how it was possible after her emotional encounter with the Ash of Ger. Such was the enigma of magic.

"Ah," she said, "the truth comes out."

"Anyway, off you go. I have work to do."

"You'll really be fine on your own?" she asked again, just to be sure.

"Absolutely," he assured her before waving his hands to shoo her away.

She bowed and turned on her heels, intent on asking her mother all her pressing questions.

16

THE DWESDAR MASSACRE

Maliah was surprised when her mother didn't jump at the chance to join the investigation into the stolen dagger. Normally, whether out of curiosity, duty, or an interest in the latest gossip, Meta would have inserted herself into the situation with fervor. Instead, when Maliah suggested they return home, Meta agreed.

"You don't want to go help Dad?" Maliah asked.

"I wouldn't want him to feel outclassed," was her mother's flippant reply. Because why be serious when you can be snarky?

So, when the morning ritual ended, they returned home and got comfortable on the rooftop patio, where the fresh, inviting breeze danced through their hair and across their skin. They sat in silence for a while, enjoying a musical performance drifting on the wind.

Maliah found it difficult to distract herself from her encounter in the artifact library, so she turned her attention to the stolen dagger. The artifact library was under constant guard, and the only access was the entrance they had used. There weren't even any windows, so a security gap didn't explain it.

She wondered how the guard had become aware of the artifact's absence without an alarm of some kind. Had they noticed something? Or was it only detected when reviewing the inventory? Perhaps she should have stayed with her father. It would have been an excellent learning opportunity, though she hoped to never have to deal with an artifact theft herself.

Finally, when the distant music had lulled, Jarith asked, "So what happened again? Something important was stolen?"

The question caught her off guard. She'd become so comfortable with his presence that it seemed absurd that he didn't understand what had happened. She reminded herself that although they could now—apparently—speak to each other in their minds, that didn't mean Jarith knew everything she did.

"Yes, someone stole a dagger," she said.

"A dangerous one," Meta added. "It's called the Dwesdar Dagger. It's a magic artifact."

"I don't remember an artifact being stolen before," Jarith said, hand on his chin as he thought.

"I'm not aware of anything being stolen from the artifact library during my lifetime," Meta replied. "Even before that, I only recall one incident, before it was guarded so heavily. But whoever stole it must be proficient with magic."

"Dad said the same thing." Maliah ached to know more.

"Only someone with magical abilities can wield it for its true purpose," Meta continued. "To a non-magic worker, the dagger is merely an instrument that never dulls."

"That's incredible." Maliah sat forward in her seat. "But that doesn't sound so bad."

"That's just the start. The dagger's creator, Exalted Grand Priest Dwesdar, was the advisor of King Priore the Third."

"I've never heard of him," Maliah admitted. She looked at Jarith, as if he would know anything more than she did. He shook his head and shrugged.

"He was only king for seven days. On the morning of the eighth day, his attendants found him in his chambers, appearing to have died in his sleep of natural causes. Yet, he was rather young.

"His heir was his young daughter. She ruled for five years before being found dead in the same mysterious circumstances as her father. The court recruited the best alchemists and priests to look into the incidents."

"Several years later, the next monarch died, but this time something was different. Exalted Grand Priest Dwesdar had become bold in his distaste for the late king, and the court and investigators found evidence that he was unhappy with how King Priore the Third and his daughter, Queen Majan, executed their duties.

"The leaders confronted him. It was then that he revealed the dagger, though its true power stayed hidden.

Its razor-sharp blade murdered ten armed guards before he turned it on his fellow priests. The priests weren't trained for combat, and none of them survived. If it weren't for a Young Priest who had hidden during the confrontation, many more would have died from the dagger's power."

Jarith was transfixed on the story, hanging on every word. Meanwhile, Maliah was wondering what the point was.

Her mother continued. "The girl told the remaining Temple priests what had occurred, and while Exalted Grand Priest Dwesdar was busy with the next coronation, they secretly called for the Ocomit Priesthood."

"What's that?" Jarith asked, excited sparkles in his eyes.

Maliah stifled a laugh. "They're the combat branch of the Huleay Temple," she said. "Priests dedicated to the art of war."

"The art of war," Jarith repeated, enamored.

It should have been a crime to be this adorable, especially for a grown man.

"Did they get there in time?" Jarith asked.

It was exactly the right question.

"No," Meta replied. "By the time they arrived, Exalted Grand Priest Dwesdar had killed the entire court. He even sat on the throne and declared himself king."

"Then what did they do?"

"They did what they were trained to do. And during the battle, they discovered what the dagger's power truly was.

"When we use our magic, we connect with Nature, with the realm of spirits. In return for faithfully serving their will, we are imbued with protection from harm."

Maliah had to work pretty hard not to raise a sarcastic eyebrow at her mother, who was as talented at wordsmithing as she was at magic. This was a fancy way of saying that the Huleay Temple provided protection charms to everyone in the spiritual caste who didn't have their own magic. These charms were to safeguard against magical threats but offered additional, although limited, protection from physical harm.

"The kings and queens of old were protected in much the same way," Meta continued. "But this dagger that Dwesdar created could pierce that magical protection. It could, from a distance, cut the cord of life to kill its victim."

This got Maliah's full attention, and her jaw dropped open. "How did they get it away from him?"

"They attacked in force. The dagger can have only one victim at any moment. So while he attacked one, the others overcame him and seized the weapon."

"Oh," Maliah said as she remembered something from her history lessons. "The Dwesdar Massacre. I knew I'd heard that name somewhere."

Before her mother could answer, the gate to the front garden swung open. Five guards stormed in, each holding a khopesh at the ready. Following just behind them, Jua entered with brow furrowed.

"What's going on?" Meta asked as she rushed over to the parapet.

"Are you all safe?" Jua asked from below.

"Yes, of course," his wife replied.

"Check the home thoroughly," Jua said to the guards before rushing around to the exterior stairs.

"Are you essence tracing?" Meta asked when he reached the rooftop patio.

"I thought Maliah told you," he replied.

"She told me someone stole the Dwesdar Dagger and that you were helping investigate. But you know how dangerous essence tracing is. Why would you—"

"Trust me," Jua interrupted. "It was necessary. And it led me here."

"What?" Maliah asked.

"Jarith," Jua said sternly. "Where were you between when you left last night and when you arrived this morning?"

Maliah couldn't believe what she was hearing. She tried to interject, but Jarith put a hand to hers.

With no hesitation, he replied. "I went home with Amun and remained there all night. When I woke up, I came straight here. I went to the guest room, changed my clothes, and then waited in the garden. I remained there until Maliah woke up."

Maliah couldn't believe what was happening.

"Is anyone able to verify that? Did you pass anyone on the street?"

"No. It was still dark when I arrived here. I'm not even sure the attendants saw me."

"We'll ask," Jua said, nodding at one of the guards who had followed him.

Just as the guard dashed away to follow the unspoken order, a voice called out from below.

"Exalted Grand Priest Jua. We've found something."

Maliah was the first to follow her father down. A guard tried to stop her from going into the home by holding out his weapon, but Meta, several steps behind her daughter, flicked her hand, and the weapon swung out of their way.

"Are you serious?" Jua was saying as they entered the home.

"We can't be sure. You tell us," a guard replied.

Jua was holding something. He closed his eyes for a moment. Maliah thought she saw a glimmer of light shine around him, but it was so faint, she assumed it was her imagination.

Moments later, Jua's eyes shot open, and he whipped his head toward Jarith. He held up his arm, and Jarith grunted with effort. Jua's power pinned Jarith's arms to his side. The Highrealmer tried to jerk free, but he only fought for a second.

Jua took careful steps forward, closing the distance between them.

"Meta. Maliah. Step away."

Maliah was pinned in place with indecision. Her mother dragged her several steps toward the wall. Her eyes wide, Maliah watched in horror as her father stepped closer.

Her horror wasn't for Jarith. As a Highrealmer, it was an everyday pastime to shape reality. Jarith may have been getting used to his new physical form, but she was not under the delusion that he was powerless.

A lump caught in her throat. She needed to warn her father, but she couldn't bring herself to speak up against Jarith. She pulled her hands up to her chest as she tried to figure out what she could do.

Jua held up a wooden sheath painted white with gold patterned inlays. "Why was this in your room?"

"What is it?" Jarith asked.

"It's a dagger's sheath. A very specific one. And it's tied to your essence trail, which was present at the location where the dagger was stolen."

"I don't know why the sheath was in that room."

Jua stepped closer, his intensity rising. "Have you ever seen it before?"

Jarith swallowed. "Yes."

He was not offering any information beyond what he was asked. Maliah recalled Jukartis teaching Jarith this strategy, preparing him in case the savage Midrealmers tried to imprison him. It was a form of emotional de-escalation that bought time to build a complex magical defense. If Jarith was acting on this advice, as he answered the questions, he was also crafting spell-s—what Highrealmers called formulae—that could be unleashed at a moment's notice. This situation, if her father wasn't careful, could turn violent.

Her mouth went dry, and she tried in vain to relax her shoulders. She clutched at the sleeves of her dress, but it didn't comfort her or make it any easier to interrupt the scene unfolding before her.

"Where?" Jua asked, drawing out the word with a sense of warning.

"When I was in Highrealm," Jarith replied. When Jua's glare made it clear he expected more, Jarith continued. "Our scientists kept records of objects that held significant power. It was in that archive of data."

"Where else?"

"Nowhere. That's the only time I've ever seen it before now."

Why was Jarith answering these questions? He could break her father's hold with ease and take control of this situation. Perhaps he was worried about seeming guilty, but she feared a deeper meaning. A seed of doubt formed in her mind.

Jarith was hiding something.

Maliah's hands trembled as she reviewed the facts. Jarith was boxed into a corner, likely forming defensive spells to protect himself. Her father had traced the thief to their home, and the sheath of the stolen dagger had been found in Jarith's room. Bile built in her throat as tears came to her eyes.

Amun's warning came to mind: "Jarith is dedicated to fulfilling prophecy."

It was a simple message fraught with meaning. If his ultimate purpose was to ensure the prophecy was fulfilled, who knew what lengths he'd go to? Maybe he'd go so far as to pretend to love her. The thought came so quickly that she struggled to push it away. Had the High-realmers controlled what she saw and heard in their reality? Had they spoon fed her the entire experience to groom her for Jarith's arrival?

Jarith could have been lying this whole time, and she'd been too caught up in her emotions to realize it. She put her trembling hands to her lips and found them cold.

The energy in the room was changing, as if sucking the heat from the air. Her mother's expression was uncharacteristically grim. She must have felt it, too.

"You're not asking the most important question," Jarith said.

"Am I not?" Jua asked. "And what question is that?"

"Did I steal the dagger?"

Maliah could see from her father's expression that he was not amused, so she was surprised when Jua humored him.

"Fine. Jarith, did you steal the dagger?"

"Of course I didn't," Jarith said with the first inflection of annoyance she'd heard him use since he arrived.

"Even so, I must detain you until we determine what's happening, or—"

The door to their home opened again, and everyone looked to see who was barging in on their little surprise arrest party.

"Release him, Jua," Amun said as ze entered the now very overcrowded common room.

Jua didn't comply. He outranked Amun, despite Amun's advanced age. But Maliah assumed her father was holding onto Jarith more as a precaution than anything else.

"He's a suspect—"

"I know," Amun said. "I heard. Let him go."

Jua looked long and hard into Amun's typical stern face and finally lowered his arm. Jarith visibly relaxed.

"Now, please review our understanding of the events that have transpired," Amun requested.

"The Dwesdar Dagger was stolen from the artifact library," Jua grumbled. "The essence left behind led us here, and the dagger's sheath was recovered from his room."

"Quite incriminating," Amun said. Ze placed zir hand to zir chin. "And what were you hoping to accomplish by restraining him?"

"To prevent retaliation," a guard spoke up, who really should have known better. At a simple glance from Amun, he shrunk back into himself.

"If Jarith is accused of a crime," Amun said, "he should be investigated. However, we can't expect to detain him as we would a normal prisoner. If he's powerful enough to steal the dagger, the only safe place to hold him is here."

The guards exchanged looks while Maliah nodded her head in understanding.

"Yes," she said. "Here, he can be watched by the most powerful priests in Ledine."

Amun gave her zir sort-of-smile and nodded. "Exactly so. To do otherwise would be negligent." Ze crossed zir arms. "The guards should focus on completing their investigation, and we will continue with our evening."

Jua looked to Meta for her opinion, but all he got was a shrug. Oh, and an equally helpful grimace.

"Very well," he said. "Guards, you're dismissed. Please allow the attendants back in as you leave."

Maliah breathed out a sigh of relief. She was comforted by Amun's ability to de-escalate what could very well have been a disaster, but she still felt on edge.

All she could hope for was that they found answers soon.

While the attendants prepared an early dinner, Meta returned to the roof for some fresh air. The sun was still out, beaming down and warming the earth as if nothing had changed. She basked in its glow, placing her hands together and praying to Asne, the spirit of sun.

Footsteps coming up the stairs interrupted her conversation, and Amun appeared moments later.

She smiled warmly. "That was quite the show you put on."

"Me?" ze asked. "Your husband was looking to start a war. Unless you expect me to believe he underestimates Jarith's power so terribly."

Ze sat next to her with care, no sign of aging in zir motion.

"He's very dedicated to protecting his people," she replied. "And when he's caught up in an essence trace, sometimes the spirit of who he's tracking affects him as well."

"Are you insinuating that Jarith is the source of Jua's pique?"

"I didn't sense any anger from Jarith."

"Nor I," Amun admitted. "But he comes from another world, and he's trained his entire life for this. Perhaps he can mask his energies well."

Meta leaned against the back of the couch and allowed her head to dangle. A pair of ibises flew overhead, gracefully gliding toward the river. As she watched them cut through the sky, she sighed.

"I'm not convinced. We've missed something. I just can't see what."

"I believe you're exhausted," Amun said, eyebrows drawn tight with worry.

"That I am," she admitted. "More and more, recently. The effects are waning faster each time." She took a deep breath. "But Maliah's powers are sure to awaken soon, so at least I don't have to worry about her any longer."

"None of that talk," Amun said. Ze hovered zir hands above her body. "Just relax, and I'll see what I can do."

17

Scorn and Offering

As Jua spoke to an attendant across the room, Jarith sat alone with Maliah. It seemed like the first time they'd had a moment to themselves in days, though it had only been hours.

Maliah had lingered near him, but her father had made it clear through less than subtle social cues that although Jarith was literally going to stay in their family home, he also remained figuratively in serious donkey poop.

Now that the heat of the moment had passed, he spoke in a low voice that his magic ensured only she could hear. "I didn't steal the dagger."

She looked at him with drawn brows and puckered lips. "I don't know how I can believe that."

"I wouldn't lie to you about this."

"And what **would** you lie to me about?" she scoffed. "What **have** you lied about, Jarith?"

He drew in a shaky breath and clenched his jaw. Fighting back tears, he searched her features for something gentle. A twinkle of understanding was all he needed, though more than he deserved. After all, he had to ritually sacrifice Maliah's mother or else face death. He struggled to contemplate the former option, and hadn't given the latter more than a passing twinge of terror.

Maliah and her family had shown him nothing but kindness. Even Amun had stood up for him. Yet he was destined to throw it all away just to infuse some Highrealm energetic DNA into their gene pool?

He deserved her scorn. He accepted that. Yet he wanted to convince her that he didn't want anything terrible to happen. No simple words existed to express the complex grief consuming him, so he stayed silent.

"I was right, then," Maliah continued when he didn't answer. "You have been hiding something."

"Maliah," he started, but there was nothing to add.

She stood and walked away, striking up a conversation with an attendant in the kitchen.

His thoughts turned to escape. Jukartis had instructed him to remain as non-threatening as possible if detained, to feign weakness until his chances of escape were optimal, but that didn't seem to be working out. Especially since, unlike his parent, he didn't see the Midrealmers as expendable.

The guards, who he could have disabled if necessary, had left the property. But he didn't know the extent of Jua's power. Meta and Amun were out of sight for now. He could sneak out the front door, but once outside, there were only a few trees to conceal himself behind. They'd spot him before he could get through the gate.

And if he made it out, where would he go?

The research team in Highrealm had discovered caves to the west that were suitable candidates for temporary accommodations. He'd still be a fugitive, but he'd be free. That is, until he dissipated and his essence returned to Highrealm in a billion pieces.

Jarith placed his face in his hands. Running wasn't an option. He either had to confront this head-on or accept his inevitable death.

Something nudged his shoulder, and he looked up to see Amun standing over him with a plate of food. More time had passed than he realized. Maliah was no longer in the common area, and Meta was reviewing a tray of food in the kitchen. Nearby, Jua spoke with a group of people, doling out orders, Jarith assumed.

"Eat, child," Amun said.

Jarith took the food and thanked the Exalted Grand Priest. He was surprised when ze sat in the chair across from him.

"What distresses you?" Amun asked.

It was the oddest question Amun could have asked. Sure, maybe not as strange as how many olives Jarith could fit in his belly button, but it was peculiar nonetheless. And it was just as effective at making Jarith second-guess whether he wanted to eat the olives on his plate.

He guessed that the question was a litmus test, which Amun would use to gauge his worthiness. But the correct answer eluded him.

"Lots of things," he said with a disbelieving look, "including being framed for a crime I didn't commit."

"Then you're innocent?" Amun asked.

Another trick question. This form of questioning reminded him of Jukartis, who had a keen interrogation technique. Jarith had rarely been able to keep up with his parent and had therefore relied on telling the truth.

"I'm innocent of stealing this dagger," he clarified. He would have included the name of the dagger to strengthen the statement, but he couldn't remember it.

The corners of Amun's lips curled upward. It looked nothing like a smile, but Jarith got the feeling that was what it was supposed to be.

"I believe you," Amun said, "and I shall do what I can to resolve this."

"What does that mean?" Jarith asked.

As he spoke, a loud clang rang out from behind him. Jarith sprang to his feet, his plate clattering to the floor. Olives danced away, but he paid them no attention. His eyes grew wide with worry as he saw Meta lying on the floor of the kitchen. Much of the food that had been on the tray was now scattered around her.

Jua rushed to her side as she pushed herself onto her elbows.

"Oh, dear," Meta said as she took her husband's arm for balance. "I merely tripped over myself, everyone. I'm fine."

The attendants hovered nearby, awaiting orders, but Jua waited for Amun. Together, they helped her to her feet.

"Really," she said, then repeated, "I'm fine."

"You should retire for the evening," Amun instructed.

She nodded, looking too exhausted to quarrel, and allowed them to walk her to the bedroom. When they emerged a few minutes later, Jua closed the door. Though he spoke softly, Jarith heard Jua ask Amun if she was "fine."

"She knows herself," Amun answered. "And I believe she'll realize she's unable to continue at her current pace."

"She's been working almost every day, even on her rest days. Today is the first she's taken off in many lunar cycles."

"And thus why the spirits have willed her to relax."

Jua sighed, and Amun put a hand to his shoulder.

"You should focus on your wife," ze said. "Allow me to host Jarith another evening."

"You think that's wise? If he stole the dagger—"

"Then your wife won't get in my way," Amun said.

Jarith couldn't tell if it was meant in jest or not.

Jua sighed again. "I don't think he's the thief," he whispered. Luckily, Jarith had already crafted amplification formulae so he could hear them better. "But I have no evidence to support that."

"He's made no move to flee," Amun replied. The statement seemed non sequitur to Jarith, but Jua understood the implication.

"Fine," Jua said with a nod. "Take him home, but monitor him. And return first thing in the morning."

Amun's hand still rested on Jua's shoulder. Zir sleeve slid down to zir elbow, revealing something far too familiar for Jarith to ignore. If he hadn't been looking right at it, he would have missed the symbol inscribed there. Jarith wasn't sure if it was a tattoo or something more powerful, but he recognized it. After all, he'd seen it every day for most of his life.

It was the Athu Aqatne, the theorem to travel between worlds, which sat above the entrance to the Ascension Project in Highrealm.

Every curve was carefully calculated. Every line was exactly etched. And every angle was perfectly proportioned. The mark's precision left no doubt: there was more to Amun than it appeared.

And the pieces were coming together.

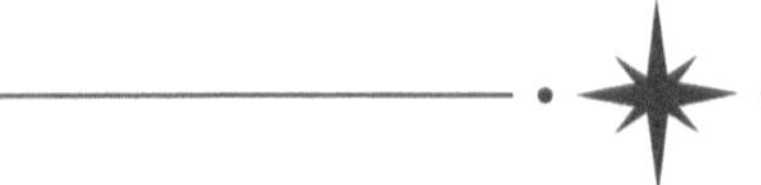

Maliah sat on the bench by her window, looking out at the sky, which was being quite the show-off as day turned to dusk. The gold accents on the statues up the hill gleamed, setting them starkly against the matte pigment that adorned the stone of the sculptures. The sky was so clear, Maliah found herself lost in its gradient of blue, pink, and purple.

She scoffed at the drama, but not because she found it any less breathtaking than ever. Instead, her scorn was toward herself.

It seemed clear that Jarith had stolen the dagger. The discovered sheath and essence tracing left little doubt. All that remained was to find where he'd hidden the dagger itself. But if Jarith was guilty, why had he done it?

She was riddled with apprehension. She knew Jarith. It seemed impossible for him to have concealed a completely different side of himself her entire life. And it was hard to believe he would steal a dagger to kill someone. Who would he even have reason to kill?

She pulled her hair around her shoulder and ran her fingers through the twisted curls. Her mind kept going in circles. Jarith had been hiding something from her. Had it been a plot to murder someone? What was his motive? And how could he have hidden this from her?

Even if he did plan to take someone's life, he must have a reason. That didn't make it acceptable, but she was certain such a task would burden him. He had no one to confide in, and Maliah had pushed him away.

Perhaps if she'd been more supportive, he would have been more forthcoming. Maybe he would have shared his plans with her, and she could have talked it out with him.

Her heart seemed heavy as her questions multiplied. It wasn't too late. She could still show him she cared. Jarith was carrying such a burden, and she wanted to help him shoulder that.

There was a knock at her door. She sat up straight before calling for them to enter. Her father peeked in and, seeing that she wasn't in bed, entered the room.

"How are you?" he asked.

"How would you be if Mom was accused of theft with intent to murder?" she said with a forced half-smile.

He nodded. "Understandable." He walked over to her and glanced out of her window. "Lovely evening to be ruined in such a way."

Maliah didn't respond. There was nothing more to say.

"I wanted to tell you," he continued, "that your mother had a bit of an incident." Before Maliah could ask, he told her what had happened in the kitchen. "She's just fatigued," he assured her. "We should urge her to rest tomorrow. I've already sent word to the Temple that we'll all be taking another day off."

"And Jarith?" she asked.

"Jarith is staying with Amun again this evening. They'll return in the morning. They left a short while ago."

"I need to apologize to him," Maliah said. "I don't want him to go to bed tonight believing I've abandoned him."

Jua placed a hand on her head and stroked her curly hair. His smile was pained but sincere. Maliah's life had been sheltered, but she now understood that her father hadn't always lived in such a comfortable environment. Even so, his warmth and sincerity shone through his complex expression.

"This is a tough situation for you both. I believe Jarith would appreciate the gesture." His face grew stern. "You should go now while it's still light out. If Jarith isn't the culprit, there remains a thief afoot with a weapon meant to harm those with magic."

Maliah smiled and threw her arms around her father. With a quick goodbye, she slipped out of the house, unaware that the drama she despised was just beginning.

As soon as Jarith and Amun entered zir home—except for a momentary pause to marvel again at how the lamps lit themselves in unison—Jarith spoke.

"Who are you?"

"That's quite an open question," Amun replied, turning to face zir guest. "Can you be more specific?"

"I saw it. On your arm. The Athu Aqatne."

Amun didn't seem as surprised as Jarith expected, although he also recognized that the Exalted Grand Priest was quite difficult to read. Still, he felt that some amount of shock should have come to Amun's expression. Either the shock of being found out, or at least a questioning look of confusion over what an Athu Aqatne was. Really, anything other than the same measured, stern gaze would have been preferable.

"You're from Highrealm, aren't you?" Jarith asked.

Amun didn't respond immediately. Instead, ze gazed into Jarith's eyes, as if searching for something.

Jarith wasn't sure if ze found what ze was looking for or not, but after an uncomfortable and awkward wait, ze replied.

"I didn't know what to expect from you, Jarith, child of Jukartis."

So, that was a yes, then.

"But I certainly didn't expect this," Amun continued. Ze moved across the room to a small table. With calculated movements, ze took off each ring and placed them in a line. "I thought it incapable for em to teach such care as you seem to have for Maliah."

"Why are you here?" Jarith asked. "How did you even get here?"

"I arrived in much the same way you did, I presume. I admit, though, I'm concerned. In order for you to be here, you must have collected the cost. Whose life did you steal to cross into this reality?"

"I haven't killed anyone," Jarith insisted.

Amun laid the last ring onto the table before turning zir attention back to him.

"So my hypotheses were correct, then," Amun replied. "You're able to defer the energetic cost. That means there's still time."

Jarith didn't process the latter part of Amun's statement because he was confused by the former.

"What do you mean, your hypotheses?" he asked.

"I hate to reveal this to you," Amun said, not sounding at all like ze hated to reveal it, "but the 'prophecy' you've been brainwashed to believe—the one which foretells the rescue of our people from extinction—is fantasy. Merely a propaganda campaign to sell my work to the people in aid of a larger plot."

Jarith correctly assumed that Amun expected him to be surprised at this revelation. So, as petty retribution for Amun's own lack of expression, Jarith remained as neutral as possible.

"I already know the truth," he said after a few moments of feeling proud of himself.

"Do you?" Amun asked, raising one eyebrow in disbelief. "Somehow, I doubt that. If you understood the full truth, I don't believe you'd be here in Midrealm."

Amun's aura began to compress—shrinking in size but becoming denser. Ze was preparing something, and a sudden pang of worry gripped Jarith. He'd thought they were having an awkward but civil conversation.

All he could think to do was keep Amun talking.

"You said these are your hypotheses, that this is your work. Who does that make you?"

"Do you not know your history?" Amun asked.

Jarith felt pretty confident in his history, but he needed to buy time to figure out what was going on.

"I'm the scientist who discovered Midrealm," Amun said.

Ze moved zir index finger in small circles. Jarith took a cautious step back. Amun was crafting formulae, but to do what?

"I'm the one who realized we could transfer discrete souls between Highrealm and Midrealm. I'm the author of the Athu Aqatne theorem. My work is the basis for the entire prophecy."

"So, I'm guessing you didn't go by Amun back in Highrealm," Jarith replied.

"I've taken many names, but that isn't important now."

"Oh, so now Amun gets to decide what's important or not," Jarith chose not to say.

The goal was to keep zir talking, not antagonize zir. So instead, he stayed silent.

"Allow me a moment of inquiry," Amun said. "Who are you tasked to murder?"

Jarith swallowed back a lump in his throat. He didn't know if the question was rhetorical or not. If Amun was really the scientist who authored the Athu Aqatne theorem, ze understood the complexity involved in the calculation to determine the sacrifice. Ze must know that not just any soul would suffice, but that a powerful individual from Midrealm was needed to balance the equations.

And that particular guest list of honor was pretty darn short.

Speaking of short, Jarith got the feeling, as Amun's aura commanded the entire room to heed zir will, that time was running short as well.

18

TUSSLE

As Amun built an impenetrable aura of energy around zirself, Jarith struggled to understand what was happening. If Amun was actually the person who created the theorem used to transfer energy between Midrealm and Highrealm, perhaps ze could help him figure out a way around murdering Meta. However, ze seemed poised to attack, and Jarith was no closer to determining how to defuse the situation.

Before Jarith could say anything in his defense, a painful stab struck his skull. He recoiled, throwing his hands up to his head. There was nothing—at least not anything physical—causing the pain. He swung his gaze back to the Exalted Grand Priest. The entire room seemed to sway as he reached toward Amun.

"Wait!" Jarith cried out.

With no hesitation, Amun threw zir arm up. Jarith flew backward. His body slammed into the floor, sliding across until he hit the far wall. Ze slashed zir hand diagonally across zirself. Jarith whipped up his arms. In a fraction of a second, the air in an arc around him froze to ice, forming a shield. Amun's attack hit it, and it shattered.

He scrambled to his feet as he wove a set of formulae into being. He formed a ball of fire in his hands. It blazed before him, rippling in a magic-induced wind as Amun tried to snuff it out. Jarith hurled the fire at Amun, but ze jumped out of the way, rolling across the room like a person half zir age.

Actually, Jarith had no idea how old Amun was. Maybe the theoretical person was only a tenth of zir age. But now wasn't the time to get caught up in the details.

It was clear the old priest was done talking, and Jarith couldn't afford to hold back. He reached into the potential energy of the room. Focusing it on Amun, he pushed his arms away from his body. Every item in the room zoomed toward zir. The space erupted with clangs, cracks, and a cacophony of din. Jarith shielded his face as splinters of wood broke off and shot across at him.

Another wave of pain exploded through him, echoing through his body. His legs gave out, and he dropped to the floor.

The room blackened. Though he fought to remain conscious, he didn't know how successful he was being.

The shield he had placed around himself the day before was taking up too much of his concentration. If he wanted more powerful attacks, he'd have to stop putting energy into it. However, if he was right about Amun's goal, he couldn't afford to do that.

The room came back into view, the ceiling glowing red from the light of growing flames. The room darkened again. Hisses and pops filled the silence. As his vision returned, he heard a crash followed by the joyous cheer of a fire receiving new fuel. Then, the room went black again.

Soft footsteps broke through the fire's unsympathetic song. Jarith's heart raced as he tried to work out how far away they were and how much time he had before the flames reached him. His vision returned, but all he saw was a blurry field of red and black—fire and darkness. Pushing himself up onto his elbows, he tried in vain to blink away the blur.

A dark figure came into view, a black smudge surrounded by red flames in the background. Ze was close, far too close. And before Jarith could muster another defense, a sharp point pushed against his neck.

"There's still time," Amun said in a heated whisper. "Don't worry. I can still save everyone."

Jarith got the feeling ze wasn't talking to him.

He didn't move. More than ever before, he was aware of how much his physical body shifted, even when he wasn't doing anything. The rise and fall of his breath forced the sharp object deeper into his skin. Despite a valiant effort to slow or stop this autonomic process, he failed.

That breathing thing was kind of important.

His vision cleared, and he saw Amun's hand holding the safe end of the blade digging into his throat. Its ornate, white handle had golden inlays of abstract patterns, which matched a certain sheath that had been found in Jarith's room at Maliah's family home.

It was as Jarith had guessed. This was the Dwesdar Dagger—the name of which he remembered at just this moment. And Amun intended to use it to pierce his shield and kill him.

He weighed his options.

The dagger was already at work unweaving the intricate defense he had crafted around himself. It didn't need to be in contact with his skin, yet Jarith surmised that the strength of its effect was proportional to its distance from the target. In other words, if he couldn't stop what Amun was doing, he needed to at least get away from it to slow its effects.

Easier said than done, especially when said blade was pushing into one's neck. The palm of Amun's free hand was facing him. If he tried to move, ze would counter with zir power.

He needed an unexpected solution, and it had to be clever. Otherwise, Amun could overcome it.

Maybe he could conjure up an illusion of Jukartis. Surely, Amun would be astonished to see Jarith's parent. Maybe astonished enough to distract zir. But that would take time and energy.

Perhaps an auditory distraction would be better. He could probably create some noise in the garden.

Jarith had just committed to his lackluster plan when he heard a gasp—a gasp that hadn't come from him or Amun.

He turned his head on instinct. Amun, at that same moment, pulled the blade away to assess the intrusion, leaving a shallow gash behind. It was a small blessing, leaving Jarith free to live another day. Well, at least another minute.

The window where the sound had come from lay empty, but a moment later, the front door flung open. Maliah rushed into the room. She took in the chaos of the situation. Her expression shifted from fear to worry.

"Come on," she said, flailing her arms. "We need to get out of here."

"Maliah, run!" Jarith called, hoping the warning would save her life.

She didn't listen.

"Let's get to safety," she said. "We can talk once we're outside."

Jarith looked up at Amun. Ze was standing stiff, mouth hung open, clutching the dagger as if zir life depended on it. Zir eyes were trained on Maliah, wide and calculating. He expected zir to attack her, but instead, ze just stood there as Maliah's gaze moved down to the dagger and then back to her mentor's face.

"Whatever is going on," she said slowly, lifting her hands to show she meant no harm, "we can figure it out."

She took a step forward. Jarith's heart raced as he tried to determine his next move. Maliah's safety was his priority, but he was conflicted between taking a defensive or offensive position against Amun. He wasn't thrilled to fight the Highrealmer-turned-Exalted-Grand-Priest again, especially while ze was in possession of such a powerful weapon.

Amun abruptly jumped away. Ze spun on zir heels and raced toward the rear door. Maliah called out to zir. She even chased zir as far as the opposite end of the common area, but Amun was gone.

She returned to Jarith, tears already rolling down her face, and came to kneel beside him.

"Are you . . . ?"

He put his hand to his throat and closed his eyes. He could sense the wound and willed the healing factors in his blood to hurry their work to seal it.

"I'll live," Jarith replied. "Thanks to you."

"Then what in the name of the spirits and the ancestors is going on?" she asked.

Though she demanded answers, she helped Jarith sit up. She was rushing him to stand, and he suddenly realized why. Smoke was building up in the room and billowing out the windows and open doors.

The flames had spread since Maliah opened the front door, climbing up the walls. Jarith took Maliah's hand and stood, wavering once on his feet.

He turned his attention to the fire. Lifting his hand and twisting his wrist back and forth, he suffocated the flames until they shrank into nothingness. Maliah's grip became less urgent, and she shifted her hands to better support his weight.

"Amun is from Highrealm," Jarith explained as they exited the home. "I confronted zir about it, and ze attacked me with the Dwesdar Dagger."

"What?" Maliah exclaimed.

As they limped back to the family home, Jarith recounted the events as best he could.

He didn't expect her to trust his words. After all, the evidence pointed to him as the dagger's thief. It made more sense to believe that Amun found the dagger hidden at zir home and overpowered Jarith when he attacked zir. Yet Maliah listened without judgment. Though the light was fading, her solemn expression radiated concern. She wasn't defensive or angry.

"This must be hard to believe," he said when he finished.

"I'm sorry," Maliah replied, "about before. About accusing you of lying to me. I'm sure you have your secrets for a reason." She paused as they reached the gate of the family home. "I'm choosing to believe in you and support you, even though I don't have the full story.

"But I know you. You're the kind of person who argued with your parent to stop lying to the people of Highrealm about the prophecy. You're the kind of person who cheerfully listened to every briefing by the scientists and analysts even when they had no updates, and who showered them with compliments to raise their spirits."

The stars reflected in her teary eyes, and a breeze tossed her curls around each other.

"I love that person," she said. "And I'm choosing to put my trust in you."

Maliah sat stiffly on the couch, holding herself and biting her lip as Jarith recounted his fight with Amun and the Dwesdar Dagger once more for her parents. Beside her, Meta sat up tall, as if she hadn't been escorted to bed only an hour or so previously. Jua was in the chair opposite Jarith, leaning forward with his elbows on his knees.

She could tell from her parents' solemn expressions that they were having a hard time believing Jarith's account. If she hadn't seen Amun run off with the dagger herself, she wouldn't have believed it either. Jarith came across as sincere and truthful, but . . .

She shook herself out of that line of thinking before it could continue. The facts were the facts. She had seen Jarith immobilized. Amun had been holding the Dwesdar Dagger to his throat. She had offered to listen to zir side of the story, but ze had fled.

If what Jarith said was true, then Amun had stolen the weapon to penetrate a magic shield he had placed around himself.

"Why would Amun go through the trouble of stealing the dagger to kill you and then defend your innocence?" Meta asked.

"It was an excuse to get me alone. Ze wanted to do the dirty deed but pin the blame on me," Jarith said with a stabbing gesture that felt somewhat distasteful to Maliah.

"Amun has no reason to want you dead," Jua argued.

"Yes, ze does. I believe Amun came to this world to stop the prophecy. Ze said—"

Jua interrupted Jarith before he could say more. "What do you mean, came to this world?"

"Like I said. Amun admitted to being from my world, Highrealm," Jarith explained, and not for the first time.

There was so much information that Maliah wasn't surprised the details weren't sticking in her parents' minds. She could barely hold on to it all.

She'd never seen Amun violent before, but she had to admit ze had been acting odd. It left so many questions, but it also answered many more. Amun was one of the few people powerful enough to enter the artifact library without detection. Ze would have had to plant the dagger's sheath, an easy task to complete while they were at morning ritual.

But then there was Jarith's essence. She hadn't known what essence tracing was before this morning, but if a person's essence was unique to them, how could her mentor have replicated it? And was there any trace of Amun being there? If Amun had the knowledge of Highrealm, it was possible ze knew how to leave a false essence residue. This line of thinking was well beyond her level of understanding, and that frustrated her.

Despite her doubts, there was one piece of evidence that she couldn't ignore. Amun's tattoo was an unlikely coincidence and all the proof she needed. She had seen Amun's forearm ink on several occasions throughout her life, and sometimes, she had been able to make out the Athu Aqatne in Highrealm. But she had never put the two together until Jarith mentioned it.

She was embarrassed to have been so unobservant but tried not to dwell.

Many things became clear when she accepted Amun as a Highrealmer: how powerful ze was, how creative zir magic was, and zir commitment to the secrecy of their abilities. Ze must be far more advanced than anyone from Midrealm, enough so that working with even the most powerful magic workers would feel like child's play.

When Maliah expressed this, Jua said, "Just because someone is powerful doesn't mean they're from another world. We're not from Highrealm, and we can perform magic."

"Your powers . . ." Jarith trailed off. When they urged him on, he explained that his predecessors had discovered Midrealm and its prophecy. "In order to trigger the prophecy's fulfillment, the scientists in Highrealm activated your latent abilities when you were young."

Maliah's parents were visibly shaken by the revelation, especially when Jarith got into the technical bits, which no Midrealmer could have understood. Maliah's eyes glazed over with boredom, despite trying really hard to pretend she was interested.

"You're saying that your people instilled these powers within us," Jua summarized.

"Sort of," Jarith replied. "You already had the capacity to manipulate your environment. They enhanced that ability."

Maliah wondered why the Highrealmers had chosen her parents, but now wasn't the time to ask. She wasn't ready for a seminar on the mathematics of multimodal variables in the stochastic characteristics of tangential realities—or any other random sequence of big words that meant absolutely nothing to her.

"Why would they act to fulfill our prophecy?" Jua asked.

"Exactly as it says in your prophecy. Ascension."

"Ascension?"

"The ascension of Midrealm souls to Highrealm."

They weren't connecting the dots, but their focus remained squarely on the present conversation, unlike Maliah's wandering thoughts of worry for her mentor.

"And you said Amun wishes to stop the prophecy," Meta asked. "So ze doesn't want Midrealm souls to ascend to Highrealm."

"Correct," Jarith confirmed.

Silence fell over the room as the two Exalted Grand Priests processed everything they'd heard. Maliah couldn't tell from their shared looks whether this was a good or bad sign.

"It's not that we don't believe you," Meta said, sounding very much like she didn't believe Jarith. "It's just very . . . sudden."

"And out of character for Amun," Jua added.

They turned their gazes to Maliah in unison.

"Are you sure it was the Dwesdar Dagger?"

"Yes," Maliah said. "It had the same shape and coloring as the sheath."

"And why target you, Jarith, instead of us?" Meta asked. "Ze has been a part of our lives for decades. There must have been ample opportunity to effect change before your arrival."

"I don't have all the answers," Jarith said. "Amun probably got close to your family so ze could take action when the opportunity presented itself. And I guess I was that opportunity."

"Even so, why would Amun wish to stop the prophecy?" Meta asked.

"I wish I knew. But yesterday, ze asked me if I understood the risks of fulfilling the prophecy. Ze must have concerns about it, about taking those risks."

"Risks? What kind of risks?" Maliah asked her parents.

"I'm not aware of any," Meta said as Jua shrugged.

Maliah couldn't shake the feeling that something was missing. There was some critical piece of information they were lacking, information that would bring clarity to Amun's actions. Perhaps it was wishful thinking, but she had to believe her mentor was acting on logic.

A memory fluttered into the periphery of her consciousness, and she grasped at it.

"I just remembered," Maliah said. "After I told Amun about Jarith's arrival, ze cautioned me about trusting him."

Had ze really been worried over the prophecy coming to fruition?

"This doesn't make sense," Jua argued. "Amun has been preparing you for your future role as heir to the prophecy. Ze has been there for us as we fulfilled our roles, as well."

"And I won't believe it was all an act," Meta added. "Amun loves us."

"I'm sure ze does. But that also explains why I'm zir target," Jarith said. "If I'm the Highrealmer bent on . . . whatever horrible thing ze believes, then I'm the one ze has to stop."

Meta sighed and leaned back against the couch.

"We're talking in circles," she admitted. "It's imperative that we locate Amun and talk this out."

"What? Talk this out?" Jarith asked.

Maliah trusted Amun. They all loved zir. And she wouldn't entertain any notion that ze was acting out of pure malice. Her mother was right. Amun held all the answers they needed.

"We know Amun," she said. "Ze wouldn't do this without good reason."

"We can't move forward without knowing the full picture," Jua agreed.

Jarith didn't seem to like the idea, judging from the furrow on his brow. "Just a reminder that the closer I get to zir, the faster the Dwesdar Dagger's power will work."

"You can stay here," Meta suggested.

Jarith let out a sarcastic laugh. "Yeah, right. There's no way I'm letting you all head into danger without me."

"Then it's decided," Maliah said. "We're going after Amun."

19

Beacon of Understanding

While her parents settled into bed, Maliah ascended to the rooftop patio with Jarith. They sat on the bench in silence as the insects of the night played their lullaby.

The weight of change felt suffocating. She might never have another lesson from Amun. The seat at their table might be destined to remain empty. And she'd be lost in her duties as a Priest without zir guidance.

Across Ar, lamps flickered as the cool breeze wound its way down streets and between houses. The air was lightly scented by flowers that bloomed at night to entice pollinators to their petals.

Jarith's muscles were tense, and she longed to go back to the previous night's levity and joy. She put her hand on his, and without looking at her, he took it and pressed it against his lips.

He was so warm that for a moment, she yearned to fall into his arms and lose herself in his love. His presence had triggered Amun's apparent desperation, and yet his presence made the thought of losing her precious mentor seem bearable.

It was a horrible, selfish thought, one she would have liked to escape from. It overshadowed her suspicions about Jarith's version of events, her fleeting lustful thoughts, and even her grumbling stomach.

She wanted to ask what Jarith was pondering. He seemed far more calm than she felt. Anxiety flowed through her. She ached to say something before she exploded with some nonsense just to fill the time. She opened her mouth, though she wasn't sure what was going to come out.

Her next statement was probably going to have something to do with fireflies having lanterns on their bums. This was a passing notion that had crept up every once in a while since she was young and that she, luckily, had never had the chance to say out loud.

"This wasn't how it was supposed to be," Jarith said just before she embarrassed herself. "I don't know how to do this."

"Do what?" Maliah asked.

"Because I'm here, someone you love can no longer be part of your life."

He was avoiding her question, so she decided to try a comforting word or two. Maybe she needed comfort as well.

"Everything will work out. We just need to talk through—"

"You're all deluding yourselves if you think we can talk this through," Jarith interrupted, letting go of her hand and standing. He paced. "Amun snuck into your artifact collection, stole a dangerous knife, planted the sheath to frame me, lured me back to zir home, and almost slit my throat. Ze is dedicated to this task, or else ze would have hesitated."

He ran his hand over his twists to pull them behind his shoulders before continuing.

"There was no hesitation. If you hadn't shown up when you did, I'd be dead, and that tells me ze is irredeemable." He looked at his hands. "I can feel my shield unraveling. I'm focusing my attention on keeping it secure, but I don't know if I can risk sleeping."

He finally looked up into her glistening eyes.

"Maliah, I can't do this alone."

"You won't have to—"

"You're not understanding," he interrupted, saying each word with intent, "and I'm not sure I can tell you."

"Tell me what?"

His gaze was intense. She probably could have listened in on his thoughts, if he was projecting any. But she was terrified of what she might hear. Plus, with everything else going on, she'd forgotten she could even do that.

"Do you know what we need to do?"

"Yes. We need to find Amun."

"How?"

"I—"

She stared into his eyes, and they seemed to transform the very world around her. Her psyche fell into a maze of probabilities, and she wandered through it, following a beacon of understanding. It led her through twists and turns, over hurdles of opaque transformations, and under baseless suspicions, toward its exit.

Every turn brought a new set of branching paths, and her connection to Jarith guided each action she made. The path narrowed and widened, and objects, like fragments of memories, littered the ground. She ignored them, staying focused on her destination until, at last, she reached the labyrinth's end.

It was unremarkable, so consistent with the maze of neural activity that she would never have recognized it if not for the beacon at the center of a grassy courtyard. A large orb hovering off the ground, it exuded a warm light as it bobbed in place. Underneath, the grass waved in a radial pattern, as if the orb was causing ripples in a pool of water.

Maliah moved closer, fear rising within her. Her hair rose from her shoulders and head, and she found herself floating. She moved closer still, pushing back her anxiety. Her fingers drew closer to the orb, and she realized it wasn't solid. Its surface wobbled like a drop of liquid, holding its form in a fragile state. She wasn't sure what she'd find, but she knew it was important.

As her hand rested on the orb's surface, she sensed what Jarith had been afraid to say aloud. It was an answer. Not a simple answer, but a complex interweaving of causes and consequences, of possibilities and realities. Yet the longer she sat with it, the clearer it became.

"You want me to locate Amun," she said, "by activating my powers."

Maliah wasn't sure which thought was more intimidating: activating her powers, or doing so in order to pursue her mentor. She had just experienced a transformative peek into Jarith's soul, the soul of a non-physical Highrealmer trapped in a very physical Midrealm body.

He had lived in Highrealm long before she was born, although she couldn't be sure how long, in part because time didn't work the same way there. His understanding of Nature was profound, and she hadn't understood most of what she had just experienced. It was very much like her time in Highrealm, watching through Jarith's metaphorical eyes, except this time she had been within him somehow.

She knew better than to think too hard about this. Not to mention, she had bigger worries at the moment.

Jarith's eyebrows were drawn down in sadness, fear, and shame. He didn't confirm her findings.

"Amun clouded zir essence, even at zir home," Maliah continued, trying to put words to Jarith's beacon. "I'm the only person who knows what zir essence feels like because I've used artifacts that ze created. But I can't trace it without my powers."

Jarith remained silent.

Maliah understood. Asking her to do this was asking her to commit irrevocably to her role in prophecy, and she was still fearful about what that commitment entailed. Jarith would never ask this of her outright, yet she understood that her inaction could mean his death.

"There has to be another way," she said. "An option we aren't seeing."

Then, like a word on the tip of her tongue that suddenly revealed itself, it came to her.

"The mirror!"

She shot to her feet before Jarith could ask what she was talking about. Grabbing the nearby lantern with one hand and Jarith's hand with her other, she pulled him down the stairs.

"I'll explain on the way," she said.

Maliah and Jarith pulled hoods over their heads as they neared the gates of the inner Huleay Grounds. A few guards were typically stationed at night, but tonight there were a dozen, likely in response to the dagger's theft.

Above them, the two massive statues stared down, but luckily not at them. Maliah knew from history lessons that their gazes were firmly set on those who would oppose the Ledine Empire and the will of the spirits. She may not have been keen on fulfilling prophecy, but she wasn't necessarily looking to anger the spirits.

Not tonight, at least.

"Can you still do it with so many guards?" Maliah asked Jarith.

"Are you kidding? The more people around, the easier it is," Jarith said with a suspicious amount of confidence. "They feed off each other."

He held up a finger and wiggled it. A fireball exploded from a nearby lantern. Maliah jumped back, running into Jarith, who laughed.

Within moments, every guard on duty was racing to help temper the flames. Jarith gave her a nudge, and they rushed past the panicked figures. Once safely in a dark alley, Jarith quelled the fire.

"Good luck doing that same trick on the way out," Maliah said, enjoying Jarith's amusement despite trying to focus on her serious task.

"Getting out is even easier," he promised her.

"Where were you sneaking when I wasn't watching?" she asked.

"Let's just say that non-physical practical jokes, especially when inflicted on my parent, are so much funnier in person than if I tried to explain it." He peered around the corner to make sure the guards were still preoccupied. "Now, where are we going?"

"This way." Maliah pointed into the darkness.

"I have to know. Can you actually see? It's so dark here at night."

Maliah grinned and took his hand. She'd taken for granted that in Highrealm, she could see no matter how dark or bright Jarith's surroundings had been. She hadn't understood much of what she was experiencing in the energetic realm, but nothing in Highrealm compared to the invisibility of darkness.

"Your eyes will adjust. Just hold on to me."

He rested his hands on her hips. She closed her eyes for a minute, retracing every step she'd ever taken through the halls and alleys of the Huleay Grounds. The light of the moon was enough to find her way, but she wanted to ensure they were taking the most desolate route, just in case.

When she began walking, Jarith followed, but he wasn't quiet for long.

"So, this mirror that tracks formulae—I mean, spells," he whispered, "you'll be able to use it to find Amun?"

"I think so," she replied in an equally quiet tone. She paused at a crossroads and, not hearing anything from any direction, continued forward.

"How do you know about it?"

"Amun periodically had me choose between different objects. I think ze hoped to gain some kind of insight into my latent ability—that's what you call it, right? So anyway, I'd choose from these objects, and then we'd follow up by doing something with the one I chose. Sometimes, nothing would happen, but I was able to use the mirror."

"Without your powers?" Jarith sounded genuinely surprised, even in his hushed whisper.

"Yes. Is that odd?"

"I don't know if it's odd, but it's definitely impressive."

Maliah rolled her eyes even though she knew Jarith couldn't see. "Why?"

"Most of your magical artifacts—those I'm aware of, at least—work through an interaction between the user's essence and a trace essence on the object itself. It's almost like instructions that are left behind by its creator. To use an artifact like that without the ability to sense those instructions means you have a pretty amazing intuition."

She didn't completely understand, but she got enough of it not to argue.

"This mirror is special for another reason," she said instead. "Amun created it."

Jarith's grip tightened on her hips, stopping her in her tracks. She wasn't sure if she'd offended him by wanting to seek out an artifact created by Amun or if there was something else going on. The quiet surrounding them was as eerie as the darkness, though she could make out the basic forms of the buildings nearby. But Jarith seemed on edge.

She opened her mouth to ask what was going on. Before she could, Jarith pulled her against him. He backed up to the nearest wall, taking her with him. She waited. The silence was pervasive. Even the wind had died down to a whisper.

Maliah looked up at Jarith, who was laser-focused on something.

Nearby rocks shifted.

"Do you sense it?" Jarith's voice echoed in her mind.

It surprised her, but Jarith held her still. She shook her head.

"There's a powerful aura just beyond this corner."

Maliah, still lacking any magic ability, sensed nothing.

She tried to lean forward, but his grip held her firmly against him. Luckily, pinching him got him to release her. He recoiled, and she was pretty sure he shot her an angry glare. Neither bothered her as she leaned to peer beyond the wall.

Pale moonlight bathed the wide pathway that led from the children's temple to a lecture hall. A nearby pond twinkled as the light danced across it. The trees, bushes, and flowers sat motionless.

Then, movement caught her eye, and she whipped her head around in time to see the mysterious creature jump from the ground onto a wall nearby. Unable to control herself, Maliah burst into a hushed laugh.

Jarith turned to follow her gaze and squinted.

"It's a cat," Maliah said between breaths, holding a hand over her mouth in a vain attempt to stay silent.

"No way. Cats are small creatures," Jarith insisted. "The aura I saw was much larger than . . ."

His voice trailed off as he identified the source of the aura for himself. He crossed his arms over his chest.

"I didn't realize cats were such mighty beasts," Maliah chuckled.

"That cat is very mighty." He was smiling now, too, and within moments, he was laughing himself.

"Come on." Maliah pulled him along. "It's just up here."

Another turn brought them to the entrance of the smallest sanctuary on the Huleay Grounds. This was where she'd trained under Amun for over six years. Where she'd likely never train with zir ever again.

She fought the nagging pang of regret as she touched the door.

Jarith placed his hand on her shoulder. "Are you okay?"

With a deep breath, she stood tall and assured Jarith that she was fine. She stepped back so he could unlock the door with his power, but he held up his hands.

"It's unlocked already," he said.

"It is?" She turned the knob and found that it was indeed open. Suddenly sure Amun was just inside, she threw it ajar and rushed in.

Four pairs of eyes peered down from the corners of the sanctuary. In the darkness, she almost sensed sadness from them, as if they felt as abandoned as she did. The emptiness and solemnity of the situation sapped the joy and hope she was grasping for.

Jarith swiped his hand to the side, and the lamps throughout the sanctuary lit themselves. He peered around several corners, ensuring no one was hiding from them. Then, he returned to the center of the chamber, where Maliah now stood.

"This entire building is enchanted with some kind of masking spell," he said. At her questioning gaze, he continued. "It's no wonder I couldn't see your training sessions with Amun. It's as if this entire temple doesn't exist."

She looked around. "What are you talking about?"

"I don't mean physically. I mean energetically. Even our auras are suppressed right now."

"Why would Amun do such a thing?"

"Your guess is as good as mine," Jarith said with a shrug. "Where's the mirror?"

"Ze kept zir artifact collection in a storage room. This way."

She led Jarith to the back of the platform, where a short ramp led to a locked doorway. Well, it was supposed to be locked, but it, too, was open.

Jarith put his hand on the door, and it let out a high-pitched creak as he pushed it ajar.

The light reflecting around them was dim, but she saw enough to make her catch her breath.

20

Mirror of Amun

"**N**o."

It was all Maliah could say. Below her, littered across the floor of her mentor's storage area, remnants of artifacts lay scattered. She brought her trembling hands up to her cheek, where tears trailed down.

Jarith lit a lamp just inside the room to get a better look. "What happened here?"

She knew he didn't expect an answer, but she shook her head anyway. Taking careful steps forward, she couldn't avoid the shards of stone and glass that cracked under her shoes. She saw what she was looking for, and she hoped beyond hope that it was still intact. Despite Jarith reaching for her, she continued through the room one crunching step at a time. She crouched and picked up the heavy silver handle, turning it over to face her.

"It's the mirror," she confirmed.

"It **was** the mirror," Jarith corrected.

The mirror's body had a long crack through it, and its glass now sat in a million pieces across the floor. However, it wasn't the only ruined item. Almost every artifact that had once graced the shelves of the collection lay broken beyond repair, destroyed. Many items were so thoroughly shattered, they were unrecognizable.

"Why would ze do this?" Maliah pulled the mirror to her chest.

"You think Amun did this?"

"There's no sign that someone broke in. The doors were unlocked, and Amun has the only key." She wiped tears from her cheeks, but they were replaced in moments. "Ze doesn't want us to find zir. But I don't understand. We're a family. Why would Amun shut us out like this?"

Anger bubbled up within her. Her grip on the mirror tightened as tears clouded her vision. Her emotions boiled over, and she threw the artifact to the floor. Glass and debris splashed up, and she recoiled.

Jarith said her name gently and knelt next to her, the glass cracking beneath his knee. He pulled her into him, and though she tossed her shoulders forward and back in an effort to escape him, he held her tightly.

Her speech became unintelligible as she wailed. She had known that change was coming. In her own way, she had prepared for the loss of her innocence, her freedoms, and her independence. But she hadn't been ready to lose her mentor, one of her closest friends, her confidante.

Perhaps she should have been focused on Jarith's waning chances of survival, her mother's strange exhaustion, or her imminent awakening. Any of these worries would have been—arguably—more constructive and maybe even more logical.

Unfortunately, grief doesn't listen to reason.

Jarith didn't need to hear Maliah say it. He already knew. She intended to awaken her powers. The grief written across her features spoke volumes, and his heart felt heavy knowing that her loss had only just begun.

She remained silent as they closed the doors to the sanctuary, snuck past the guards, and returned to the family home. It was probably better that way. As long as she said nothing, he wouldn't need to lie to her. He wouldn't have to pretend she wouldn't soon lose someone else she loved. He wouldn't feel forced to act as if he was innocent.

Jarith was tired of lying, but he couldn't confess the truth right now. That would be totally inappropriate.

"Oh, hey. I know you just lost your mentor—who was kind of a jerk, by the way—but I gotta kinda sorta kill your mom now. 'Kay?"

No, that wouldn't go over well.

Even so, as exasperated as he was of lying, he was also physically exhausted. Every step was harder than the last, and a buzzing sensation penetrated his essence. He couldn't tell if that was the dagger's creeping influence dismantling his protective shield or if his essence was losing cohesion.

Neither was good news.

When they entered the family home, Jua and Meta were on the couch, having been unable to sleep. They turned their attention to their daughter and someday-maybe-son-in-law. It was obvious they were in no better spirits.

"We're going to awaken my powers," Maliah said without prelude. "Then we'll find Amun and figure out what's going on."

Jarith could only imagine what was going through her parents' minds. He imagined they had planned out a joyous event for her awakening. They had probably expected to hold a private celebration and perhaps even make a public announcement. There were supposed to be hugs and presents, community and tears of happiness.

Their expressions, instead, were somber and tense. They waited in silence for Maliah to continue, but she didn't. As the quiet dragged out, they turned their attention to Jarith for further details.

He couldn't think of anything comforting to say, so he just said, "We should begin the preparations."

It didn't take long for Maliah's parents to gather most of the items needed for the Awakening Ritual. The most critical aspect was the collection of crystals for Jarith to charge, but their supply of ink was low as well. Jarith also required a writing implement with a sharp tip, which they didn't keep around the home.

While Jua went to the Huleay Temple to obtain the last supplies, Jarith returned to the rooftop patio to examine the gardens below. They were spacious and opulent, but that wasn't what he was interested in.

He was looking beyond the physical, at the energetic potential of the earth, air, water, and fire. Dewy flowers swelled with power as they funneled their energy into fresh growth. The kinetic energy of the central fountain undulated outward from where the water trickled down. Lamplight danced with dynamic movement. And a gentle breeze swirled over him, bringing with it the scents of a desert night.

Everything was alive with potential, and he suddenly didn't feel that Midrealm was all that different from Highrealm. The two worlds had always seemed incompatible to him, with Highrealm being a universe of energetic beings and Midrealm being so corporeal. But as he watched the ebb and flow of Nature, he saw an underlying truth that tied the two worlds together.

Having selected a spot in the garden for the ritual, he descended the stairs. Voices drifted out from the rear door of the home, which he'd left open.

"It may not seem like it right now, but this is the right decision," Meta was saying.

"I know," Maliah replied. "I just wish it felt like I had a choice."

Jarith peered around the corner as silence fell between the two women. Meta and Maliah were sitting at the table.

"Have I ever told you how I found out about the prophecy?" Meta asked.

She tilted her head to the side and waited until Maliah shook her head.

"I was a person of interest for the guard because I always seemed to be nearby when trouble was afoot. When they escorted me to the Huleay Grounds, I thought, 'This is the day. I've finally gone too far.' I was sure I was in for a punishment. Although I don't recall what for, I was confident they'd put me away for good.

"They brought me before the most senior priest of the time, Exalted Grand Priest Rubei. Exalted Grand Rubei had me do three tasks. They laid several trinkets before me and bade me to select one. I instinctively took hold of an artifact. Then they requested I describe a scene as vividly as possible. I proceeded to describe exactly what Exalted Grand Rubei was imagining.

"For the third task, they asked me about dreams. I had never heard the word before, but as soon as they explained the concept to me, I understood their meaning. I knew I experienced something rare as I slept, but I'd always been called a liar when I revealed my dreams. At Exalted Grand Rubei's insistence, I described the visions I had seen of your father and the things that had happened before and would happen after. The Temple had conscripted Jua several years earlier, and I described his arrival as if I had been there myself.

"I was quite proud of impressing the Huleay Temple. But once they told me what the tasks meant— part of a prophecy in which I'd been named—I tried to escape."

Maliah perked up. "You did? Why?"

"I'm not certain." Her mother paused to think while she ran her hands along her hair to flatten any out-of-place strands. "But it was terrifying. I'd never been responsible for anyone or anything other than myself. Yet here was this powerful person explaining how important I was."

"It's overwhelming," Maliah said.

Meta let out a quiet laugh. "Yes, I suppose it is." She placed her hands on Maliah's.

"If I'd awakened my powers when I was younger—like you and Dad—could I have avoided all this? Everything happening with Amun right now?"

"I don't know, love. No one can be sure of that. As difficult as these trials are, we must concentrate on the present because we can't change the past."

Maliah didn't have a response, so her mother continued.

"Prophecy has brought us together, all of us. It has given us immeasurable gifts of love and joy. Our duty isn't easy. However, it is immensely rewarding. Very few people in this world can claim to have a divine purpose. It's a scary and overpowering concept, but it's also a rare and beautiful thing."

She ran a hand through Maliah's hair. Jarith could tell from Maliah's wandering gaze that her mother's words hadn't convinced her.

"I believe in you," Meta said. "I know you'll bring miracles upon our people."

"No pressure," Maliah mumbled.

"No pressure," her mother assured her with a smile.

Jarith interrupted Maliah and Meta's heart-to-heart to collect the materials that were sitting on the table. Meta watched him with intense concentration, and he wondered if she realized that he'd overheard their conversation.

"Perhaps we should perform the ritual in one of the sanctuaries in the morning," she recommended. "And we could all provide our energy to the purpose."

"This is a ritual only I can perform," Jarith said.

Meta raised an eyebrow.

"My people locked Maliah's power," he added, as if that explained everything.

Both Maliah and her mother looked quite ready to shoot the messenger as they vocalized their disbelief. They followed him out to the garden, and he placed each item on the ground with careful attention. The positioning needed to be precise, but more important was the order in which they were charged.

Meta asked him questions without leaving time for him to answer. He nodded patiently at each concern. It wasn't like he had much information to share. No one had ever told him why they'd restricted Maliah's power. He didn't even remember when he'd been informed about it. It was just another decision made with no concern for how it would impact Maliah.

He wondered whether it had been decided by Jukartis or the scientific team. Quickly abandoning that line of thinking, he assigned the blame to Jukartis. That felt right, so it was good enough for him.

"How will this work?" Maliah asked when her mother's questions waned.

He took a few steps back to admire his handiwork. The stones were arranged in a radial pattern, and each stone's highest point was facing outward. The motif was intricate, with smaller stones used in areas of greater detail. At the center was a large, empty circle.

"I'll charge the stones," Jarith replied. "Once they're charged, you'll come into the circle with me, and I'll inscribe a pictorial representation of the equations and formulae into you."

"Into?" Maliah asked.

Jarith lifted his shirt and turned away from them, revealing his side, where a complex pictogram—a derivative of the Athu Aqatne—was etched into his skin. It was healing, though it still looked pretty rough. The area ached sometimes, more so now that most of his concentration was on his shield.

"By the spirits and ancestors," Meta said.

"When did this happen?" Maliah reached her hand out to touch it, but stopped short.

"It was inscribed into me as part of the transfer process," he said.

Maliah's hand finally reached him, and he remained steady despite the burning sensation that came with her fingers sliding across the dried blood and ink.

"It's a physical manifestation of the spell required to take a physical form and transfer me to Midrealm."

Maliah was concerned for him, but she removed her gaze and stood back up to face him.

"I understand," she said, "though we will discuss wound care when this is over."

He smiled.

"We should have asked your father to acquire a numbing salve," Meta said, "though I'm uncertain how effective it would be."

"I can dull her nociceptors before I begin," Jarith offered.

The look the two women gave him reminded him that their biological understanding was limited. The people of Midrealm hadn't yet discovered the myriad of receptors that allowed them to sense the world around them.

"It'll help ease the pain," he added.

Meta nodded in agreement.

"How long will it take?" Maliah asked.

"I need a few hours to charge everything, but doing the inscription won't take long." The formulae were etched into his mind, and he was confident in what needed to be done. But he could only guess how long it would take.

He asked her to consider where she wanted the inscription placed before making his way into the radial design. Sitting cross-legged at its center, he took several deep breaths. His head was aching, and the energy required to keep his shield up was draining him. The power of the dagger was pulling apart his protection as if cutting the individual fibers of a cloth. It was already in a poor state, but it was holding . . . for now.

"Can we provide any assistance?" Meta asked.

"Just bring me the supplies as soon as they arrive," he requested.

Amun paced from one side of the cave to the other. Nearby, on a large, flat rock, sat the Dwesdar Dagger. It looked innocuous enough, just sitting there with big, innocent gems adorning its white hilt. Yet its power remained honed on a target, and it was ever so slowly weakening the intruder bent on completing a fool's errand.

"Even at the end, I sensed no ill will from him," Amun said.

There was no one else in the cave. At least, no one physically.

"Is it possible that he is a pawn?"

Ze picked up a piece of chalk and returned to the cave wall. It was full of writings: formulae, proofs, equations, diagrams, and strange swirling doodles.

"No. No."

Ze scribbled a line of math. Frustrated, ze struck it out once, twice, a third time before drawing a new swirling doodle just beside it.

"No. He knows what he's doing. They didn't extract the cost when he was transferred. That means he must murder someone to stay. He must."

Ze resumed zir pacing. Each step echoed around the empty space, the only sound except for the fires burning in nearby lamps. It was dry and cool, but that didn't distract zir.

"She's fading. There must be a connection. You see the correlation, don't you?"

With another glance at the wall of scribbles, ze pointed.

"No!" ze yelled. "I'm not wrong. The evidence and proofs are unmistakable. You can't argue with facts."

Pausing to listen to something that wasn't there, Amun shook zir head.

"I wish I was wrong. This would be so much easier if I was wrong. I've done the calculations more times than I can count, but no matter the parameters, fulfillment of the prophecy will cause catastrophe."

Ze waved zir arms at the wall as if it explained the truth ze was so sure of. But Amun's writings would have been incomprehensible to most of the Ascension

Project's scientists. They certainly weren't clear to the nothingness that ze was speaking to.

"If I stop him, I can save her and avoid the coming end. If I choose to let him live, I can return . . ."

Zir brow furrowed. Clutching the chalk with fervor, ze slammed it against the wall and swirled it in circles.

". . . at the cost of my people's existence and the life I've built here."

Round and round, the chalk spun. The tip broke, and Amun watched it drop to the ground. Ze put zir hands against the wall.

"Will you be there when I'm gone, my friend? Or will I be forced to roam this vast realm devoid of free souls?

"Will you?

"Will you?

"Will you?"

21

Running Out Of Time

At the center of Jarith's pictogram now sat two stools, a small bowl of newly enchanted ink, a knife, a candle, a writing utensil made of stone with a sharp tip, a dish to capture blood, and several cloths. Meta and Jua stood together outside the spell across from Jarith, waiting for Maliah to return.

Their daughter had gone inside to change, and only her father had lingering concerns that Maliah would attempt to flee. Meta was worried for her daughter, but she still managed to make a bet with her husband that Maliah would go through with the ritual.

Any remaining doubts were allayed when Maliah crossed the threshold wearing a long white ritual dress, a headdress, and an array of jewelry on her arms, waist, ears, wrists, and fingers.

The morning sun's rays grazed the edges of the sky, so they couldn't see her painted face, but her message was clear to her family, to Jarith, to the spirits, and to the ancestors. She now faced her fate head on.

Jarith held his hand out to her. She walked to the edge of the circle and placed her hand in his without hesitation. As soon as they were both within the bounds of the pictogram, a buzz rippled through him. His shield was gone, having been drained away by the Dwesdar Dagger and his split attention. The air seemed to vibrate, leaving a sensation of small pricks all over his body.

He was running out of time.

Leading her through the stones, Jarith wondered where she had decided to place the inscription. Before he could ask, she took a long strap that hung on the skirt and pulled it around her, exposing her thigh.

His entire body felt hot as he stared at her delicate hands, which were securing the strap to her waistband. Regretting being unable to touch her thigh prior to etching a pictogram into it, his jaw went slack.

Maliah's hand reached up to his face and lifted it to meet her eyes. The determination he saw there sobered him, and he put his hands on her jawline. He brought their foreheads together.

"Are you sure?" he whispered.

"Yes," she replied.

Her voice betrayed her fear, but he trusted her.

"*I'm sorry,*" he thought.

He guided her to sit on the central stool, then took up a position on the ground next to her. With one more check to ensure that the supplies on the second stool were complete, he picked up the knife and placed it in the candlelight's fire.

Speaking the words of the formulae in a soft, pained tone, he brought the inscription to the forefront of his mind. He needed to reduce the flow of blood, which he would do by cauterizing the wounds as he worked, and he wanted to provide Maliah relief from the pain. He couldn't make it completely numb—he just didn't have the spare concentration to hold the formulae in place.

Placing the knife on her skin, he looked up at her. Her attention was fixed on the sunrise, its bright pinks and reds just beginning to grace her soft features. It was time to begin, and there was no more room for hesitation.

He returned his gaze to her leg and, concentrating heat and pressure through the knife and into her skin, began carving into her flesh with his power.

Jarith stood by the window of Maliah's bedroom as her parents hovered over their daughter, who was in her bed assuring them she was fine.

The sun was up, and the enormous statues at the top of the hill stared down at him. He leaned against the wall and crossed his arms. If he wasn't so sure these spirits weren't real, he would definitely have been worried about possible retribution from them for carving up Maliah's leg.

The knife had glowed with heat, the dish had filled with blood, and the ink had sparkled with golden power. Maliah had clutched the sides of the stool with pain, but her leg hadn't even flinched the entire time. It hadn't eased his guilt, but it had quickened the process.

Though they were now outside the pictogram, the prickling throughout his body continued. He could sense that his energy was being sucked away from him. It was a new sensation, and one that he didn't enjoy one bit. But he told himself it was a valuable reminder of his limited time.

While Jua inspected Maliah's wound for the millionth time, Meta asked for the millionth time, "How are you feeling?"

"I'm fine," Maliah answered, annoyance thick in her tone.

"It isn't bleeding any longer," Jua said in amazement.

Jarith decided not to explain for the millionth time that the enchanted ink assisted with the coagulation of blood, resistance to infection, and recruitment of healing factors.

"We need to find Amun," Maliah argued.

"Do you know where ze is?" her mother asked.

Maliah paused and shrunk into herself. "No. Not yet."

She lifted her hands as if to check whether they were showing signs of increased power. Jarith could confirm that such a thing was highly improbable, but Maliah didn't need to know that.

"I don't feel any different," she said, looking to Jarith. "Are you certain you did it right?"

"I'd hate for you to experience such a process again," Meta cooed, running her hand over Maliah's head.

Jarith could see the difference in her aura, shining and spreading throughout the room. As soon as the last line had been etched, her aura had expanded rapidly, filling the entire garden. He hadn't mentioned it yet because—well, no one had asked.

"Yes, I'm sure," he replied.

Meta sat on the bed. Jarith suddenly realized that while Maliah's aura was brighter and larger than ever, her mother's appeared dimmer than usual. None of them had gotten any sleep the night before, but she looked pale. And despite the mild temperature, she glistened with sweat.

"How do I make it work?" Maliah asked him, pulling him from his distraction.

Jarith shrugged. "I was able to use my powers as soon as I was born. I just visualize the scientific principles, and it works."

Maliah rolled her eyes and looked to her parents for guidance. They walked her through their favorite exercises and meditations, but none made a difference.

"This is great," Maliah grumbled. "Awakened my power, and now I'm exactly as useless as before."

"Don't be so hard on yourself," her mother said. "It takes time to learn how to—"

"Time?" Maliah asked. She looked at Jarith again. "Jarith, how much time do you have?"

He couldn't bring himself to answer, in part because he didn't know and in part because the room was starting to spin.

"We need to find Amun today," she demanded. "The longer we wait, the less likely we'll find zir."

"Stress will only make this more difficult for you," Jua said.

An electric shock raced through Jarith's body. He dropped to his knees. Maliah called out his name, and she sat up as her father rushed to his side. The pain eased, and when he looked back up at Maliah, her eyes were wide.

He tried to think of something comforting to say, but his mind was foggy. His legs shook as Jua helped him back to his feet.

"Wait. What's that?" Maliah asked, pointing at him.

He looked at himself, and seeing nothing, gauged the expressions of Meta and Jua. When they were all satisfied that none of them knew what she was talking about, they returned their attention to her.

"What are you seeing, Maliah?" Jua asked.

"It's a . . ." Her voice trailed off before she jumped to attention—as much as one can while in bed. "The mirror! It's like the power of the mirror."

She swung her legs off the bed—the side closer to Jarith and opposite her mother—and jumped to her feet. At the sudden pain in her leg, she buckled over and fell. Jarith caught her, and Jua braced them both when they wavered.

Her eyes moved down Jarith's body and across the room. Everyone followed her gaze, but whatever her gaze was locked upon, it was invisible to the others.

"I'm seeing the link between you and the dagger," Maliah said, "which means we can follow it to Amun."

One might assume that a magic string connecting a magical item to its intended target would be a straight line. After all, if one was a magical object, one would presumably want one's effect to take the shortest route. However, magical items aren't sentient—except for, according to legend, two artifacts created by Exalted Grand Priest Nirishava that grew old and died. Interestingly, Exalted Grand Priest Nirishava's scrolls on the nature of sentience suggest that at the very moment someone—or something—becomes able to think, they begin making decisions that are nonsensical.

The string that Maliah claimed to see—and that Jarith was feeling sore about not being able to see— wound around the city of Ar in a circuitous route. Jarith hypothesized that it was following the path taken by Amun.

He was wrong.

The flow of magic was actually dictated by the complex mechanics of a particle field whose interaction with the physical world was integral to the use of magic in Midrealm. Jarith was coming to understand that his power's limitations were tied to his connection to this field of particles. It was an understanding that, while irrelevant to the task at hand, was a useful distraction from the life force being drained ever so slowly from him.

He followed Maliah, ignoring the pain as best he could. Now that they were out in the open, her aura beamed with radiant brilliance. He'd never seen a Midrealmer with such an expansive presence, and part of him wanted to believe it was because of that Highrealm touch—his Highrealm touch. However, he was a sensible kind of guy and was pretty sure her brilliance had more to do with the alterations the Highrealm scientists had made to her parents.

Meta and Jua had insisted on joining them for their less-than-joyful jaunt. Jua looked no worse for wear, but Meta was struggling. Despite her refusal to slow down, she was pale and sweating profusely. By the time they'd trekked through most of the city, her breathing was labored. The others took turns glancing back at her with worry, and she gave them each equal glowers of annoyance.

The invisible path eventually led them out of the city and to the west, where a seldom trodden trail led them up onto a ridge. As they reached the top, they turned back to look at Ar. The river glistened in the distance, and homes seemed piled on top of each other. The Huleay Grounds rose from the chaos, bright walls glaring. And the statues guarding the inner walls commanded attention, a constant reminder of the protection offered by the Temple.

"How far could ze have gone?" Meta asked.

"If ze obtained a horse or camel, we could never find zir," Jua replied.

"Maybe we should return home and organize a plan."

"I'm inclined to agree."

Jarith turned his attention westward at a landscape more familiar than it should have been, given that he'd never left the city before. The sand dipped into a valley bordered further west by rocky cliffs that jutted up from the ground. And like pockmarks across the stone, caves dotted the cliffside.

"Caves," Jarith said to himself.

Jukartis had instructed him to head to these caves if he found himself in danger. Whun Miu had harassed the scientists until they provided a visual of the outside of the caves and of the layout of their interior. Whun Miu had then been voluntold by Jukartis to help Jarith memorize the caves' layouts. At the time, he hadn't understood what caves were, but now that he saw their pattern against the cliffs, it all made sense.

Maliah followed his gaze.

"Those are the Huleay Caves," she said. "The Temple was founded by a secret society of magic workers working to hone their understanding of Nature and the spirits. They carved out those caves."

"You don't think . . ." Jua asked.

"It's a maze inside. One could get lost and never return," Meta added.

"Which makes it the perfect hiding place," Jarith insisted.

"Is that where Amun went?" Jua asked his daughter.

She shook her head as she squinted, as if that would help her see better. "I'm not certain. It's too far. It's the right direction, though. And there isn't much else out here."

"I say we check it out," Jarith voted, though no one asked for his opinion.

They all considered him with long, unimpressed gazes.

Jua let out a sigh. "Once we get closer, it'll become clear whether or not ze's there. If necessary, we could bring in the guard to help us hasten the search."

"But they'll arrest zir." Maliah was stating the obvious, but her tone made it clear that she hoped they'd resolve this with no further arrests.

Jarith couldn't believe she still wanted to defend zir. He was literally dying here, and he couldn't help but think that Meta's poor condition had something to do with Amun as well.

"You're the one with the vision," Meta said to her daughter. "It's your decision."

Maliah looked from one pair of eyes to the next. Jarith could tell she wasn't thrilled to have this weight placed on her shoulders, but she was the only one able to lead them to her mentor. Her gaze drifted to the city, the capital of Ledine, where the enormous statues of the Huleay Grounds glinted in the sunlight. It was her legacy, one she'd agreed—however reluctantly—to take hold of.

Then she looked back toward the caves, where her mentor was probably scheming how to get close enough to Jarith to finish the job. Not that Jarith was bitter or anything—just terrified and annoyed and exhausted and maybe a bit hangry.

Maliah was leaning on one foot, trying to keep as much weight off of the leg he had etched into. Jarith wondered if she was thinking about all the responsibility she had agreed to when he awakened her power. She wasn't broadcasting her thoughts, so for all he knew, she could have been measuring the distance against her own level of hunger.

They waited as Maliah weighed the options. The sun beamed down on them, its heat dulled by a gentle breeze that lifted sand into the air. Jarith raised his sleeve over his face to fend it off, but the quick motion made him dizzy.

They were still quite a distance from the base of the cliff. Had he been in a better state, he could have concocted some innovative way to hasten their trip. But as it was, he struggled to keep his vision from doubling.

The wind picked up, sand swirling from the ground. What began as a gentle breeze now gusted in violent bursts.

"The spirits are directing us," Meta yelled to be heard above the wind.

Jua put his fists together in front of him, and a shield of air whooshed around them, fending off the building barrage of sand. It was a sudden show of power Jarith hadn't been ready for, and he found himself exhilarated by it. Enough so that he was happy to play along.

"Which way do they want us to go?" Jarith asked with a hint of sarcasm that, luckily, no one picked up on.

"Maliah?" Jua yelled.

The sands lifted higher, surrounding them on all sides, and Maliah took a step toward the group as her father's power pushed back against the force of it.

Jarith's confidence faltered. This sandstorm had come out of nowhere. Its dynamic whips in every direction seemed to have sentience. He didn't believe in their spirituality, but for a brief moment, he wondered if the spirits were real. A wisp of sand darted across his face. He recoiled as it cut into his skin.

This was getting a little too intense for his liking.

22

No Other Choice

The sandstorm raged around them, stopped only by the barrier of air Jua was holding steady. It was dark, with only a dim glow of sunshine making it through the debris. Maliah seemed paralyzed with indecision, unsure whether to go back toward the city or onwards to where they believed Amun was hiding.

A powerful gust of wind penetrated Jua's shield, knocking everyone to the ground. But the sand continued swirling around them instead of overcoming their position. Jarith hurried to his feet. A tunnel of sand appeared nearby, leading toward—if his internal compass was correct—the caves.

His questioning gaze met similar looks from Jua and Meta.

"I guess we're going that way," he yelled, pointing to the tunnel within the swirling dust.

They all looked at Maliah, who nodded and led the way in. Above them and on every side, walls of earth swarmed around them, yet not a speck penetrated them. Somehow, this barrier was even more effective than Jua's had been.

Jarith had a hunch that this strange sandstorm wasn't the work of the spirits, as Meta hoped. Though he had no evidence, he believed it to be Maliah's doing. It echoed her inner turmoil over whether to face Amun and potentially save Jarith or return to the safety of her home and seal Jarith's fate.

The tunnel lengthened as they walked, leading them onward to a destination that was masked by the thick cloud of sand around them. It remained dark, but the noise of the wind was deafening. Maliah's aura pulsed, something he'd never seen before. He was no closer to understanding what it meant when, abruptly, the air cleared. The wind calmed to reveal that they were moments away from the nearest cave entrance.

They had traveled the great distance in far less time than normal. He scanned Maliah's aura for clues to how she'd done such a thing, but found nothing. Even so, he was as confident that she had caused the sandstorm as he was terrified by the thought of such a powerful ability being wielded unchecked. On any other day, the thought wouldn't have concerned him, but his vision was blurred and his hands were numb.

Maliah led them up an ancient ramp to long wooden switchbacks. Her confident strides led them past several openings until she came to one that was different somehow. It looked the same as all the others to Jarith, but he hoped the dagger's magic string was leading into it. They didn't discuss what they planned to do, nor did anyone ask for confirmation of the dagger's location. With no ceremony, they followed Maliah into the cave, presumably toward a would-be murderer and zir weapon of choice.

After a twist and two turns through branching paths of the cave, Jarith saw light. Lamps were lit in the distance, and as they neared, Jarith realized the flames were steady and didn't let off any heat. Instead, a set of formulae excited electrons which—once returning from the atomic equivalent of the zoomies—caused the emission of photons.

In other words, they were on the right track. The path remained convoluted as Maliah approached each branching with firm resolve. It wasn't long before she threw out her hand to instruct them to stop.

In the distance, Jarith heard a song. He recognized the melody despite the poor technique of the singer. It was a lullaby from when Maliah was a baby, long before he could detect auras, when her life was simple and sweet and sometimes stinky.

The lullaby told the story of a person who wandered the desert looking for companionship. They came across different varieties of animals, hoping each would make them feel at home. But they still felt empty. Until one day, the person came across a little boy and a little girl. The children brought such joy to their life that they stopped searching and settled in one place.

Jarith couldn't remember if the person died at the end or if their death was a morbid joke he'd made up when the song got stuck in his head.

Maliah held up her hand and made eye contact with each of the others in turn. She wanted them to stay hidden. Jarith noted that none of them nodded their agreement, but Maliah didn't seem to mind.

She then walked around the corner and out of their line of sight.

He heard her soft footsteps revealing her position and could only hope that was part of her plan. Rocks crunched under her shoes, and the sound seemed to carry much further than he expected.

"Maliah?" Amun's voice was crisp and clear, as if ze was only a few spans away. "What are you doing here?"

"I'm here to bring you home," she replied. "You can still stop this, and we can go back to normal."

"That isn't possible," Amun insisted.

"Then explain why. Why are you killing Jarith? Why are you trying to hurt someone I love?"

"If I don't act, this world shall be torn apart."

Jarith's body tensed. He didn't understand Amun's concerns, but whatever they were, he didn't like the implications.

There was silence. Jua made eye contact with Jarith and Meta and motioned for them to move forward. There was a corner just ahead, which led into a narrow passageway. Somewhere beyond, Maliah and Amun continued their conversation as the trio crept closer to the source of the voices.

"I don't understand," Maliah replied. "Are you speaking ill of Jarith?"

"You're asking the wrong questions, my dear."

"Amun, please. Stop talking in riddles. I'm here. I care. But I can't understand if you don't speak plainly."

"The truth is," Amun said with reluctance, "I created a solution to a problem. It wasn't until later, until Emin, that I realized the repercussions. But in connecting to Emin, I set in motion events I could no longer control."

"Emin?" Maliah asked.

Jarith could see Maliah's shadow now, cast in the wavering light of a lantern.

"It doesn't matter," Amun continued. "What matters is that everyone will be safe."

"Except Jarith."

"Jarith is a fool. A fool for believing the lies of Jukartis. A fool for risking everything to come here. And a fool for thinking he could get away with murder."

Jarith had already been tense, and if someone had asked him moments before whether he could get more tense, he would have said no. Yet he did become more tense, so tense that his muscles spasmed and a cramp pained his leg. The thought of bolting full force from the cave to the open air of the desert was overwhelming, but he was too terrified to move.

Suddenly, he regretted not making the time to share his fears with Maliah. Wishes raced through his mind: to hold Maliah again, to share one more meal, to see the people cheer for her, to see her adored as she should be. But those wishes soon turned cold.

Dread was filling him faster than the warmth of the sun on a clear day. Was he going to be forced to act? If Amun revealed his secret, he may need to kill Meta immediately. But he hadn't arranged anything he needed for the ritual. The ritual to transfer her to Highrealm would take time, and it might not even work without the appropriate preparations. No, there was no way he could do that, and it wouldn't stop the dagger's effects anyway.

The only other option was death. The tingling in his body from the dagger's power had progressed to burning, like a thousand needles being raked across his skin. If he didn't do something soon, he would die by Amun's hand.

This was a lot to think about in the few seconds between Amun preemptively accusing Jarith of murder and Maliah letting out a confused, "What?"

But Jarith was a quick thinker.

"It's true," Amun said. "The transfer requires a sacrifice, so Jarith must kill in order to remain here."

"There's no way—"

"Even if you deny it, it is so."

Maliah was quiet.

"You're wondering who the victim is, hoping it would be someone despicable. Would that comfort you, Maliah?" When she didn't answer, ze continued, "Unfortunately, the requirements are far more specific than that. Jarith doesn't get to choose who will be sacrificed." Ze spit the word "sacrificed" out as if it was a bad joke. "And given that he remains here in Ar, the target must be close."

"What are you saying?" Maliah asked. Her voice trembled.

Her fear ripped at his insides, overpowering the pain even being made by the dagger.

"He's going to kill your mother," Amun said. "He must if he wishes to survive."

Jarith dove into action. Rushing into the open space, he threw a wave of force at Amun. The Exalted Grand Priest was caught by surprise as the force pushed zir to the ground. Jarith didn't wait for a reaction. With a clap of his hands, he commanded lightning to flash toward Amun, striking zir with a deafening boom.

Maliah screamed as the magic lamps in the room went dark. Jarith raised his hand again, glowing red in the remaining fire from one lone lantern. Amun wasn't moving, so he took a moment to look around. His priority was the dagger.

He felt Jua's power surround him as it had when he was arrested, trying to restrain him. With little effort, he shook it off. He took careful steps toward the fallen priest.

"Where's the dagger?" he boomed.

A hand grabbed his arm, and he raised his arm to force its owner back. His gaze met Maliah's desperate eyes, her curls falling from their pins. Her eyes looked black in the dim light, yet the sparkle of the fire revealed tears.

The air grew thick, and he pulled Maliah from her position just in time as a blast of force sliced through where they had just stood. Amun was on zir feet, rushing toward a leveled boulder Jarith hadn't seen. On it, he saw a thin line of red.

Recognition washed over him. It was the dagger reflecting the light of the fire. He lifted his hand again, slicing the boulder into two clean halves. Amun jumped backward and turned to Jarith and Maliah. Jarith held his arm out. Electric sparks filled the gap between Amun and the dagger.

Jarith was acutely aware of everyone in the room. Amun's brow drew down. Maliah's grip on his arm tightened. Jua and Meta stood behind them, widened stances but without the knowledge to harm him.

"Step away from the dagger," Jarith commanded.

In his mind, he crafted an electric cage around Amun with a complex set of formulae. He would need to spring the trap at just the right moment, but he had to prepare it first. Quickly, he calculated the necessary arcs and contact points. He wove together a series of formulae.

But his preparations came too late. Amun was gone.

Many years prior, before Maliah was born, before Meta or Jua were born, before Amun came to Midrealm, there lived an Exalted Grand Priest named

Emin. Xe was a soft-spoken person, a thoughtful being who epitomized what it meant to serve xir people as a priest of the Huleay Temple.

Living a quiet and uneventful life, xe spent xir days leading rituals, managing disputes, and meditating. Xir abilities were stronger than many who had come before. However, xe used them only on rare occasions. To Exalted Grand Priest Emin, the powers were a beacon—a calling to the Temple—not a tool to be abused.

Xe believed that if the power manifested itself through xir, it was a sign from the spirits and ancestors. A sign of what? Well, that is unclear, but definitely a sign of something.

The only surviving evidence of such an omen was a prophecy, which came to Exalted Grand Priest Emin in a series of dreams over five consecutive nights. The prophecy told of four generations of a family. Each generation would command more powerful magic than the last until their power would manifest something unimaginable: spiritual evolution for all.

This was the Ascension Four Prophecy, the most important prophecy of the Ledine people, and the most relevant prophecy to the current conflict.

Despite being the origin of this prophecy, Exalted Grand Priest Emin was equally well-known for the circumstances of xir end. Legend had it that in xir final years, xe grew erratic. One day, xe appeared during an evening ritual at the main temple. At the climax of the ceremony, xe stepped up onto the stage and into the reflected light of the sunset.

Xe killed xirself in front of the entire congregation.

Witnesses claimed that over the following days, they saw xir body dissipate, and by the third day, xir corpse went missing. It was never found, and its location remained one of the biggest mysteries of the Huleay Temple.

This information may have been of particular interest to Jarith in this moment if he hadn't been laser focused on the Dwesdar Dagger, which was still sucking the life from him. He could feel it tugging at his very being as he crossed the cavern toward the flat rock where it sat. Behind him, Jua conjured multiple spells meant to intercept him, but he continued on.

His mind raced, trying to figure out how to stop the dagger. The closer he stepped, the faster it worked. Yet he assumed the weapon was driven by the will of its last handler. If he picked it up, he didn't know if it would kill him or obey him.

There wasn't time to ask the priests in the room, and he doubted they were in the mood to chat right now.

He reached toward the dagger. His hand was on fire with pain. Every span felt like an invitation to death, a moment that could be his last. Yet he crept forward, wishing and hoping and wanting and regretting. His legs gave out, and he dropped to his knees. His vision clouded. Stabbing spasms erupted in his muscles. Yet his hand reached, grasping for the dagger's hilt.

Without warning, Maliah's hand shot in front of him, grabbing the dagger from its rocky pedestal. In an instant, the pain was gone.

Most of it, anyway.

He slumped against the stone and rested his upper body on it. He still felt a tingling sensation, which he now understood meant he must pay the cost of transferring to Midrealm soon or be dissipated. Despite that, the immediate threat was gone, and so he breathed a sigh of relief

The air was tense, and Jarith half-expected to look up to see Maliah brandishing the blade in his direction. As he straightened, he made no sudden movements. Much to his surprise, Maliah was holding the dagger in a relaxed grip at her side, and her expression was drawn with worry, not fear.

Her parents didn't look as comfortable with the situation. They were stiff and didn't close the distance to join Maliah.

"How do you feel?" Maliah asked.

"That's a hard question," Jarith replied. "But the dagger isn't active anymore. Thank you."

"That's good."

Jua finally broke his silence. "Maliah, bring me the dagger."

Maliah's eyes seemed to ask Jarith if doing so was acceptable, so he nodded. Not that he felt he needed to approve. She just appeared so unsure.

Jarith leaned against the cave wall and slid down until he was seated on the ground. Every muscle ached with exhaustion, but he couldn't rest easy yet. Maybe if he just closed his eyes for a minute.

Maliah placed the blade in her father's hand. His eyes still betrayed uneasiness, but his threatening grip on the dagger was confident as he sharpened his attention on the former Highrealmer.

"Jarith, you owe us an explanation."

Jarith rested his head in his arms, and he propped them on his bent knees. "What would you like me to explain?"

"Are you here to kill Meta?"

Jarith forced himself to lift his head and make eye contact with the man, who had taken several steps closer. Meta and Maliah remained a few spans behind him.

"No. I'm here for Maliah." Jarith sighed. "But it is true that, in order for me to stay in Midrealm, Meta must die."

Maliah was indignant, her worry for Jarith replaced by fear and anger. "When were you planning on doing it?"

"Honestly?" Jarith replied. "I thought I'd figure out some way to avoid it. I mean, I hoped I would."

His gaze lingered on Meta's. She was unusually quiet and extra-unusually somber.

"I don't believe you," Jua hissed. "You knew what had to be done. Surely you were willing to do it or you wouldn't have traveled here."

"I'm sorry," Jarith said. "I've never wanted to kill anyone. I still don't. But even now, I don't know any other way to survive."

Jua turned to his wife. "Can you believe this?"

She didn't reply.

"Mom?" Maliah asked.

Meta stepped in front of her husband, her determined eyes flickering in the lamplight.

"I'll be your sacrifice," she said.

23

Meaningful Death

Jua and Maliah raised their voices in argument above Meta's acceptance of becoming Jarith's sacrifice. Talking over each other, they asked questions without providing time for answers. They objected and even berated her for accepting such a fate.

To Jarith, their cries seemed distant. He'd only known Meta for days, but already, he knew she was magnificent. In Jua's harsh words and Maliah's heartwrenching sobs, he heard the entire Ledine Empire cry out in fear and sadness. Meta wouldn't be leaving behind just a husband and daughter. She was agreeing to leave behind a nation who loved her.

Jarith shook his head from side to side as Meta maintained her eye contact with him. He had never wanted to take her life, but somehow, her agreement made the act even more horrendous. In her eyes, he saw wisdom and beauty, tenacity and patience. Her aura was fierce yet gentle.

A lump built in his throat. He fought the urge to throw up. His mind raced for answers, but none came.

Meta opened her mouth to speak, and Jarith suddenly remembered Jua and Maliah were there, still begging for answers while not waiting for them to be given. Meta lifted her hand, and her family paused their ramblings.

It was magic, hanging like a breath in the air before settling on its targets like a suggestion. It was simpler and more subtle magic than what Amun had used to control Maliah and Jarith's actions. Yet it was more powerful than Jarith thought Meta capable of.

Once their voices quieted, she said, "Let's sit down."

Jarith wasn't sure if Meta coerced them or not, but soon they were seated on the cool, hard rock lining the cave floor. Jarith relit several magic lamps so they could see better. Their unnatural white glow eased the ominous mood of the fire, though it didn't reduce the tension in the air.

Jua began, "You can't just concede your life without question."

"Allow me to explain," Meta insisted.

"No reasoning could be enough," Maliah cried, her face drenched in flowing tears that were becoming far too frequent for Jarith's liking.

Meta didn't honor the statement with a response. Instead, she began her explanation, making intense eye contact with her daughter.

"I've always believed we exist with purpose," she said. "Each of us lives to affect the world, and sometimes we affect the world in the way we die."

Jua opened his mouth to speak, but when she turned her gaze to him, he paused.

Jarith had been unable to see auras while Amun was here. Meta's aura revealed she was struggling to hold back powerful emotions, though the swirls of intermixing color made it difficult to distinguish which were most potent. Despite this, her expression was gentle, and her voice was steady.

Jarith could tell by Jua's reaction that he recognized her struggle, too. He honored her strength by listening, despite his own intense emotion.

"I've been afraid for several lunar cycles, believing my life would end without purpose."

Maliah and Jua were focused on her words, but Jarith found himself distracted, trying to find an alternative—any alternative—to this amazing woman's premature death.

"The truth is," she continued, "I've been unwell for some time. With Amun's assistance, I've continued living as usual." She paused. It must have been difficult to say the words, but her strong facade didn't falter. "I'm dying."

"What?" Jua asked, eyes wide in terror. "Since when?"

"I don't understand it myself," she admitted. "Amun detected it before I even knew to be worried. Ze tried to treat it, but it has continued to progress."

"Why didn't you tell us?" her husband begged.

Meta didn't answer the question, instead continuing her explanation. "I don't want to die. With Amun's help, I've reviewed our literature, looked at every option available. But we just don't have the power to heal me."

"We're just supposed to let you die, then?" Maliah asked with bitterness sewn into every syllable.

Meta didn't respond.

"Jarith," Maliah said in a panic, her teary eyes almost too much for him to handle. "Tell her she's mistaken."

A nagging voice tried to pin the blame for Meta's condition on Amun, but he dismissed it. The old priest didn't understand the concept of subtle, and ze had shown no violence toward anyone other than him. A knot formed in his stomach. He didn't know enough about human physiology to understand what was causing her illness, but his gut told him Amun had done everything in zir power to help her.

Jarith shook his head. His voice cracked. "I don't know how to help her. I can't even detect anything wrong."

"This is why you've been so tired," Jua said.

His eyes pleaded with her, but he held back his questions. Her aura was dim but not weak, and she sat up straight, as if unaffected by her symptoms. However, tucked behind her were trembling hands.

"If I must die," Meta said, her voice still not betraying her, "I'd prefer to pass with purpose. I accept the will of the spirits and ancestors."

Jarith hated the spirits and the ancestors. He hated the Highrealmers. He hated science. He hated Nature. He hated himself for being too inexperienced to help her. He hated Amun for not having all the answers.

How could she say such things with a straight face? Her commitment and bravery made him feel childish. He had never truly accepted that he would have to take a life. All he'd done was put it off and ignore it, hoping it would never happen.

He couldn't help but wonder if he could have done more while in Highrealm. He should have researched deeper, pushed harder. Perhaps he would have the answer if he had just dedicated himself to finding it instead of relying on Highrealmers, who never showed concern for the Midrealmers.

Maliah begged her mother for more information and pleaded for her to change her mind. She responded in a level, patient tone. As far as Jarith had seen, the only thing Meta took seriously was her duty, and she saw this final act as an obligation.

Jarith expected Jua to reach out for his wife, even to hold her hand, but he didn't. Knowing his wife as he did, he must have known that Meta's disdain for showing her own weakness meant she wouldn't accept any coddling.

When an awkward silence lingered, Jua finally asked, "You're sure there's nothing we can do?"

Meta nodded.

Maliah stood in outrage. "You're giving up now, too?"

"This is your mother we're talking about," Jua said, wiping away tears that came right back with stubborn abandon. "She cherishes life more than anyone. If this is her destiny—"

"Don't you dare!" Maliah screamed.

A wind rushed out from her, snuffing out every lamp in the room, even the magic ones. An eerie glow emanated from the thin hallway they'd traversed to enter this chamber. Maliah spun on her heels and rushed out.

"Maliah!" Jua called before rushing after her.

Meta sighed and reached out for Jarith's hand. They supported each other as they stood, and as they passed each lamp toward the cave's exit, he couldn't bring himself to extinguish them. When they reached the final lamp, Meta gave him a pat on the hand. Then, she stopped walking, turned, and quenched every flame at once before taking his arm and leading him out into the desert.

Her death was imminent now, and he was sorely unprepared.

Maliah rushed toward home ahead of her family. Jua trailed behind her, trying to speak to her.

Jarith's muscles still ached, and his skin still tingled. As he and Meta took their time, he eased their effort by making the sand firmer and thus easier to walk on. The afternoon sun hung behind a lone cloud, giving a slight chill to the weak gust of wind that happened by every few minutes.

"I'm sorry you've had to shoulder this alone," Meta said abruptly.

Jarith hadn't expected Meta to want to talk to him. It seemed awkward to strike up a conversation with your executioner, even if you agreed to the execution.

"I remember when I first came to live at the Huleay Temple," she said. "I felt out of place, very alone. My mentors put the weight of the world in my arms. I was certain I'd ruin everything somehow." A smile crept onto her face. "I used to have dreams of horrible things coming to pass, and I'd blame myself for them. How powerful I must have thought I was." She chortled.

Jarith didn't find it funny.

"You don't have to do this alone, Jarith. Tell me your worries."

"You're kidding," he replied. "I agreed to do a terrible thing. I'm an awful person."

Meta nodded absently—not in agreement, but in acknowledgment—as he continued.

"You've done so much good for your people, and they love you. Now I'm supposed to end that. There has to be another way. Maybe I should resign myself to dying instead."

"Jarith."

"I think that would be better for everyone," Jarith continued.

"Jarith," Meta tried again.

"I should never have even come here in the first place."

"Jarith!" she said in a raised voice as she smacked him in the chest. He stopped walking. She placed her hands on her hips and waited for a gust of wind to die down before continuing. "You're here by prophecy. No matter what your people did to intervene, the wheels of fate are turning with every moment of every day."

"I don't believe in prophecy," Jarith stated.

Meta smiled again and put her hand out. Even though he was bigger and taller than she was, he somehow felt like a child when he placed his hand in hers. Her grip was firm in a protective way as she led them forward.

"If you had never arrived," she said, "my illness would still have spread. Amun's treatments would still have failed. I would have died without meaning, and my soul would have been trapped in my body forever."

He snapped his gaze to hers.

"Did you think I don't know?" she asked with her wry smile. "How could I not notice the plight of my people?" She gave his hand a gentle pat. "Now, because you are here, my soul will be freed. I can serve a new purpose. My husband and daughter will be able to join me someday, and you as well. We'll all be a family again.

And every family alive today in Midrealm will have their families.

"Because you're here, my daughter—who has struggled with her personal life, if you haven't noticed—now has a partner who understands her. Someone who can appreciate her brilliance, who can foster her growth, and who can be her greatest friend.

"Because you are here, I can smile knowing I leave this world to leaders with beautiful hearts. And I'm thankful to your people for allowing me this time to treasure you."

"Even if they didn't have a choice because it was fated," Jarith said with thick sarcasm.

She squeezed his hand and laughed. "Exactly so."

"Thank you," Jarith added. "I'm sorry it has to be this way."

"Me, too," she replied.

Another gust of wind blew over them, and they arrived at the peak of the hill, beyond which stood a spectacular view of the glorious city of Ar. The river beyond gleamed in the sunlight as boats passed along its surface. Flags near the city's entrance waved with strength. Oxen, donkeys, and camels brought pilgrims from faraway places. There was so much to discover about this place.

"I've had a recurring dream for some time now, since I first found out about my condition," Meta said. "You and Maliah and Jua are gathered around the dinner table, laughing and eating and drinking. You're telling stories and sharing frustrations and learning from one another. I know this won't be easy, but you'll get through it. As a family."

Jarith saw Maliah up ahead, still angrily pushing herself forward, as if running away from the inescapable problems before her. How he wished she was here, sharing this moment with them. He cherished the motherly tenderness in Meta's voice, the softness of her hand in his, and the simple elegance she carried herself with.

Much like he had been refusing to face his destiny, Maliah was fighting against hers. He understood it, and part of him still wished she could refuse it, even if that meant rejecting him.

He understood now, he didn't need to relish what had to happen next. As Meta descended the hill with her chin raised to her beautiful city, he steeled his heart.

If she could face her destiny with such grace and dignity, so could he.

24

A Day In The Market

Maliah stood on the rooftop patio, leaning against the parapet and looking out over a city still unaware of the tragic loss to come. She had many reasons to retreat to the roof. She could have come up here to cry more, as she'd done in bed the previous night. This was even a suitable spot to direct her resentment at the city her mother was so dedicated to serving.

However, she'd come up here to escape Jarith. He'd been waiting outside her room when she awoke, which wasn't creepy at all. Though he hadn't been pushy, he'd wanted to speak with her, "about everything."

She didn't want to talk to him. As a matter of fact, she was pretty sure she never wanted to talk to him again. If they had a conversation, how would she stop herself from blaming him for her mother's death? It wasn't his fault. She knew it wasn't. But he had agreed to it, which sort of, almost, maybe did make it his fault.

As she had eaten breakfast, Jarith and her parents conversed in low voices. She heard every word. They hadn't spoken **that** quietly. But they were trying to be discreet in their own way. In order to perform the ritual, Jarith needed to prepare. Her mother wanted the ritual to take place on the Huleay Grounds. Before they could rope Maliah into anything, she had excused herself and retreated here.

It was a beautiful day. Soft clouds dotted the rich blue sky. The sun gleamed off the mudbrick homes. In the distance, the market was teeming with activity, and beyond, the river pushed its way toward the coast. She took a deep breath as a warm breeze tossed her hair into her face, tickling her nose.

It all felt pretty rude, and she scoffed at time for not stopping, at the world for not dimming its brilliance, and at her curly hair for not staying behind her shoulders.

She rolled her eyes as she heard someone walking up the steps behind her. Was she going to lash out at Jarith or just run away again? Her heart raced as she tried to decide. She was surprised when she heard his voice below her, where Jarith and her father were exiting the front door. She turned to see her mother, whose smile was as genuine as ever.

"Your father is escorting Jarith to the Huleay Grounds to prepare," she said, as if they were getting ready for a party instead of her death.

"I don't want to talk about it."

Maliah spun back around in time to see her father exit the gate. Jarith's gaze met hers, and he lingered until she looked away.

"Oh, me neither," Meta scoffed. "I've had enough of the drama."

Maliah glanced back. What was her mother trying to do?

"No," Meta continued. "I was thinking of heading into the market today, since Jua has put me on leave."

"I think he wants you to rest."

"He's not here."

Maliah turned and had to fight a smile at seeing her mother's sneaky grin.

"Even so," Meta continued, "I don't believe being alone is the most prudent course of action."

"You want me to come with you?"

"Your father has put you on leave as well."

Maliah shook her head and rolled her eyes. "Fine."

The market was even busier than usual. Even so, the crowd parted to allow them through. Most denizens knew Meta's face, and those who didn't at least recognized her garb.

Over her stark white dress, she wore an overlay made of bright, colorful beads. A golden chest piece matched armbands and ankle bracelets. Her hair was pulled back into a bun, and she had a linen hood pulled up to shield her from the sun. Its golden embroidery sparkled in the sunlight.

Maliah was used to the people's stares, but that didn't make it any more comfortable. Her mother held her arm gingerly as they walked through the crowd, each step bringing more people to a pause.

A man stumbled out in front of them and fell to his knees at their feet.

"Please," he cried. "Exalted Grand Priest, I beg you. Heal me." He pointed at his own feet, which were swollen and bruised.

Several men stepped out from the sidelines. They grabbed the man and began to pull him away.

"Please," the man begged. "I can't work. I can't feed my family."

Maliah looked up at her mother, who already had a hand raised to stop the men. Yet, despite her gesture, they were still dragging the thrashing man to the side.

"You there," Maliah yelled.

The men looked back. Panicked at Meta's raised hand, they froze. Maliah felt sorry for them. The entire crowd seemed to hold its breath as they waited to see what the Exalted Grand Priest would do.

Her mother slipped her other hand from Maliah's arm and walked over to the babbling man. She knelt beside him, her intense stare stopping his begging.

Meta whispered, and with a mere thought, Maliah could hear her. "Have you visited the Grounds?"

He mumbled a response.

"What is your name?"

He told her and gave her his address when she asked. Maliah looked around. To the crowd, Meta exuded an air of commanding intensity. Somehow, Maliah knew that the denizens weren't seeing the truth. They saw the man being reprimanded by a powerful priest.

Her words, audible only to the man, were anything but admonishment. She provided him with a set of ingredients to soothe the pain and promised him a priest would visit him to provide treatment. Then, she instructed him to attend a series of services at the Huleay Grounds upon his remission.

He promised her he would heed her words and thanked her profusely.

"No need," she said. "Now, be on your way."

The man stood and took a step away from her. He paused, and Maliah saw surprise in his eyes as he looked back at her mother. Then he rushed away, his gait much less pained than it had been minutes before.

Meta returned to her daughter's side and took her arm.

"You healed him?" Maliah asked in a whisper as they continued their way through the crowd.

"Numbed the pain for a while, is all. I learned that one watching Jarith," she said with a grin.

She'd seen her mother help people before, but never outside of the Huleay Grounds. At least, she thought not. However, perhaps her mother had helped many people who approached them in the past. Maybe Maliah had just been unable to see it, like the other citizens had been unable to see it.

Now that her powers were awakened, Maliah experienced the world differently. It was difficult to pinpoint, but there seemed to be another layer to the world, subtle but discrete. By shifting her perception of this layer, she had made her mother's words audible and detected the improvement in the man's condition.

"I thought you weren't allowed to provide services outside the Grounds," Maliah said.

There were exceptions to this rule. For example, the Temple regularly held public visitations and gatherings, where they provided services to the people. But Amun had taught her that using their true magic outside the Huleay Grounds was taboo.

"My dear," Meta replied with a wry smile, "I'm an Exalted Grand Priest. I can do whatever I want."

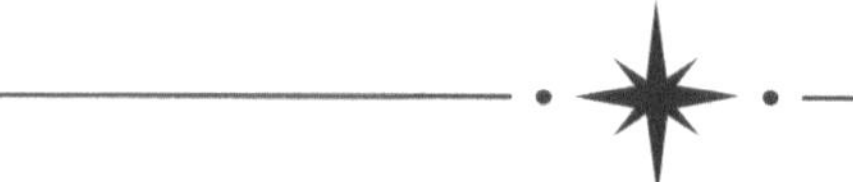

Maliah and her mother weren't interrupted again as they continued through the market. They turned a corner and entered a small herbal store.

"What are you getting here?" Maliah asked.

Meta gave her arm a pat. "Don't worry about it. I'll find it. Why don't you wait by the door?"

Maliah wasn't fooled. Meta was buying materials for the ritual. A knot formed in her stomach as she watched her mother peruse the store's goods with a far too cheerful comportment and make conversation with the shop owner. Meta had said she didn't want to die, yet she was shopping with levity, as if perusing ingredients for a meal.

She thought back to the man who had stopped them earlier. As soon as she'd seen his feet, she had known what ailed him. No, not known. Sensed. She couldn't describe it with words, but she'd detected it.

Yet she didn't sense anything wrong with her mother. Amun had identified the cause of her illness, so it must be possible. Maybe if ze was here, they could find a solution together. Maliah brought a new perspective, and perhaps that's what they needed to heal her mother.

She longed to speak to her mentor, then she longed harder to go to a place where all was well. Where her mother could live. Where she could be with Jarith. Where Amun didn't feel threatened. Did such a place exist? Maliah figured that if a place like Highrealm existed, there must exist somewhere they could be a complete family.

She cleared her thoughts. If she could detect her mother's illness, she could find a solution. Jarith had told her she had a good intuition. Her father had been impressed with her capabilities before her powers were awakened. Amun believed in her, too.

"Are you well?"

Her mother's voice surprised her, pulling her out of her meditative state.

"Yes," Maliah said. "Did you find what you need?"

"I did. Irdayus is always well-stocked."

Meta caught her up on the gossip from the herbal shop's owner as they browsed the market's offerings. Her mother stopped to purchase a new rug for their home and bought a replacement bouquet of dried flowers to replace those that hung in their common area. She was baffled as her mother acted as if nothing was wrong, as if she wouldn't be gone very soon.

Maliah's arms were full by the time they headed back home, but she couldn't hold in her questions any longer.

"I don't understand how you do it. How can you act as if everything is fine?"

"I'm with my favorite woman in the world," Meta replied. "And we're enjoying our time together."

"You bought things for the house. Things you won't get to enjoy."

"I thought you didn't want to talk about it."

"I don't." Maliah paused. "But why buy something when you'll be gone?"

"Maliah. Dear." Meta sighed. "Don't you see? It's because you won't be." She bumped Maliah with her hip. "And because I don't want you stuck with that rug we've intended to get rid of for a year."

Maliah could think of nothing else to say. Her mother's smile, the scent of her perfume, the sound of her laugh—it all made the knot in her stomach tighten even more. She soon realized her mother had been waiting for the crowd to thin. When they turned off of the main road, they were mostly alone, so Meta took her chance.

"There's something important I must ask of you." She didn't wait for Maliah to deny the request. "I don't want you to blame Jarith."

Maliah swallowed back a retort.

"It would be easy," Meta continued, "to saddle him with the blame. He's already feeling such shame. But if you look within and allow yourself to remember your dreams, you'll know there's no other way."

Maliah tore her gaze from her mother's. She didn't want to relive those dreams. Each night since the first, she suspected the dream had returned, and she'd done her best to block it out. But the pieces all suddenly made sense.

The dreams had started with fire, representing a new life brought into this world: Jarith. The flames searched for something, for her mother. Then, representations of the spirits of earth, sky, sun, and river had swirled together, divining their intention. The words of a spell followed, the spell that would take her mother's life, as intended by the spirits. The words marked the ending, a sacrifice, as foretold by the prophecy. But they also marked a beginning.

"You knew?" Maliah asked, eyes brimming with tears.

"I sensed we were sharing the same dreams," her mother replied. "Jarith is going to need you, and I think you'll need him as well. He's a wonderful person who will make a tremendous impact on our world and our society. But more so, he'll provide the support you deserve to flourish into the Exalted Grand Priest you'll soon need to be.

"Maliah, I believe in you with all my heart. You are kind and fiery and incredibly talented. But you can't get through this alone. Please, let Jarith be there for you. Process your grief together, and grow stronger because of it."

"Jarith doesn't have to do this," was all Maliah could force out without breaking down in sobs.

"No, he doesn't."

Meta's gentle smile told Maliah what her words didn't. Her mother saw Jarith's actions as a gift. Jarith planned to do something he feared in order to provide meaning for Meta's end. Even though she had said this in the cave, Maliah hadn't understood it.

This time, she could sense her mother's complex emotions. Her fear of leaving this world. Her pride at everything she'd accomplished. Her sadness at losing her family. Her joy at giving her life to save Jarith's.

Abruptly, her mother's shining aura appeared, stretching outward in glorious beams of light. Maliah's jaw dropped as the golden radiance forced her to squint her eyes, but she was sobered as she turned her gaze to its core. Though Meta shone with blazing splendor, a thick, white webbing covered her body. It was concentrated at her chest, stomach, and hips, but its tendrils stretched across her extremities. The web seemed alive and dynamic, gradually spreading even further.

Maliah looked for a weak point. Amun had taught her how to do this, and although she'd never been able to try it, she understood what she was looking for. She combed through her mother's physical and metaphysical being, analyzing every physical and metaphysical property she'd ever been taught and even some she discovered by chance.

There had to be something she could do. Every problem had a solution. She only needed the smallest of chances.

"You see it, don't you?" Meta asked. "What Amun calls the webbing."

"We can cut it," Maliah said, though she knew it wasn't possible. "We can peel it from you. Surely there's an artifact—"

"There's not. We tried."

Maliah kept looking, but her mother and Amun were right. She'd never seen or heard of this before, and she could probably spend her entire life trying to understand it. But neither she nor Jarith could prevent its inevitable result.

25

ACKNOWLEDGMENT

When Maliah and her mother arrived home, Jua and Jarith had returned. While Jua reminded Meta of the definition of rest, Maliah looked around for Jarith. She found him on the rooftop patio, almost exactly where she'd been when her mother had come to her earlier that day.

He turned his gaze to meet hers, eyes sparkling with tears, though he wasn't crying. She opened her mouth to speak, but no words came out. What could she say? With a deep breath, she went to his side.

Her arm rubbed against his, and she laid her head on his shoulder. Gazing up at him, she understood the endless ways she needed him. It tore at her because if she needed him this much, how could she handle him hurting her?

He really was a jerk for being so wonderful. With just this look, her heart softened, and she found a place of forgiveness. She wasn't so far gone that she could forgive him just yet, but she saw the path ahead. Her heart yearned for that path. In his eyes, she could almost see their future of honest laughter, angry spats, and loving nights.

His full lips looked enticing. She wanted desperately to embrace him, lose herself in his kiss, and escape the painful reality. But before she could even complete her fantasy, he spoke.

"I'm so sorry."

It was a quiet whisper, and though his voice trembled, the words were clear. He hadn't whispered because it was difficult to say, but because he was terrified of how she'd respond.

"I'm sorry, too," she replied.

"What do you have to be sorry for?" he asked.

"So, so much."

"It's okay if you don't want to tell me."

She lifted her head from his shoulder and looked down at her hands.

"When I was growing up," she said, "your world was an escape. It was someplace where I didn't have to be the child of prophecy, the future Exalted Grand Priest. I associated you with a sense of freedom. Every day, my life here was so focused on my duty and all these things I'm supposed to achieve. But I didn't have to worry about any of that in Highrealm. I was able to just exist.

"I hate this prophecy. Really, I do. I've been so afraid of this destiny ruining my life, but I've also been frightened I won't meet everyone's expectations of me.

I'm terrified of losing Mom and Amun, but I'm terrified of starting something with you."

"Terrified of me?" Jarith asked.

"Yes. You're pretty scary. Didn't you know that?"

He let out a pained laugh before reaching out and tucking a stray curl behind her ear. His hand paused on her cheek.

"Jarith, I'm tired of being afraid. So, I'm just going to ask you. Can I trust you?"

"That's quite a loaded question," he replied with a forced smile. "Let's see. You can trust me to stay by your side as long as you'll have me. You can trust me to support you through hard times."

"To help me with my makeup?" she asked.

His smile became more genuine. "Yes, absolutely."

He leaned down and placed his forehead against hers, and she reveled in the feel of his breath on her skin.

"In Highrealm, Jukartis and eir Ascension Project decided every part of my life. My very existence was forged for prophecy. There were so many times when I thought I couldn't go on. Times when Jukartis was so cruel that I ached to end it.

"Maliah, I love you. I admire how thoughtful and passionate you are, and how committed you are to your own values. I love that you're willing to look prophecy in the eye and ask if it's the right thing to do.

"I'm tired of being scared, too."

He reached out and took her hands in his, lifting his head away from hers to meet her gaze with intense determination. It was all she could do to avoid crying as she cupped his face in her hands and wiped tears from his eyes.

"If you tell me right now not to go through with this ritual," he continued, "I'll stop. I won't fear the future that awaits me because I'll know I've done what's right. Not because my people told me to or because a prophecy foretold it, but because we see the good in each other and made the best decision we could."

Maliah gazed up into Jarith's eyes. A lump caught in her throat, and the knot in her stomach returned. His expression was unreadable, and she knew he was avoiding swaying her opinion.

Fear had ruled her for so long. Because of fear, she'd struggled to make friends, failed to come into her own as a priest, and pushed Jarith away. If she was going to push aside that fear, she couldn't stay stuck in her head any longer.

She went back to her conversation with her mother, who was dying with or without Jarith's intervention. If she didn't stop the ritual, her mother would have the meaning she wanted. Jarith would live. But she would be cutting short her remaining time with the most important woman in her life.

If she stopped the ritual, she could have many lunar cycles left to spend with her mother. Meta would weaken and dull until, finally, she'd pass on, trapped in her body for eternity without purpose. And, of course, Jarith would die as well.

No matter when she lost her mother, the remaining time would never be enough. No amount of stalling would change that.

Jarith had said he wanted them to make the best decision. He understood that there was no appealing choice. Either way, Maliah was going to lose more than she could bear. Jarith didn't offer this opportunity lightly. She believed him when he said he wouldn't go through with the ritual.

She wanted to delay the inevitable for as long as she could. Desperately, she wished not to face the loss of her mother, the loss of her mentor, or the loss of Jarith.

But that was fear talking, and she didn't want it to control her any longer.

"No," she finally said, her voice cracking. "We should continue with the ritual."

Jarith's expression shifted, but was just as unreadable. He threw his arms around her and pulled her tight against his chest. When she felt his jerking movements, she realized he was crying. She held him tightly as he apologized over and over again.

How she wished he didn't have to shoulder this burden. Yet she wouldn't allow him to face it alone. Comforting him provided little solace to the deep pain in her heart, but even so, she was thankful for it.

Amun slunk through the shadows, darting from one alleyway to another. The sun was below the horizon, but ze couldn't risk being seen. If ze was going to stop the cascade of events, everything had to go according to plan.

Ze had spent most of the day obtaining intelligence. It was easy enough. After all, it was something ze'd done for many years under many names after arriving in this world. The adjustment to a physical body had been troublesome, but more concerning had been zir detachment from zir powers.

Ze had been weakened by zir time imprisoned by Jukartis. Even the memory of eir name brought a snarl of disgust to Amun's lips. The being had used eir power to bind zir to one place, and ey had tortured Amun to further zir research.

It had taken several lunar cycles in Midrealm for Amun to command the smallest spark of zir power. Years had passed before ze had mastered it again. Yet even now, too many limitations came from being trapped in a physical form.

But it had all been worth it. Ze had methodically built the framework to stop the plans of Jukartis. Ey had been selfish and willing to risk far too much. Amun knew ey saw the Midrealmers as inferior and expendable, and it was that hubris that allowed Amun to prepare.

Jarith was preparing a ritual in a small temple on the Huleay Grounds. Based on the time Jua had requested space for, they were planning to complete the sacrifice ritual the day after next. That meant there was still time.

It concerned Amun that Jarith had somehow convinced the family of his goodwill. Despite zir warning, they had been fooled into believing the ritual was innocuous. Maybe he'd even told them this ritual would save Meta.

"We can save her," Amun whispered. "We merely need more time."

Ze neared the river's edge. Boats lined a nearby dock, but they were empty of people. Amun could hear voices, likely a party on one of the boats. Ze paused to rest on the riverbank and drank the rest of the water ze had obtained.

As ze refilled zir earthenware jug in the river, ze whispered, "Our priority is to halt the solidification of Jarith's transfer. He mustn't be allowed to fracture this reality. We'll figure out how to heal Meta once he's dealt with."

Pain overwhelmed zir stern features, and ze laid zir head on bent knees.

"How have I become so like em? This cruelty feels so foreign. But the visions you send me are clear. If Jarith isn't stopped, both our worlds will fracture."

The evening breeze danced across the water, bending the reeds along the bank as the last light of the sun faded. Amun fought back tears. Ze feared ze would be found, yet ze feared being alone.

"Emin, my friend, you're still out there, aren't you?"

Only the silence replied.

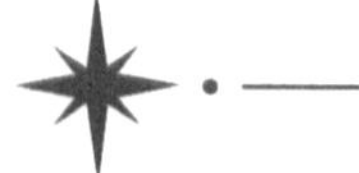

Jua pushed open the door to their bedroom. The tray he held had a variety of choices from the dinner their attendants had prepared. Closing the door behind him with his foot, he shared a long look with his wife.

He laid the tray on the bed and then reclined next to her. She thanked him and gave him a kiss. He watched as she picked at the food, choosing only her favorites.

"I think Maliah and Jarith made up," she said between bites. "I gave her a stern talking-to."

"I'll bet you did," Jua replied with a grin. "And Jarith?"

"That boy needed a gentle talking-to, which I'm not as good at."

Jua laughed. "We had some time to talk today."

"That's true. And what knowledge did you bestow upon him, my love?" Her wry smile was infectious as she plucked out her favorite berries from the mix.

"I believe he merely humored me." Jua shrugged. "His only lacking appears to be his relationship skills."

"Oh?"

"Indeed. We shared fond memories of Maliah's youth, and I counseled him not to remind her of a few of those stories."

"Oh," she said in a knowing tone. "Thank the spirits and the ancestors that he has you to guide him."

She picked up a handful of nuts and a slice of prepared meat. "And how did the preparations go?"

"Jarith said our preparations were well past the limit of overkill."

"Just how I like it."

"You're certain the day after tomorrow isn't too soon?"

Meta gave him a smile that meant, "Don't ask me again."

"I know," Jua said. "Jarith informed me he isn't aware of how much longer he has, but it's likely not more than a couple of days." He turned more toward her. "I just keep thinking, what if the sacrifice isn't necessary? What if they miscalculated? What if we have more time?"

"That's good, love," she said, giving him a pat on the leg. "You're working through the stages of grief."

"Meta . . ."

She groaned. "Jua, if I hadn't dreamt of my passing, and if Maliah hadn't experienced the same vision, maybe then—maybe—I'd entertain some hope. But we both saw this, and we both interpreted it the same way."

He took her face in his hands, and though she tried to pull away, he clung to her. "I know. I'm sorry. But with everything happening with Amun, and now this . . ." He trailed off.

"I wish ze was here as well," Meta said, her expression gentling.

"It feels like just yesterday, you showed up at the Huleay Grounds covered in dust and clay. You used to offer me stupid bets. And I fell for them every time."

"You still do." She dropped what she was holding onto the tray and put her arms around his neck.

He moved his hands to her waist. "I asked Jarith what life was like in Highrealm," he whispered. "He described a magical place, a place worthy of the spirits. It's a place where your power will be at your fingertips, except you'll no longer have fingertips. You'll be boundless, able to mold your reality with no effort."

"Sounds . . ." She stopped.

"What?"

". . . terrifying," she finished. She pulled him closer until their foreheads were pressed together. "What will I do in a universe so vast, so endless, but without you in it?"

"I'll join you someday," he promised. "All we must do is wait." He ran his fingers through her long hair. "Perhaps we'll remain connected in our dreams."

"I'd like that."

Meta had never wanted Jua to be strong for her. She'd never accepted his pity. Maybe it was because of her unyielding resilience, or perhaps her incredible stubbornness. But in doing so, she had also never fully acknowledged his strength.

Jua had never wanted Meta to show her weakness. He'd never accepted platitudes from her. Maybe it was because of his trusting nature, or perhaps his sincere kindness. But in doing so, he had also never fully acknowledged her struggles.

That all changed tonight.

26

Strands Of Reality

Sharp pain woke Jarith from a dream, surging through him like lightning. If it weren't for the pain, Jarith would have, immediately upon waking, realized this was his first prophetic dream. He would have celebrated it before realizing the details were quite fuzzy. In his excitement, he may have gone to wake up Maliah, perhaps interrupting her own prophetic dream. And by the time he got her attention in something resembling a wakeful state, he would have forgotten what the dream had contained.

As it was, the sharp pain he awoke to had interrupted the dream, and, as any Exalted Grand Priest would have advised him, an interrupted dream is as useless as no dream at all. Not that Jarith had the time to consider any of this. The intensity of his agony occupied his thoughts.

He heard a voice screaming and, moments later, realized it was his own. His body convulsed as an unseen force tried to rip him to pieces. He couldn't force his eyes open. It was all he could do to remain conscious.

A soft pressure touched his face, but it felt like needles pressing into his skin. He reflexively jerked away. More hands pushed down on his ankles, wrists, and throat. A thousand spikes seemed to pierce through to his muscles. His mind and body were enveloped in torture, and he couldn't fight back.

A warm, white light appeared in his mind's eye, hovering in place. He tried to focus on it, but a surge of stabbing tore his attention away. The light grew brighter, and its reach extended. With each passing moment, it crept through more of him.

The pain subsided in his hands and feet, then his legs and arms, then his torso, his neck, his head, and finally, his mind. Exhaustion weighed on him, making his body seem heavy. Beads of sweat dripped over his skin as he pulled in labored breaths.

"There, now," a voice said. "Can you hear us, Jarith?"

His eyes snapped open, and he found Meta, Jua, and Maliah at his bedside. He tried to sit up but couldn't work up the strength. And even if he had, Meta's hand on his chest would have knocked him back down. Rude.

"What happened?" Maliah asked.

The tingling throughout Jarith's body was a worrying sign. At first, he wondered if Amun was nearby, but this wasn't the dagger. Either Amun had concocted an even stronger spell than the Dwesdar Dagger, or . . .

"Do you sense Amun's presence?" Jarith asked, his voice hoarse.

Maliah opened her mouth, probably to argue, but stopped herself. She closed her eyes, and Jarith saw her aura expanding in waves of energetic connections. Its ripples reached beyond the walls of the room, and prismatic colors pulsed through it.

"No," Maliah said, her aura settling down. "At least, I don't sense zir power. This isn't Amun."

"That's what I was afraid of," Jarith said.

"What do you mean?" Jua asked.

"It's the transfer. It's collapsing," Jarith replied. He looked at Meta for guidance. "What did you do? How did you stop it?"

Meta looked him squarely in the eye, not wavering. "I sacrificed some of my energy in hopes of anchoring you here temporarily."

Maliah and Jua shared a grim look. It was clear from their gazes that they didn't like where this conversation was going.

"I didn't know that was possible," Jarith said. He tried to sit up again, and this time, Meta put a hand on his back to help him.

"Me neither," she replied. "We can't postpone any longer. We must complete the ritual."

"In the morning, we can—" Jua began.

"Now," Meta interrupted.

"Now?" Maliah repeated.

"I don't know why feeding Jarith my energy was successful, but I'm certain it won't last long. If we don't take action, Jarith may not make it through the night."

As they climbed the hill toward the inner Huleay Grounds, Maliah's arm steadied Jarith. He still felt weak, and the tingling sensation across his body was a sore reminder of their impending, though vague, deadline. A few paces in front of them, Meta was leaning into Jua as he supported her weight.

It would be several hours before the sun rose, so each pair carried a lantern to light their path. Their crunching footsteps in the sand interrupted the silence of the night. In the distance, the river tended to its business as most of the world slumbered dreamlessly. Enchanted by underlit statues that framed the enormous gates, Jarith was almost able to distract himself from his task.

However, distraction wasn't what was required right now. He needed to focus on the transfer formulae. Though he tried to concentrate, his mind flowed back to his lessons from Jukartis.

"Remember," ey had said on more than one occasion, "in Highrealm, we can morph our reality to create and cast formulae. You won't have that luxury in Midrealm. Their primitive physical limitations may require that you create a tangible pictogram before you can manifest its effect. As barbaric as it seems, the more complex the formulae, the more likely a corporeal rendering will be required."

Though Jarith had never needed to be reminded of this, Jukartis was always happy to repeat emself. Happy was probably the wrong word, as Jukartis made sure Jarith knew ey did not relish the role of educator.

"Do not take chances with the transfer formulae," Jukartis had warned. "Before you complete it, you'll need to create the rendering. The ideal plan is to begin with reconnaissance to identify your point of attack. Next, procure materials by any means necessary. Tracking formulae will help you locate them. Then, disable your target and draft the rendering on its skin. Once complete, proceed with the ritual as soon as you can."

Jukartis hadn't been satisfied with just one plan, and so, ey laid out a slew of contingencies for Jarith to follow. A non-zero number of them involved killing the sacrifice first, then preparing and executing the ritual sometime after. The only reason Jukartis didn't favor these plans was because ey believed it would negatively impact the efficacy of the spell. Unsurprisingly, none of eir contingencies had included getting to know the target or coming to love her.

When they reached the inner Huleay Grounds, Jua and Meta spoke with the guards. Maliah and Jarith held back. Maliah's eyes glistened in the fire's light, and her mouth hung open, as if she was about to say something. She noticed Jarith watching her and lowered her gaze, pulling her hair over her shoulder with her free hand.

Only then did she speak.

"I'm sorry you had to go through that pain."

"I'm sorry we don't have more time," he replied.

"Are you going to be able to complete the ritual? You're shaking."

"I can do it," he promised her.

"Is there . . ." She paused, and her parent's voices murmured in the background as she considered her words. "Is there anything I can do to help?"

The sting of her offer was obvious on her face, and Jarith wished to spare her. But he couldn't afford to make any compromises.

"Maybe, if you think you're up for it."

She nodded. "I can support you, and I'd be glad to ease her transition to Highrealm."

"Thank you," Jarith said. "I understand how difficult this must be for you."

"I don't know that you do," Maliah said with gentleness. "But I appreciate it."

Jua turned and waved for them to follow. Through the twisting passageways of the grounds, they made their way to the smallest sanctuary of the Huleay Grounds. Maliah paused when they approached.

"Here?"

"I know," Jarith said, "but since Amun is missing, it was the ideal option to prepare something with the flexible timing we required."

She hesitated, and Jarith didn't rush her to continue inside. But she took a deep breath before pushing forward. He couldn't help but be in awe of her, and he promised himself he would stay present and focused. He'd do what he came to do.

Once inside the small temple, Jarith looked around for his supplies. Near the door, he found what he was looking for. On a pedestal sat a large bowl that held several items. He picked the bowl up, but Maliah snatched it from him.

"I've got this," she said and left his side to go toward the stage platform.

The torches around the periphery of the sanctuary were already lit, and shadows danced on the walls as the flames flickered. The statues at each corner of the room looked solemn, as if each felt a twinge of guilt for leading events to this moment. Jarith was glad he didn't believe the spirits were real. Otherwise, he would have been angry at them for watching the events unfold without intervening on behalf of one of their most loyal followers.

Jarith made his way to the platform where Amun had masked Maliah's lessons from him in Highrealm. Although he'd been here once before, it still seemed surreal, as if he was once again peering through Maliah's eyes. He was in control, yet a sense of dissociation separated him from his body. Again, he pulled himself back into the present. He was taller, he assured himself as he stretched his spine. Definitely taller.

At the center of the stage was an altar that had been in storage for over a decade. Jua had remembered its use in an overcomplicated ritual intended to bless the new king of a neighboring nation with a son. According to Jua, the king had made the lunar cycle-length journey to Ar with his wife, who was pregnant with their fifth child. He had heard stories growing up of the power of Ledine's priests, but had never ventured this far beyond his empire's borders.

Because they were pretty sure altering a child's sex after conception wasn't possible and being very sure it wasn't ethical, several of the Huleay Temple priests had tried to rein in the king's expectations. The king insisted they try anyway and had assured them he wouldn't blame them if it didn't work. After all, he already had four daughters, all of whom he loved dearly. What was one more?

Prince Dracaen was born several lunar cycles later, and Ledine's priests weren't sure whether to feel far too powerful or favored by coincidence. They agreed never to speak of it again and placed the custom-crafted altar in storage, never to see the light of day.

Luckily, Jua had visited the storage area recently, noticing the golden detailing that decorated the base. When Jarith had requested a surface for Meta to lie on, Jua insisted on doing better than a blanket on the floor and had requested the altar be retrieved from storage.

As they prepared for the ritual, Jua covered the altar with a blanket that was folded at one end and then helped Meta up onto it. He slid a small pillow under her head and neck. Meta's stiff motions betrayed her exhaustion, and Jua's trembling hands betrayed his fear.

Jarith watched, transfixed, as the couple shared a long look. A part of him was still looking for a way out, but there was no more time. The tingling sparks across his body were a constant reminder of the urgency to complete the formulae. As Jua and Meta clasped each other's hands, Jarith tore his gaze away. He sat at the edge of the stage and held his arms out to Maliah.

"What's all this?" she asked as she handed the bowl over.

"Once it's mixed, it'll be a paste to use as ink. Similar to the one I used for your spell." He gestured at her thigh, where he'd etched the pictogram to awaken her powers. "It'll be thicker this time so it doesn't run or spread, and we'll be able to wipe it off afterwards to prepare her body for burial."

"You don't need to cut into her?"

"No, thankfully," Jarith said as he poured an ingredient into a small mortar that had been sitting in the bowl. He held it up to Maliah. "Would you mind?"

She took the mortar from him and, after locating the pestle underneath a pouch in the large bowl, started grinding. The other materials were already prepared, so he emptied the bowl and started mixing. Once the consistency was right, he added in the ground powder from Maliah.

He placed his hand over the bowl and spoke precise, intentional words. The air thickened, and the dark ink glowed. Strings of light appeared, stretching from the floor upward.

These were the strands of reality, a negligible fraction of the endless connections between realities. Each strand glistened in vibrant colors, as if diluting an entire world into a wavelength of light. Though the filaments were transient and dynamic, Jarith's words wove meaning from them.

He held up the bowl, and as he spoke the final words of the formulae, the ink changed. Its black color faded to white, then it glistened with color just like the strands of reality. He tilted the bowl in a circle, checking its viscosity and glisteniness, which is the scientific term for it.

Satisfied, he stood and faced the family. "I'm ready to begin."

27

Transfer Formulae

Maliah stood apart from the others at the edge of the stage. She'd spent hours here almost every day for many years, learning the magic of Nature and the nature of magic. However, only now did she understand the immensity of the power they could wield.

A memory came flooding back of a lesson between Jarith and Jukartis, one she hadn't understood at the time. They had been discussing a spell they called the transfer formulae, based on the Athu Aqatne, the theorem to allow a soul to move between realities.

"The elegance of the transfer formulae is that their core relies on stochasticity," Jukartis had said.

Stochasticity was a word they used often in Highrealm and a word she'd never heard anyone other than Amun utter in Midrealm. She understood it as having to do with randomness, but her culture had little knowledge in this area of mathematics to give her context.

"If you think of the formulae as a graph," Jukartis had explained, "at its center you'll find the stochastic element, a field of probabilities, which we cannot predict. It's connected to four components. Once you've begun the first component, it's imperative that you continue. Do you remember why?"

Jarith had responded, "Because we have anchored the realities together."

"And?"

"And distant realities don't align well enough for a single anchor to remain stable."

"And," Jukartis continued, drawing out the word, "once you've created an anchor, even once it's collapsed, it forms a scar between realities. It's then more difficult to create an anchor near the same location.

"After the anchor is in place, you'll move on to the second component, destabilizing the boundary between realities. The third component will plot the path for the transfer, and the fourth will release the soul from its ties to its home reality.

"Only then can you initiate the core component. Remember, the transfer isn't instantaneous, but it is imminent. The core component will resolve itself."

Jarith had stated that he—ze, at that time—understood, even though Maliah had been overwhelmed by the instructions. Now, as Jarith announced he was ready to begin the ritual—the transfer formulae, as Jukartis had called it—she wished the explanation made sense.

Jarith looked over at her, and she recalled that she'd offered to help with the ritual. Her feet felt stuck in place. At her hesitation, his gaze softened.

"You don't have to do anything," he said.

"No," she replied, her voice cracking. "This is something I need to do."

Before he could say another word, she approached the altar where her mother lay, careful not to cross any of the thread-like strands stretching vertically through the room. Maliah didn't know if she was supposed to avoid them, but disturbing them didn't seem like a great idea. Her imagination ran away with her as she wondered if they were physically there and worried that they'd split her in half.

Her heart was racing, as were her thoughts, but she took a deep breath in, held it, then let it slip out. Meta's gaze met hers, offering a calm, determined expression as an example. Yet even her mother, as strong and dedicated as she was, clung to her father's hand.

Jarith joined them and placed his utensils and bowl next to Meta. "Once I begin, it will be difficult to stop. If we stop, it will be hard to try again. So, are we all sure we have to do this?"

Meta nodded, then Jua. When Jarith turned his gaze to Maliah, she gave the weakest nod possible. Jarith waited. Frustrated, she nodded more enthusiastically. Damn this man and his dedication to her consent.

"Alright. Here goes nothing," he said.

He raised both his hands and held them over Meta.

"Bilewo, wo woat."

His words seemed to echo through the chamber deeper than they had just moments before. The bass boomed, and Maliah could feel the vibrations run through her body. He pushed his hands down until he was almost touching Meta. Then he flipped his palms upward and began raising his hands again.

"Cihu atme ne atas bias asatat."

The strands of light became more concrete. They glowed brighter, still sparkling with dancing colors.

"Cineneciat at ayar pearlelele."

As Jarith continued, more strands appeared. They grew even brighter, dazzling light shining from them.

"Huledi fiasat ase ay ar bi'le."

Suddenly, the strands of light all went white at once, and everything alive in the room—Jarith, the three priests, and even the potted plant in the corner that looked like it really needed watering—seemed to glow in ethereal light.

"With this, our worlds are anchored," Jarith said.

And there was the first component. Anchoring the two worlds.

"My brother, Jua. My sister, Maliah. Witness the boundary of worlds dissolve. Feel the connection of your essence. Every particle of your being is tied to a particle in Highrealm. Take hold of that link."

She wasn't certain what a particle was. Jarith's words shook the air, so she decided the details couldn't matter too much. Though the air trembled, the stage was steady beneath her. She widened her stance, just in case, then turned her attention to the connection Jarith was talking about. She felt nothing—until she did.

"Arlexo. Aratarciat. Meledi. Meargu."

The sensation was just a passing thought at first, not even a fully formed one.

"Leasne athu binediar biatwone ar woarledias filexobileat ne athu pearmebileat."

Jarith continued to chant, and the sense grew stronger. She could only describe it as another part of herself, like her body and soul.

"Arlexo. Aratarciat. Meledi. Meargu."

As if a dull reflection in a glass pane, another place appeared several feet above the ground. There was a floor or ground of some kind, pillars, and walls that stretched upward, through the ceiling of the sanctuary.

Though the view wasn't as solid as the world she existed in, she knew exactly what she was looking at.

This was Highrealm.

Maliah was peering into another world. Though it sat above Midrealm's plane of existence, its glistening facades and exotic architecture were unmistakable.

Even now, Highrealm didn't have a physical nature. However, Maliah's brain was interpreting the messages being sent across the membrane between worlds. It was eerie, but it meant the second component of the transfer formulae was complete. The boundary between their worlds was destabilized.

Maliah now understood what that meant. It was as if she could reach out and touch Highrealm. The veil between their two worlds was thin, thin enough to allow her mother to pass through.

She looked back at Jarith, who was holding the bowl of glowing ink and a writing stylus. After dipping the stylus, he began the next part of the spell. With each word, he drew symbols on Meta's flesh that plotted a path through the boundary for her soul.

"Jarith!" Jua exclaimed the warning, but it was too late.

Before Maliah could follow her father's gaze, Jarith's arms were pinned to his side. The bowl dropped to the floor, landing upright with only minor spillage.

Out of the shadows, Amun took a few steps forward, hands extended toward Jarith. Amun lifted Jarith from the stage with zir power. Though Jarith thrashed and kicked, his effort was in vain.

"Stay here, and do what Jarith asked of us," her father said.

Maliah whipped her head to argue with him, but he was already around the altar. He threw out a hand toward Amun. A spark struck zir in the arm, and ze winced. Jarith dropped to the ground, landing on his feet as his bent knees absorbed the shock.

"Amun, please stop," Jua commanded.

"You're murdering your wife, and you're telling me to stop?" Amun spat the words. Zir eyes were wide, and dark bags hung below them. "You're tearing a hole in your reality, and you're telling me to stop?"

Her mother grabbed Maliah's hand. Maliah looked down at Meta, whose eyes fluttered open. She squeezed her mother's hand.

"I'm here," she said.

Her mother tugged on her.

"No matter what." Her mother's voice was soft and her breath labored, so Maliah bent down to hear better. "Proceed with the ritual, no matter what."

A loud bang echoed through the sanctuary, and Maliah snapped her head up. Her father had been thrown backward, and a large vase lay broken on the floor.

"This is what she wants," Jua said through gritted teeth. He got to his feet and blocked the altar with his body, and though she couldn't see it, Maliah could sense that her father was shielding them from Amun.

Jarith returned to Meta's side and picked up the bowl. He rushed his words as he continued drawing symbols down her arms. When he dipped the stylus to replenish its ink, his hands quivered, but as he returned to her skin, the strokes were steady and precise.

"No," Amun argued, pushing a wave of pressure toward Jua that pushed him back another step. "She doesn't want to die."

Jua crossed his arms in front of his face. "She said you looked and found no answers."

"Yet. No answers yet."

Ze shifted zir gaze back to Jarith, but Jua waved his arms out to return Amun's attention to him.

"He's lied to you," Amun scolded. "At this very moment, he's sealing the fate of everyone in this universe."

The words caused Jarith to pause. Maliah reached across and touched his wrist.

Suddenly, the world was silent. Her mother's breathing paused, as did Jua's counterattack at Amun. It was as if she and Jarith were the only beings in existence. Jarith looked up from his writing.

"How are you doing this?" he asked.

"Me?"

"You've created an isolation bubble."

"I have? What's that?"

He shook his head. "It doesn't matter. But you've given me the time I need."

"Jarith," she said as he returned to his task. He looked back up at her. "No matter what, you must finish the ritual. So, keep working. We'll protect you."

His eyes widened, and he whispered her name.

"Go on," she added.

With a nod, he began once more, chanting and drawing his spell. When Maliah withdrew her hand, everything returned to normal. Well, everything returned to chaos. Maliah kissed her mother. Then she slipped away to stand at her father's side.

"Amun, don't make us do this," she said.

"Maliah, you must believe me," Amun begged. "There's still time to avoid a tragedy."

"I know you're speaking your truth," Maliah replied. "But that doesn't mean I'll let you harm Jarith."

She put her arms out to her sides, then brought them together. Amun seemed to be pulled by an invisible rope, arms and legs drawn against zir body. Ze twisted. Maliah took a step forward, and her mentor flew backward. With a loud thud, ze hit the wall of the temple.

Ze stared at her, as if examining her. And a few seconds later, ze flung zir arms out, breaking Maliah's invisible bonds.

"Let the path be clear," Jarith said from behind her.

That meant the third component was complete.

Pure anger seemed to bubble up on Amun's face. It reddened as ze grit zir teeth. Without warning, ze clenched zir fists in front of zir, and an invisible force grabbed Maliah's hair. She screamed as she was thrown to the ground. Her father cried out as his body slammed down beside her.

The invisible force plastered Maliah's face to the floor, threatening to crush her. It took a concerted effort to draw in each breath. She could barely move, but with effort, she was able to wiggle her fingers.

Not exactly useful, but it was a start.

Footsteps approached. Amun was walking toward her. She frantically tried to open her eyes, at least the one that wasn't squashed against the cold, hard floor.

"Child of Jukartis, stop," Amun commanded.

Jarith continued his chanting. It was quiet and rushed, but exact in its execution.

Maliah racked her brain, searching for a solution to free herself. She raced through years of training, every magic spell she'd learned about but never had the power to practice. There had to be something she could do.

"Child of Jukartis, you will discontinue your ritual this very instant."

Jarith didn't discontinue anything.

The footsteps grew closer. Maliah didn't know how much longer Jarith needed. But if she could buy him even a few seconds, maybe it would be enough.

"Drawing worlds together in this way causes a chain reaction," Amun continued. "A cascade that, at best, ends with the destruction of Midrealm but, at worst, threatens to destroy many worlds."

Why wasn't Amun simply stopping Jarith by force? Ze appeared to be stronger than he was, so what was holding zir back?

Finally, her eyes opened. Nearby, her father's gaze was on hers. His expression was grim and determined, and she knew that he'd be ready as soon as she figured out how to free them.

Motion caught her attention, and she strained to look toward the source. It was Amun, who was mere steps away. Each step ze took was labored, and clarity came to her mind. Ze was using most of zir energy to hold her and her father in place, not leaving enough to attack Jarith from afar.

She needed a distraction, something to break zir concentration, even for a moment.

"I told Jukartis of the danger, and ey silenced me," ze continued. "Don't be like em, child."

Maliah turned all of her attention to her arm. She willed the fingers to move, but she couldn't summon any power to her command. Amun had to be suppressing her, just as the Highrealmers had done all her life. Without her magic, what hope did she have of stopping zir?

Ze held incredible power, more than either of her parents. She'd never seen zir use it, so there was no way she could have known ze wasn't who ze appeared to be. Yet she still felt foolish. What else had ze been hiding? Obviously, some convoluted plot to kill Jarith when he arrived, but was that all?

And what about destroying their reality along with others? Was ze telling the truth about that, or was it a fabrication?

She re-centered herself.

None of that mattered right now. This was her mother's choice and the only way for Jarith to live. They could deal with all of her questions later.

She hated it. She wished it could be different. But she couldn't second-guess the decisions she'd already made, not if she wanted to save Jarith's life.

"Ayar asle ne leneguar atdi huar," Jarith said. "Voneatar fiarathu woathuat fi'ar."

As Amun's foot stepped into view, she threw her arm out. Grabbing zir ankle, she pulled. Ze fell backward, losing zir magic hold on them.

Maliah rushed to her feet to face Amun, who was already getting up. Jua wasn't far behind.

"Athu pearbinileatas legune ne athuas memeneat mekunegu ne atarathu legune atwo woardias." Jarith placed his hands on her mother's chest. "The road is open. All you need to do is take it."

"No!" Amun yelled.

Faster than Maliah would have thought possible, ze charged between her and her father toward Jarith.

Jua and Maliah both reached out with their powers to stop zir. Amun froze only a step away from zir target, letting out a gasp that seemed to echo through the entire chamber. Unsure of what had happened, Maliah relaxed her magic's grip on her mentor.

Ze stumbled back a few steps.

A knife clamored to the floor, dropping from Amun's hand and splattering blood across the stone tiles.

"Meta," Amun cried.

Ze collapsed. Only then did Maliah see the Dwesdar Dagger plunged deep into zir. Maliah rushed to Amun. Just as she reached zir, the light of life snuffed out, trapping zir soul within the dead husk of zir body.

Jarith fell to his knees, and Maliah whipped her head around. Blood ran from his own knife wound.

28

Aftermath

Maliah began trembling the moment she saw Jarith's blood. Tears she had been fighting escaped her as she closed Amun's empty eyes. Ze was still in there, trapped in a lifeless husk, and more than ever, she could sense the depth of that isolation. She desperately wanted to free zir, but she knew only one way: the prophecy.

She ripped her eyes away and turned her attention to Jarith, who Jua had already reached. Blood seeped from the wound at his side, and she struggled to pull her gaze away. Jarith was covering the gash with his hands, but his expression betrayed immense pain.

"I finished the ritual," Jarith said.

"Good man," Jua replied as he knelt. "Now, let me see."

"Did it work?" Jarith asked.

"We can worry about that later. You've been stabbed," Jua said.

"You know? I noticed that."

"How bad is it?" Maliah asked as she reached them.

"It'll heal," an all too familiar voice said.

Maliah snapped her head up to the altar. Her mother sat on the edge, her legs dangling off. Except her mother was also still lying on the altar.

"Mom?"

Jua and Jarith looked up, too, but she could tell from their wide-eyed expressions that they couldn't see her.

"We did as you asked," Maliah said. "We finished the ritual."

"Yes," Meta replied. She stood, and a motion trail drifted behind her, echoing her movement until it caught up with her several seconds later. "You were splendid."

She looked down at Amun with a furrowed brow.

"Maliah," her mother said, "soon I'll be gone. Before that, I need to borrow your power." Meta held out her hand even though she was too far away to reach. "May I?"

Maliah didn't understand, but she nodded. Her mother—and her motion trail—floated to Amun. She began to glow, and soon, the surrounding air sparkled.

"Meta?" Jua asked as she became visible to everyone. "You're still here?"

"The transfer isn't immediate," Jarith explained as Jua helped him sit up. "But what's happening?" He groaned with the pain of it.

Meta knelt beside Amun, placing her hands on zir chest and head. She spoke gentle words of a spell Maliah had never heard before.

Amun's spirit jerked up from zir body, zir motion trail following. Ze looked down at zirself with surprise before gazing up at Meta.

"You live!" ze exclaimed, then realized ze was wrong. "No. No." Ze turned to Jarith. "What have you done?" ze asked.

"I've freed your soul from your body temporarily," Meta replied.

"Not that," Amun scoffed. "Of course, that's what you've done. I mean the reckless action your daughter and future son have taken. Despite my warnings, they—"

"Amun," Meta interrupted. She waited until zir attention returned to her. "I've called you forth from your prison. You must respect my wishes."

Maliah had never heard of such a rule before, and she wasn't sure if her mother had made it up or if this was something dead people knew the moment they kicked the bucket. Her bet was on the former.

"And what do you wish of me?" Amun asked.

"I merely wish to know you. Tell us how you came to be in our world, which you kept from us all these years."

Amun stared at her as if she'd said something ze could not fathom. "You . . . wish to know my story?" ze asked. "After what I've done?"

"Yes," Maliah chimed in. "We wish to know the real Amun."

"Share lessons that we can take with us now that you're gone," Jua said.

Amun looked between them as if gauging their honesty.

"Please," Jarith added. Maliah hadn't heard him saying a spell or anything, but she could sense his energy shifting. "I swear, I didn't know about the potential to destroy our universes. Maybe we can avoid it if we know more. Jukartis never told me about you. Ey never told me that everything we accomplished was thanks to you."

Their eyes were all trained on zir. All curious. All patient. All waiting. And slowly, zir stern expression shifted to one of—still stern, but also deep love, appreciation, and acceptance.

"Very well." Ze crossed zir legs and held zir arms out in front of zir. "I'm an old soul. Almost as old as Jukartis, though it's difficult to remember."

The image of a young four-legged creature appeared before them. Its face was as fierce as a cat's, but Maliah would recognize those stern eyes anywhere. This was Amun.

"I was the first of our kind to realize our numbers were dwindling," ze began. A million points of light appeared around the chamber, and then faded one by one. "There was a time when new beings appeared often due to the coagulation of latent energy gaining sentience."

Maliah had no idea what that meant, but it sounded equal parts neat and gross.

"But over time, new beings ceased to form, and existing beings sought to join the Source in greater numbers.

"For a long time, I sought a way to mend whatever had been broken. But my studies revealed that nothing was broken in the first place."

The points of light drifted toward a central ball of light, which strobed every few seconds. Each point left behind a trail of light, like the wake of a comet, before dimming to nothingness.

"In our universe, Highrealm, energy flows one way: toward the Source. We entities were just disparate souls that were scattered at the creation of the universe. And we were all ever so slowly wandering back toward the Source.

"When I realized this, it was obvious we wouldn't find the answer to our population crisis in our universe. We needed to look to another. By the time the others accepted this truth, I had already been searching for a solution for a long time.

"My study led me to my greatest discovery: the ability to peer into other realities. The more similar the reality, the easier it was to view, but these realities were experiencing the same problem.

"So I reached farther, and that's when I stumbled across a dream."

Maliah stared in wonder. It seemed unreal that with all the technology and power at the Highrealmers' disposal, a simple dream had brought Amun answers.

"It wasn't so unlike a normal dream," Amun continued. "The only difference was whose mind I was looking through.

"You see, in most dreams, we are ourselves. However, in a minute percentage of the dreams where we are not, we are actually experiencing another reality. I learned that, of the realities I peered into through my dreams, most were too similar to Highrealm."

"And then I dreamt of Midrealm."

A young priest appeared above them with olive skin and dark black hair pulled back into a long braid.

"This was who I experienced Midrealm through, and xe commanded powerful magic, most notably the magic of clairvoyance. Xir name was Emin."

"Emin?" Jua asked. "The Exalted Grand Priest who spoke the Ascension Four prophecy?"

"Yes," Amun replied. "But this was long before that. As soon as I realized Emin was from another reality, I began work on a prototype device to reliably peer into xir world.

"Emin and I shared a connection. It was a connection I hadn't known was there, but which solidified once the device was ready. Emin and I were able to see into each other's lives through our dreams. At first, this happened sporadically, but as I refined the technology, I could do so at will.

"When Emin divined the Ascension Four prophecy, we both understood the implications—Highrealm and Midrealm were destined to come together. But as I did the calculations, I found an incredible flaw. Anchoring our realities would result in disaster."

"Did you tell Jukartis any of this?" Jarith asked.

"Yes, of course. As soon as I had the first dream, I told Jukartis and the others. I told them I believed the answer to our problems was to escape to Emin's reality.

"Unfortunately, Jukartis had other ideas."

"That's Jukartis for you," Jarith said with an eye roll.

"Ey seized my research and used eir influence to silence me. When I spoke out against em, I was ridiculed and rebuked." Amun's eyes sparkled with ghostly tears as ze looked into the cheerful gaze of young Emin. "But Emin always understood me. We found ways to communicate despite being unable to have a proper conversation."

"So when did you come to Midrealm?" Jarith asked, breaking Amun's daydream.

The projection of Emin disappeared.

"And why?" Maliah added.

"I was still researching when Emin spoke the Ascension Four prophecy. Foolishly, I believed it validated my theories, so I took my proposal to our leaders. They twisted my vision into a plan of conquest, and Jukartis forced me to work on the calculations.

"While conducting that research, I discovered that a transfer demands a sacrifice." Amun's lip curled in disgust. "Jukartis saw the Midrealmers as pawns. Ey bound me so I couldn't travel freely in Highrealm. I needed a way out. I was a prisoner."

"So you came here?" Jua asked.

"Not yet."

Amun's eyes were closed, and Maliah longed to hold zir. How alone ze must have felt. She wanted to cry, to punch a wall, to find Jukartis and do . . . well, she didn't know what she'd do, but she'd do something. And Jukartis wouldn't like it.

"I used every spare thought to craft the spell, the formulae," Amun said. "And it wasn't until I had already delivered it to Jukartis that I realized what I'd done. I'd empowered Jukartis to end a universe."

Maliah opened her mouth to ask more about this, but Amun continued before she could.

"Emin became more erratic. And then xe . . ." Ze couldn't finish the sentence. "It was my only chance, so I used xir energy as a sacrifice and transferred here."

"I'm so sorry you had to go through that," Jarith said, bowing his head.

"You can make amends by ceasing your involvement in the prophecy."

"Why?" Maliah asked. "What is Jukartis's plan?"

"Jukartis intends to anchor Midrealm and Highrealm. As souls die in Midrealm, they will be transferred to Highrealm, where they'll live as second-class citizens under the scrutiny of Jukartis."

"How does that help Highrealm?" Jua asked.

"Because souls gravitate toward the Source," Amun explained. "If not by choice, then by force. Jukartis plans to live as long as possible outside the Source, instead feeding souls from Midrealm into it."

The family shared worried gazes, and Maliah wondered if sending her mother to such a world had really been the best decision. Not that she'd had any say in the matter.

"Anyway, the danger lies in the anchoring. Realities aren't meant to be anchored together," Amun spat. "Realities aren't perfectly parallel. Higher dimensions such as time and space are contorted when you view another reality, and when you anchor them together, they don't harmonize. Over time, the anchors will twist and pull until they eventually rip apart the realities they're attempting to hold together."

"Then we won't place anchors," Jarith stated. "And we'll ensure our descendants don't either."

"Right," Maliah agreed. "If we don't place anchors, they can't rip our world."

Amun smiled in that scary way ze always did. "It would be better if you didn't have descendants. But I suppose that will do. However, Jukartis can't learn of this, or ey will find some way around it."

"I'll handle Jukartis," Meta said with confidence. Her crooked smile was accentuated by her hand on her hip, a hand that was looking more transparent than it had a few minutes earlier.

"You don't even know what you're saying," Amun grumbled. "But you're our only hope in High-realm."

The knot in Maliah's stomach returned with a vengeance. Amun must have realized it, too, because ze looked down at zir disappearing legs.

"What will become of me?" Amun asked, looking at Meta.

"I don't know," she replied. She knelt next to zir and placed her forehead against zirs. Maliah found herself envious that the two could still touch. "Thank you for sharing this with us."

"It has been an honor knowing you, my dear." Amun's ghostly tears escaped down zir transparent cheeks. "Jua, I'm sorry for the pain I've caused you. And you, Maliah. How I yearn to see you come into your own in the priesthood. I love you, my family."

"Amun!" Maliah cried out.

She scrambled toward zir, but ze was gone before she reached zir. Her gaze shot to her mother, whose spiritual self was fading as well. Meta blew a kiss toward her before turning her attention to her husband.

Jua took cautious steps in her direction, and Meta reached out to touch his face. Her hand went through him.

"I love you," she said. The words were so raw, so fragile, so vulnerable that Maliah barely recognized them.

"We'll be together again someday," her father replied.

Meta leaned toward him to kiss him. Before her lips could pass through his, she was gone.

Jua stood still, though he was unable to hide his trembling.

Highrealm faded away.

The silence was numbing. Interrupted only by the occasional popping of a flame, it penetrated every iota of the room. It seeped through the physical world and squirmed into the recesses of their spirits, leaving a scar in their hearts that would never heal.

They would laugh again. Meta had foretold it, so it must be true. But in this moment, it seemed like eternity was passing in every instant, ripping every bit of joy from their existences as it flowed.

They would love again. Though they hadn't always been gentle, the lessons they had learned from Meta and Amun prepared them for loss. But in this moment, the pain felt like the weight of the world was resting on a single pin, stabbing them each in their hearts.

Someday, they'd look back on this day and wonder how they'd been so brave. But today, they felt as powerless as a grain of sand caught up in a windstorm, as empty as the space between atoms, and as weak as a newborn left naked in the snow.

29

A Child In A Forest

There was a child. In a forest, it sat in the dark. Among crackling leaves and dying grass, xey clung to xemself. Under a black sky, xey shivered.

Would the ball of light return? The ball of light had come before. It brought warmth with it. But every time it left, xey became a little colder. Xey jumped at a loud pop. It was too dark to see. The child was vulnerable.

It was dangerous to move in the darkness. The child had tried. Today's tumble down a steep hill of brambles was lesson enough. The chill against the wounds burned, a painful reminder.

The child could barely think. Xey knew a plan was needed. A crafty plan to stay warm. A plan to survive the night.

In a burst of energy, the child pulled dirt and leaves towards xem. Xey gasped at the sudden wave of frigid cold on xyr chest. Xey buried xemself under the detritus. The child's muscles twitched as a shiver stretched from xyr head to xyr extremities.

This wasn't a plan. Xey couldn't bury xemself night after night. Not with the dark getting colder. Not with the ball of light leaving earlier each day.

The child pulled more leaves toward xemself. Xey covered xyr head, then tucked xyr arms under the dirt. The wind whistled, shaking more leaves from the trees. Gusts blew over the child, taking leaves with them.

Wishing to cry, the child fought back tears. They would only make it colder. Hard lessons learned from previous nights alone. If only xey could sleep. Then the ball of light would arrive more quickly.

But it was too bleak to sleep.

This would not do. The child needed a better answer. When the ball of light came back, xey would find a better option.

As the child's thoughts drifted back to the bitter wind, a whisper echoed through the trees.

"The third will carry the darkness. Creation of nothing among the everything."

30

BROKEN PROMISES

It was a clear morning, and Jarith dragged himself out of bed like a champ. He washed his face with the soap and water someone had brought into the room as he slept. The fact that he hadn't detected them still freaked him out, but he was learning to deal with it. With considerable effort, he shuffled into the common area, only to find the doors to both other bedrooms open.

How in the world had Jua and Maliah gotten up before him?

The tray of food for their morning meal was on the table, and he picked out a few dates and a handful of nuts and shoved them all into his mouth as if he hadn't almost choked to death a few days earlier. He was past that now.

As he peered out the front window at the gardens, birds chirped and insects buzzed, but there was no sign of the others.

They had been interrupted in the small temple's sanctuary by an attentive attendant, who had noticed the unusual lamplight. Within an hour, there were priests of all ranks and officials of all officiality asking them questions and speaking to them in low, gentle voices.

Unknown to Jarith, Jua and Meta had devised a cover story to share with the Huleay Temple about her death. He felt silly for not thinking of that, but Meta had been very aware of how her death would impact her people.

Their story was that Meta had foreseen the theft of the Dwesdar Dagger in a vision. This vision had also told her that a deceitful presence would possess a powerful priest, influencing them to do evil. Because evil is as evil does.

Anyway, by their falsified accounts, Meta had been attempting a ritual to cleanse the Grounds of this evil. The ritual forced Amun—who was under the control of the aforementioned evil—to reveal zirself as the dagger's thief. Unfortunately, the ritual also trapped the evil within Meta. Once inside her, she was able to banish it from the world, but not before it condemned her to death.

Jua had embellished the tale to explain Amun's death, but Jarith was far too tired by that point to care. The priests and officials took Jua at his word and proceeded to transport both Exalted Grand Priests' bodies to be prepared for ceremonial burial.

Some very awkward guards had escorted them home around midday, and neither Maliah nor Jarith had said a word before going to bed, where Jarith had fallen asleep as soon as his head hit the pillow. He felt rested and energetic, plus a pang of guilt for feeling relieved.

His big secret was out, his sin was over, and he was eager to begin the next chapter of his life. Meta's devotion to her people inspired him. There were many ways he could improve their lives, and giving back to the people who loved Meta seemed like the best way to preserve her memory.

He went out the back door and ascended to the rooftop patio two steps at a time. As he neared the top, he saw a head of curly hair leaning against the parapet, looking out over the capital city of Ledine. Maliah glanced back at him when she heard his steps, but only for a moment.

A warm breeze pushed coils of hair into her face, and she twisted it around itself and pulled it over her shoulder. The blue sky stood in stark contrast to her golden skin and dark locks, and as he leaned on the parapet beside her, he wondered how she could be real. He considered pinching himself, but he figured the pain from his stab wound was proof enough of his wakefulness.

"How are you?" he asked, knowing it was a dumb question but feeling it was far too important to go unasked.

"Strange," she replied. She looked down at her hands for a few moments before looking up into his eyes. "It's as if I can still sense her, as if she's standing just out of reach. But she hasn't shown herself to me again."

He put his hand in hers. "You have a connection. Even if she's in another world, you'll always be connected to her."

Her eyes glistened, but she didn't cry. "There's so much I want to say to her. So much I should have said. Can she hear me?"

"I don't know. Maybe not. But maybe she can feel you."

"I can't believe they're both gone. Just a few days ago, everything seemed fine. Better than fine." She squeezed his hand. "Wonderful." They both managed small smiles.

"I can't know how you're feeling, Maliah, but I understand loss."

"By the spirits." Maliah let out a small self-deprecating grunt as she hurried to wipe away tears. "You've seen your people gradually die off, and you left everything you've ever known to come here. I'm so sorry. This is so insensitive."

"No." Jarith's voice was low as he leaned closer to rub his head against hers. "If you need to talk, I'll always be here for you. This loss weighs heavily on us both, and we'll get through it together."

Maliah said, "Tell me about someone you lost."

Her request surprised Jarith, as she'd never asked him anything about his time in Highrealm before. He'd lost many people in his lifetime, but it didn't take long for him to think of someone.

He said, "I had a mentor in my early days, Tsi Gen. Xe was strict. I think xe was stricter with me than with anyone else. I always assumed it was because of the prophecy, but maybe it was because I was xir favorite. Xe would go on these tangents sometimes about destiny, and, now that I think about it, I'll bet xe wished they had chosen xir for the Ascension Project."

Maliah laughed at Jarith's grin, and he found himself grinning even harder.

"Xe taught me the importance of history. During assessments, I was required to consider in my decisions how the past informed the current state of affairs. I was never very good at it, but I think about xir whenever I have a tough decision to make."

"What happened to Tsi Gen?" Maliah asked.

"I don't know. One day, I had lessons with xir. It was a normal session. I was stuck on something—I don't remember what it was. But xe was patient with me and suggested we pick up the topic the following day. But when the next day came, xe was lost—joined with the Source. I've always assumed Jukartis had something to do with it, but xe wasn't the first or the last person to disappear like that."

"What did Jukartis say about it?"

"You know, now that I think about it, Jukartis acted odd after Tsi Gen's disappearance. That may be the only time I ever saw Jukartis quiet in a pensive way. Tsi Gen had always been critical of em, though I didn't understand why at the time. Jukartis made it clear to me that ey was never wrong, but Tsi Gen wasn't shy about speaking up against em.

"I was angry when Tsi Gen disappeared. Angry at the entire universe, really. I didn't believe Tsi Gen would choose to join the Source without telling me." He shook his head. "I still can't believe that's true. And I regret not having worked harder. There's so much I didn't get to learn from xir."

"Xe would be proud of you," Maliah said.

"Yeah?"

"Definitely. You've become a kind, thoughtful man who thinks before you act."

"Hmm," Jarith said. "About that. I don't think 'man' is the right path for me. I've tried to live up to the Midrealm standards so I can be a proper husband for you, but it isn't who I am."

Maliah didn't skip a beat. "I'm sorry. I should have known the transition would be difficult for you. You're a kind, thoughtful **person** who thinks before you act."

Ze—Jarith, that is—grinned at how hard she stressed the word person and decided not to interrupt her with a snide remark.

So, she continued. "You accomplished what you set out to do for your people, Jarith. That should make you feel proud, too."

"Maybe," ze said with a laugh. "You, too." Ze bumped zir hip against hers.

"I don't know if I'll ever live up to my mother's legacy."

"You don't have to. You only have to live up to your own."

Maliah bumped her hip back against zir so hard that ze almost lost zir balance. "Has anyone ever told you that you're corny?"

"No, I don't think anyone's ever mentioned that."

They both laughed, but it only lasted a moment.

"Jarith, I owe you another apology. I spent my whole life imagining how you'd be instead of seeing you as you were."

She turned and put her arms around zir waist. Pulling zir close, she laid her head on zir shoulder.

"That doesn't seem like something you need to apologize for," Jarith said.

"Oh, it is," she insisted. "Because you're so much better than I ever imagined."

"Huh, that's odd. Because you're just as perfect as I always thought," ze added.

She rolled her eyes, and ze pulled her into an embrace. After a moment, ze looked down to see her gazing up at zir. Her eyes were hauntingly beautiful, as if she could peer straight into zir soul, and ze wanted that more than anything. Her hand moved up zir chest to cup around zir neck.

"May I kiss you?" ze breathed.

She pulled zir down toward her. "Thank you for being here," she whispered.

Ze had no words to describe the elation in zir heart, so ze just remained silent. They shared breath for a long moment until they were in total sync. Her aura pulsed with life, and zir heart fell in line to follow. Every cell of zir body became tuned to Maliah.

Her heartbeat and breathing were all ze could hear. The perfume of her scent was all ze could smell. Her soft skin and silky, wind-blown curls were all ze could feel. Her beautiful essence was all ze could see.

Ze lowered zir head until, finally, their lips met.

Their kiss lasted only a moment. Just after their lips touched, the sound of footsteps on the stairs echoed up to them. They parted, holding hands but stepping away from each other. Jarith's heart was pounding, and ze admonished zir mind as it tried to dive into a rabbit hole.

Jua had bags under his eyes, but he wore a strained smile on his face. He greeted them, then shuffled over to the couch and sat down, leaning against the back.

"Did you go to the temple?" Maliah asked as she joined him.

Jua nodded and said, "Her body has dissipated, just like Emin's. They're calling it a miracle."

"And Amun?" Jarith asked as ze sat at the other end of the couch, Maliah sitting between them.

"Still there. The Huleay Temple will hold the memorial ceremony for them both tomorrow at sunset with only Amun's body presented to the people. The Temple is worried about a public outcry. Grand Gurean even suggested we mock up a fake body to avoid a scandal." He shook his head and clasped his hands together.

The silence between them drew out. The city was quieter than usual, and Jarith wondered if the news of Meta's passing had spread already. The wind blew over them, but the usual sounds of carts and people didn't come with it.

"I've been thinking," Jua said without preamble, "about the prophecy."

When he said no more, Maliah said, "Me, too. We told Amun we wouldn't create anchors, but I don't really know what that means."

They both looked at Jarith, who raised zir eyebrows. "Why are you looking at me? I have no idea."

"Didn't you have to create an anchor for the transfer spell?"

"That was a temporary thing," ze assured them. "It only lasted as long as the ritual. I don't know much about more permanent anchors."

"Do you think Amun's fears were warranted?" Jua asked.

Jarith couldn't believe Jua was asking this question. Maliah didn't seem bothered by it. Truth be told, she looked just as interested in the answer as her father.

"That's a very complicated question," Jarith said.

That answer didn't satisfy them, if their eerily similar head tilts meant anything.

"A long time has passed since Amun came to this world," Jarith explained. "And ze hasn't had the technology to continue zir research. Meanwhile, in Highrealm, all our scientists have been working tirelessly to understand the complexities and implications of transference between realities."

Jua and Maliah's expressions were screaming, "Go on."

"It's just that, in all the time I lived in Highrealm, I never heard anyone reference a long-term destructive effect of connecting our realities via anchors. And they were looking. We had a team of researchers on the Ascension Project who were primarily concerned with its potential downstream implications."

"Does that mean Amun was lying?" Maliah asked.

"No, I don't think so. But the technology our researchers intend to use to connect our realities could be operating under different principles and parameters than those Amun originally envisioned. The technology could very well be entirely distinct. Zir worries could be a moot point."

"So you think it's safe," Jua said.

Jarith couldn't bring zirself to answer. While it was possible Amun's information was out of date and inaccurate, it was also possible that ze had discovered something that the other Highrealmers missed. After all, Amun had been the first to discover their population issues.

"Dad, are you suggesting we fulfill the prophecy despite what we promised Amun?" Maliah asked.

Jua sighed and shook his head. "I don't like our position. We'll have to second-guess every decision we make instead of just living our lives." He was visibly perturbed, fingers scrunching up the hem of his tunic, then releasing it only to begin again. "And it may be that the very act of denying it is what allows the prophecy to fulfill itself." His gaze dropped to his hands. As if seeing what he was doing, he placed them together and forced them to behave in his lap.

"So, what do you want us to do?" Jarith asked.

Jua looked back up at Jarith. "Live your life." His brow was drawn tight, and his nervous hands rolled over each other. "Meta believed this prophecy was unavoidable. If that's true, then it's better not to worry about what will come." He moved his gaze to his daughter. "And if your mother was right, then we'll all see her again someday."

Maliah seemed just as speechless as ze was. Jua's proposal seemed straightforward and favorable. Perhaps more pertinent was that Jua needed a morale boost, even something tiny. So, ze returned zir gaze to meet Jua's and nodded with a thin-lipped smile.

The relief that settled on the man's face was worth it.

As if noticing how awkward it had become, Jua changed the subject to something just as awkward. "You've reached the kissing stage of your relationship, I see."

Jarith hoped zir dark skin didn't reflect the heat ze felt in zir face, though Maliah's embarrassment was obvious.

"Dad!"

"Are you finally accepting Jarith as your partner?"

Maliah covered her face as she said some very unladylike things that Jarith was confident she had learned from her mother.

"Was that your first kiss?" When Maliah didn't answer, Jua turned to Jarith. "Hm?"

Jarith nodded, afraid zir voice would do something embarrassing if ze tried to speak.

"That reminds me of my youth," Jua said with a sigh. "You know, when your mother and I discovered we were named in prophecy, we didn't want to accept it. We were friends, and though we were furtively captivated by each other, we fought against it."

"No way," Jarith said just as Maliah asked, "What?"

Jua nodded, his usual glow sneaking back into his face for a few moments. "It's true. But one thing led to another. Once we accepted our roles, Amun came to us. Ze taught us a bonding ritual, which we performed."

Jua lifted his tunic to reveal a tattoo above his knee. Jarith's eyes widened. It was a Highrealm pictogram based on formulae used in the distant past. Its purpose was to bind two or more entities together in order to create a synergistic boost to their power.

"We grew more powerful after the ritual," Jua said once they'd gotten a good look at it, "and we effected a much larger change when we worked together. That's why we almost always do—did rituals together."

He pulled his tunic back down. "I think you should do the bonding ritual, too," Jua continued.

Jarith wanted to agree, and ze almost let zir excitement overtake zir. But before ze spoke, ze noticed Maliah's hesitance. Ze put a hand in hers.

"We'll take our time with things," ze said. "And if we're ever both ready for such a big step, we'll do it."

Maliah snapped her gaze up to meet Jarith's, and her worried expression warmed to a thankful smile. She laid her head on zir shoulder. Her aura—which had grown turbulent—calmed, gentle ripples emanating through it.

Jua was satisfied with the answer and returned his attention to the hem of his tunic.

"I . . ." Maliah started to say, but she paused. Jarith stroked her hand with zir thumb, and after a moment to build up her courage, she began again. "I had a dream last night."

"Do you remember it?" Jua asked. "You can tell us if you'd like."

"You don't have to, though," Jarith added.

"There was a child," she said, closing her eyes as if to recall the details. "Xey was in a forest surrounded by magic. I think xey was trapped there. I mean, I think someone trapped xem there. Xey wanted to be free of it, but xey couldn't leave."

Jua stopped playing with the hem, and his gaze became distant.

"Then there was a girl, a very young girl. She and the child played, and they were happy. They laughed together and shared stories. But something forced the girl to leave."

Jua's gaze shifted to his daughter.

"And then . . ."

"And then?" Jua echoed.

Maliah swallowed. She sat up straight and looked between them. She took a deep breath and squeezed Jarith's hand for comfort.

"And then flames engulfed the child. Xey burned. The smell was awful. But xey smiled and looked peaceful."

"Meta had that dream," Jua said. "Two, maybe three times before. She told me a name always accompanied the dream, but she could never recall it after she awoke."

His eyes were hopeful, and Jarith wondered if he was seeing Meta as Maliah spoke.

"Jaalam."

At the sound of the name of the Last Child of the Highrealmers, Jarith tightened zir grip on Maliah's hand. A child in a magical forest, a pocket reality that sat between Midrealm and Highrealm.

The pang of guilt returned, but Jarith said nothing. Ze didn't mention that ze had allowed them to send the child to that in-between space. Ze didn't tell them the child would be all alone until zir counterpart, their offspring, was born.

Instead, ze remained silent, collecting all zir guilt and self-loathing, and compartmentalizing it to the recesses of zir mind. Jarith needed time to heal. They all did. There would be time for sharing later, just as there would be time for laughter and joy.

It wouldn't be long. They would learn of Jaalam's fate soon enough.

Thank You

Thank you for taking the time to read Manifestation of Prophecy! You've made a big difference in the life of this indie author.

Your support means the world to me. **Please consider leaving a review** of this book on retailer websites or on book sites such as Goodreads or Storygraph. I'm a small indie author, so every review will help other readers find my work. Even one or two sentences is enough.

Want to read more from me, or get access to exclusive content? **See the next page** for ways to connect with me!

You can find me on social media as gaiusjaugustus.

Connect With Gaius

Become part of the magic at my Magician's Club HQ. Join for free to get access to exclusive stories, regular updates, and behind-the-scenes peeks. Or upgrade to a premium plan for early access and additional rewards. New episodes are released regularly!

Sign up for the MCHQ at
https://gaiusjaugustus.com/mchq/

Get 20% off premium plans with the code MANIP25.

Want less frequent updates of my ongoings? Sign up for my newsletter at
https://gaiusjaugustus.com/signup/

GLOSSARY

Formula: (plural: formulae) The meaning, logic, and principles used to enact a change in Nature. Also used to describe the spoken shorthand used to convey the meaning, logic, and principles necessary to enact a change in Nature. This is primarily used by Highrealmers. The Midrealm equivalent is "spell."

Huleay Grounds: The center of power in Ar. It is split into two parts: the inner and the outer Huleay Grounds.

Huleay Temple: The ruling spiritual caste of the Ledine Empire.

Pictogram: A graphical symbol that conveys the meaning, logic, and principles equivalent to one or more formulae. In Midrealm, formulae often require a pictogram to enact a change in the physical world. This is primarily used by Highrealmers. The Midrealm equivalent is "spell."

Spell: A magical word or phrase, or the physical representation of a magical word or phrase, which holds the intention of bringing about some change in the physical world.

Theorem: a statement that can be proven by means of a set of logical arguments, postulates, or formulae. This is primarily used by Highrealmers.

Spell Translations

CHAPTER 10:

Spell: Woathu athuas woardias m'e bidi m'e wolele, leat athuguhuatas bi fiar at fil'e. Athune asatatle ne'at ciniciarat peleatas nedi asnedi dias bi.

Translation: With these words I bind my will, let thoughts be free to fly. Then settle into concrete plots, and send ideas by.

CHAPTER 27:

Spell: Bilewo, wo woat. Cihu atme ne atas bias asatat. Cineneciat at ayar pearlelele. Huledi fiasat ase ay ar bi'le. Arlexo. Aratarciat. Meledi. Meargu. Leasne athu binediar biatwone ar woarledias filexobileat ne athu pearmebileat. Arlexo. Aratarciat. Meledi. Meargu. Ayar asle ne leneguar atdi huar. Voneatar fiarathu woathuat fi'ar. Athu pearbinileatas legune ne athuas memeneat mekunegu ne atarathu legune atwo woardias.

Translation: Below, we wait. Each atom in its base state. Connect to your parallel. Hold fast as you are able. Relax. Retract. Meld. Merge. Loosen the boundary between our worlds. Allow flexibility in the permeability. Relax. Retract. Meld. Merge. Your soul no longer tied here. Venture forth without fear. The probabilities align in this moment, making one truth align in two worlds.

Read More From Gaius

The Magician and the Mechanical Doll, Tales of a Vernian Youth Volume 1

Octavian, a promising graduate student of magic, is about to have his dreams shattered. As he activates his magical robot, Replika, the duo finds themselves thrust into an alternate reality of stuck doors and steam-powered tech. Little did Octavian know that his enigmatic research advisor, Teacher, held the technology to traverse realities! Octavian and Replika embark on a quest to uncover Teacher's hidden secrets and find their way back home.

Get ready for a whimsical, magic-filled adventure that spans time and space, transporting our travelers to fantastical destinations. Are you ready to traverse the boundaries of our reality? Don't miss out on this epic journey!

Learn more at https://gjabooks.com/ToVY

THOSE WITHOUT WINGS

Adams and his 10-year-old niece, Illeina, are in an accident that kills him and leaves her in a coma. As an angel, there is still a chance to save her life. But to do so, he will have to enter the forbidden space between the human realm and the realm of the angels, a place called Darkrealm, where creatures called Whispers corrupt souls. Adams is willing to risk his existence, but when his new friend, Casey, insists on joining him, will it be worth it to risk zir life as well?

Those Without Wings is a story of love, sacrifice, and new beginnings. Dive into the immersive world of the angels, a civilization in a universe where once-living individuals live in a place between our world and the world of energy and gods. Discover the secrets of souls, which are tethered to our world through Darkrealm. Keep a strong heart as Adams fights the odds to save the life of his beloved niece.

Learn more at https://gjabooks.com/TWW

ABOUT THE AUTHOR

Gaius (they/them) is a transgender, queer, disabled author who writes magical stories with diverse characters. In their work, they aim to convey immersive plots with unique worlds and irreverent humor. They have a distinctive background, going to university for film & television before later returning to school to complete a PhD in Cancer Biology. This colors their storytelling as they blur the boundaries of dichotomies such as magic & science, drama & humor, and good & evil.

Learn more about Gaius at gaiusjaugustus.com